Serbian
Folktales

Serbian
Folktales

Introduction by Margaret H. Beissinger

General Editor: Jake Jackson

**FLAME TREE
PUBLISHING**

This is a FLAME TREE Book

FLAME TREE PUBLISHING
6 Melbray Mews
Fulham, London SW6 3NS
United Kingdom
www.flametreepublishing.com

First published 2024
Copyright © 2024 Flame Tree Publishing Ltd

24 26 28 27 25
1 3 5 7 9 8 6 4 2

ISBN: 978-1-80417-783-9

All rights reserved. No part of this publication may be reproduced,
stored in a retrieval system, or transmitted in any form or by any
means, electronic, mechanical, photocopying, recording or otherwise,
without the prior written permission of the publisher.

The cover image is © copyright 2024 Flame Tree Publishing Ltd, based
on photograph courtesy of Wikimedia Commons/Tillman

All inside images courtesy of Shutterstock.com and the following:
darsi, Eroshka, Lililia, and VladimirProkopovic.

In addition to the new introductions, the text in this book is
selected and edited from the following original sources:
Fairy and Wonder Tales selected by William Patten and written by W. S.
Karajich (Harvard University: Harvard Junior Classics, 1917), *Serbian Fairy
Tales* translated by Elodie L. Mijatovich (New York: Robert M. McBride & Co.,
1918), *Serbian Folk Songs, Fairy Tales, and Proverbs* by Maximilian A. Mügge
(London: Drane's 1916), *Hero Tales and Legends of the Serbians* by Woislav M.
Petrovitch (London: George G. Harrap & Co. Ltd., 1914), and *Sixty Folk-Tales from
Exclusively Slavonic Sources* by A.H. Wratislaw (London, Elliot Stock, 1889).

Printed and bound in China

Contents

Series Foreword

STRETCHING BACK to the oral traditions of thousands of years ago, tales of heroes and disaster, creation and conquest have been told by many different civilizations in many different ways. Their impact sits deep within our culture even though the detail in the tales themselves are a loose mix of historical record, transformed narrative and the distortions of hundreds of storytellers.

Today the language of mythology lives with us: our mood is jovial, our countenance is saturnine, we are narcissistic and our modern life is hermetically sealed from others. The nuances of myths and legends form part of our daily routines and help us navigate the world around us, with its half truths and biased reported facts.

The nature of a myth is that its story is already known by most of those who hear it, or read it. Every generation brings a new emphasis, but the fundamentals remain the same: a desire to understand and describe the events and relationships of the world. Many of the great stories are archetypes that help us find our own place, equipping us with tools for self-understanding, both individually and as part of a broader culture.

For Western societies it is Greek mythology that speaks to us most clearly. It greatly influenced the mythological heritage of the ancient Roman civilization and is the lens through which we still see the Celts, the Norse and many of the other great peoples and religions. The Greeks themselves learned much from their neighbours, the Egyptians, an older culture that became weak with age and incestuous leadership.

It is important to understand that what we perceive now as mythology had its own origins in perceptions of the divine and the rituals of the sacred. The earliest civilizations, in the crucible of the Middle East, in the Sumer of the third millennium BC, are the source to which many of the mythic archetypes can be traced. As humankind collected together in cities for the first time, developed writing and industrial scale agriculture, started to irrigate the rivers and attempted to control rather than be at the mercy of its environment, humanity began to write down its tentative explanations of natural events, of floods and plagues, of disease.

Early stories tell of Gods (or god-like animals in the case of tribal societies such as African, Native American or Aboriginal cultures) who are crafty and use their wits to survive, and it is reasonable to suggest that these were the first rulers of the gathering peoples of the earth, later elevated to god-like status with the distance of time. Such tales became more political as cities vied with each other for supremacy, creating new Gods, new hierarchies for their pantheons. The older Gods took on primordial roles and became the preserve of creation and destruction, leaving the new gods to deal with more current, everyday affairs. Empires rose and fell, with Babylon assuming the mantle from Sumeria in the 1800s BC, then in turn to be swept away by the Assyrians of the 1200s BC; then the Assyrians and the Egyptians were subjugated by the Greeks, the Greeks by the Romans and so on, leading to the spread and assimilation of common themes, ideas and stories throughout the world.

The survival of history is dependent on the telling of good tales, but each one must have the 'feeling' of truth, otherwise it will be ignored. Around the firesides, or embedded in a book or a computer, the myths and legends of the past are still the living materials of retold myth, not restricted to an exploration of origins. Now we have devices and global communications that give us unparalleled access to a diversity of traditions. We can find out about Native American, Indian, Chinese and tribal African mythology in a way that was denied to our ancestors, we can find connections, match the archaeology, religion and the mythologies of the world to build a comprehensive image of the human experience that is endlessly fascinating.

The stories in this book provide an introduction to the themes and concerns of the myths and legends of their respective cultures, with a short introduction to provide a linguistic, geographic and political context. This is where the myths have arrived today, but undoubtedly over the next millennia, they will transform again whilst retaining their essential truths and signs.

Jake Jackson
General Editor

Introduction to Serbian Folktales

How Serbia Fits In

THE BALKANS HAVE always been a rich arena for oral traditions and folk culture. Serbia lies in the heart of the Balkans, a crossroads between east and west; Byzantine, Ottoman and European influences have determined much of its character. Written in the Cyrillic alphabet, Serbian is one of the South Slavic languages and, as elsewhere in the Balkans, most of the country's inhabitants are Orthodox Christians.

Medieval Serbia was governed for two centuries by the native Nemanja dynasty, followed by 500 years of Ottoman rule. From the early decades of the nineteenth century, liberation from the Ottomans became a fervent national cause, with local folklore providing potent emblems of Serbian identity. Serbia gained its independence in 1878. Four decades later the Kingdom of South Slavs was established; it was renamed Yugoslavia in 1929. After the Second World War, the Socialist Federal Republic of Yugoslavia was created. Then, following the break-up of Yugoslavia, the independent Republic of Serbia was established in 2006.

Nation-Building and Folklore

While a written Serbian literature lay dormant during the period of Ottoman rule, the oral literary forms that circulated, enriching the lives of the largely rural, non-literate population, flourished. These included an extraordinary culture of oral poetry and prose. Serbian culture was kept alive by ordinary people during the oppressive centuries of Ottoman rule precisely through oral traditions. Indeed, it functioned as an effective local form of resistance to foreign domination. As the nineteenth century unfolded in Serbia, folklore served as a powerful means to express the nation's hopes and 'the voice of the people'. Moreover, it inspired the local intellectual elite to collect genres of oral literature as 'precious' national artefacts, especially epic poetry and folktales.

Vuk Stefanović Karadžić

Vuk Stefanović Karadžić (1787–1864), a linguist and folklorist, became the most influential cultural figure of nineteenth-century Serbia. So important was Karadžić, and so beloved by his fellow Serbs, that he remains known even to this day as simply 'Vuk'. Meaning 'wolf', the moniker was given to Karadžić at birth to protect him from evil forces at a time when infant mortality was widespread.

Vuk was an active rammarian who advocated for the use of the vernacular and thus reformed the Serbian language, normalized the Serbian Cyrillic alphabet and produced the first Serbian dictionary. In addition, however, he collected, published and promoted folklore, and was responsible for laying the groundwork for modern Serbian literature. Due in part to his own peasant background, Vuk was particularly drawn to folklore. His first volume of Serbian oral texts was a small book of folk poetry issued in 1814. Vuk went on to become an avid collector of Serbian oral literary forms, including narrative, lyric and ritual poetry as well as narrative prose and proverbs. Indeed, his publications constitute the canon of Serbian folklore.

Vuk's Collected Folktales

Vuk's collections and publications of Serbian folktales were seminal. The first, issued in 1821, contained 12 humorous tales. Another, *Srpske Narodne Pripovijetke (Serbian Folktales)*, published in Vienna in 1853, consisted of 50 tales; it was Vuk's most significant collection of traditional prose narratives. He dedicated the tome to the linguist and folklorist Jacob Grimm, whom he knew; Grimm indeed inspired and urged Vuk to collect and publish Serbian folktales. Vuk edited these tales considerably (a common approach among the publishers of 'folk' texts in the nineteenth century), aiming to establish useful models for the creation of a Serbian prose literature. An enlarged second edition of the 1853 volume was published posthumously in Vienna in 1870.

Vuk also inspired other local folklorists to gather and publish Serbian folktales, which is particularly evident in collections issued during the twentieth century. The majority of the folktales in the present volume, *Serbian Folktales*, appear in Vuk's 'classic' collections.

Storytellers and Folktale Sources

Vuk amassed folktales from a variety of different sources. Some he personally collected from storytellers while others were tales that were sent to him, often by other folklorists who had gathered them. They included storytellers from all backgrounds and social classes. The folktales were gleaned from storytellers both young and old, living in rural and urban communities, as well as from both uneducated and educated Serbs.

In the highly patriarchal world of the traditional Balkans, it is perhaps not surprising that the majority of these storytellers were male. This is also a result, at least in part, of the fact that all of the collectors were men. Male storytellers included peasants, shepherds, millers, masons, fishermen and soldiers; others were merchants, beggars, schoolteachers and priests. However, Vuk did also publish folktales told by women and girls, both in person and second-hand, such as the famed magic tale rendered to the young Prince of Serbia (Mihailo Obrenović III) by his nurse and later sent to Vuk for his collection. Furthermore, over one-fifth of the folktales that Vuk published were stories that he recalled from his own childhood in Tršić, the village in western Serbia (then part of the Ottoman Empire) where he grew up.

Occasions for Storytelling

Folktales can be told virtually any time and anywhere; they need no 'props'. And while folktales convey profound meanings as well as reinforce codes of behaviour and values, they are above all a source of entertainment.

In Serbia, folktales have been told for generations as forms of diversion and distraction. Storytelling traditionally took place during cold winter evenings, when family and friends gathered around the hearth after a long day. Similarly, travellers listened to the tales of coachmen or shared stories with one another as they journeyed from one place to the next. Tales were told for the pure pleasure of a good yarn or simply to while away the time.

Historically, gendered work-oriented gatherings, where various types of labour were performed, were particularly fruitful times for telling tales. For men and boys, this meant while working in the field or mill, tending sheep, practising masonry, fishing on a boat or serving in the army. For girls and women, storytelling happened in domestic settings, a diversion while they spun, knitted, mended clothes or worked at other crafts for the home. Children were told tales by the nurses who cared for them – not to mention, of course, by their mothers and fathers. Tales were also spun at communal events such as wakes and burials.

The Types of Serbian Folktales

Serbian folktales (*narodne pripovetke*) are traditional, fictional narratives in prose; they feature quotidian characters and are meant to entertain. These stories include several generic categories. The largest, best-known and most popular Serbian genre of folktale is the magic (or fairy) tale, called *bajka* (pl. *bajke*). This form of folktale is distinguished by the presence of magic. Realistic tales are another type of folktale, primarily romantic in content but not usually featuring magic.

Another form is the religious tale, featuring a narrative in which the involvement of God and/or the Devil in the lives of ordinary people is key; these are often morality tales. Tales of everyday life or anecdotes (often humorous) are also a genre of folktale. So are legends, which are traditional narratives of an explanatory nature. All of these folktale genres are represented in this book.

Magic Tales

Serbian magic tales are, by nature, stories in which the family and family relations, as well as the anxieties surrounding life-cycle transitions, are central. They are tales primarily about parents and children, siblings and marriage. A few magic tales focus on children and their transition to adolescence. However, most concern protagonists who, as young people, are seeking their place in the world, usually including finding a spouse. Indeed, the majority of Serbian magic tales chart the passage of protagonists from adolescence to marriage; most of these tales end with a wedding.

In traditional Serbian society, getting married is equivalent to an initiation. The vast majority of magic tales thus follow young people who must 'gain knowledge' in order to become adult and marry. Some *bajke* also relate to couples' adapting to major changes in married life (for example, becoming parents and/or coping with in-laws), such as in 'The Golden-Haired Twins' – a classic tale of the slandered wife.

The World of Bajke

Places and times in magic tales represent an indefinite, unreal world. Magic as an essential property is taken for granted within the narrative; it may appear in things, animals and characters (for example, golden apples, curative ointment, hair, special horses or dogs or the fairy-like figures of Serbian folklore or *vile*). Gold indicates the Other World: an alternative kingdom or distant, enchanted location far beyond the protagonist's familiar whereabouts and representing the proverbial destination where knowledge may be gained. Threes are also a part of the magic tale lexicon: three brothers or sisters, dragons, impossible tasks, magical objects, even three times three or nine peahens.

Moreover, good and evil are sharply demarcated, forming unambiguous categories of right and wrong that typify both characters and deeds. The hero may be the youngest of three sons as well as the humblest and most diligent; he contrasts with his indolent and vindictive older brothers. The heroine, also typically the youngest, may be the kindest and most self-sacrificing of her sisters, who are ugly and hateful. She is often a stepdaughter, to whom her stepmother is unfailingly malicious. Kind animals, 'female helpers' (young maidens or old women) or some other figures whom protagonists encounter test their individual compassion; if they 'pass', the characters go on to aid them in their quests or journeys. Antagonists are also tested, but they invariably fail and are castigated.

Magic Tales with Male Protagonists

In the gendered, patriarchal world of traditional Serbia, coming-of-age tales focus for the most part on male protagonists. Youths, be they noble princes or humble shepherds, leave home to embark on quests to find and marry an 'exceedingly beautiful princess', such as in 'The Trade that No One Knows', which entails a series of gruelling tests involving shapeshifting. Heroes may be the youngest in a trio of brothers who help each other out, as in 'The Three Brothers'. More often, however, the siblings must compete with each other as they all attempt to rescue three princesses kidnapped by dragons, as in 'The Wonderful Kiosk' and 'Bash Chalek'.

In the compound tale 'The Golden Apple Tree and the Nine Peahens', the two older sons of the king plot against the youngest. However, it is the youngest who manages to discover the thief stealing the special apples from his father's golden apple tree: the queen of the peahens, whom he marries after first failing, and then successfully passing, impossible tasks. The tale then continues, focusing on the adult prince and his wife, including new challenges which they confront and resolve together. In another magic tale, 'One Good Turn Deserves Another', a humble prince is tricked by his evil servant to switch places with him. Ultimately, however, after many difficult trials, he wins back his true identity – not to mention the princess of his dreams.

Magic Tales with Female Protagonists

Magic tales with female protagonists are much less common and less spectacular than those featuring males. Heroines also are tested, but not by leaping on magnificent horses over massive ditches or high walls, as the heroes who win them must. Instead of physical prowess the women must rather display generosity and compassion, such as in 'The Stepmother and her Stepdaughter'.

In 'Pepelyouga', the Serbian 'Cinderella' (named Marra in the tale), accidentally drops her spindle into a ravine. This, as she has been warned it will, causes her mother to be turned into a cow, albeit a magical one who still looks after her. The familiar tale continues with three consecutive Sunday morning church services (instead of royal balls) which the king's son attends and at which he falls in love with Marra. The heroine's 'journey', enabling her to embrace marriage and adulthood, entails her internalizing compassion through her own suffering, acquiring domestic skills and sharpening her resourcefulness through some of her own disguise and deceptive storytelling.

Realistic and Religious Tales, Anecdotes and Legends

Narratives in the other categories of Serbian folktales are generally shorter and less complex than the *bajke*. Realistic tales revolve around romantic relationships between men and women, but the element of magic is absent. Nor are they based on displays of courage or valour, as in magic tales. In 'A Trade Before Everything', for example, the male protagonist learns a occupation in order to win the hand of the shepherd's daughter-cum-princess. In 'The Maiden Wiser than the Tsar', wisdom and ingenuity combine to enable the daughter of a poor man to outwit the tsar, causing him to fall in love with her. Religious tales in Serbia often include biblical figures who interact with ordinary people. Such is the case with 'He Who Asks Little Receives Much', a morality tale concerning the righteousness of generosity, in which an angel visits three brothers.

Anecdotes, frequently meant to be funny, are relatively short and sometimes have punchlines. They often exploit ethnic or social stereotypes, as in 'The Era from the Other World', in which a Turk is parodied. Era, who appears in other similar anecdotes, is a trickster.

Finally, legends are explanatory and etiological, sometimes with religious or historical themes. 'Saint Peter and the Sand', for example, explains why a particular village is quite sandy, while 'Why the Serbian People are Poor' offers to explain exactly what the title promises. Legends often involve the element of belief.

Margaret H. Beissinger (Introduction) teaches in the Slavic Department at Princeton University. Her field is Balkan oral literature and traditions, especially epic poetry and Romani music-making, topics that she has published widely on. She has written and co-edited several books and is currently editing the *Oxford Handbook of Slavic and East European Folklore*.

Quests, Challenges & Schemes

MOST OF THESE STORIES are magic tales involving quests and challenges for male protagonists who seek beautiful maidens to marry. Such is the case with 'Satan's Juggling and God's Might', in which a prince receives help in locating his bride from several knowledgeable old women. 'Clothes Made of Dew and Sunrays' tells of a suitor who, unlike hundreds of others before him, is able to tell the princess's father where and what shape her birthmark is, thereby winning her as his bride.

Another tale, 'About the Maiden Swifter than a Horse', features a maiden with special powers who is forged out of snow by a *vila*, a fairy-like figure in Serbian folklore. She sets a challenge: a race will take place between her and all the men who wish to marry her. She will run, while they ride on their steeds. The prince casts a spell on her invoking God's name, which permits him to capture her, but later she is unwilling to submit to him and disappears.

Satan's Juggling and God's Might

ONE MORNING the son of the king went out to hunt. Whilst walking through the snow he cut himself a little, and the drops of blood fell on the snow. When he saw how pretty the red blood looked on the white snow, he thought, "Oh, if I could only marry a girl as white as snow and as rosy red as this blood!" Whilst he was thus thinking, he met an old woman, and asked her if there were such maidens anywhere to be found. The old woman told him that on the mountain he saw before him he would find a house without doors, and the only entrance and outlet of this house was a single window. And, she added, "In that house, my son, there is living a girl such as you desire; but of the young men who have gone to ask her to be their wife, none have returned."

"That may all be as you say," answered the prince. "I will go, nevertheless! Only tell me the way that I must take to get to the house." When the old woman heard this resolve, she was sorry for the young man, and, taking a piece of bread from her pouch, she gave it to him, saying, "Take this bread and keep it safe as the apple of your eye." The prince took the bread and continued his journey. Very soon afterwards he met another old woman, and she asked him where he was going. He told her he was going to demand the girl who lived in the doorless house on the mountain. Then the old woman tried to dissuade him, telling him just the same things as the former one had done. He said, however, "That may be quite true, nevertheless I will go, even if I never return." Then the old woman gave to the prince a little nut, saying, "Keep this nut always by you; it may help you some time or other."

The prince took the nut and went on his way till he came to where an old woman was sitting by the roadside. She asked him, "Where are you going?" Then he told her he was going to demand the girl who lived in the house on the mountain before him. Upon this the old woman wept, and prayed him to give up all thoughts of the girl, and she gave him the very same warnings as the other old women had done. All this, however, was of no use; the prince was resolved to go on, so the old woman gave him a walnut, saying, "Take this walnut, and keep it carefully until you want it."

He wondered at these presents, and asked her to tell him why the first old woman had given him a piece of bread, the second a nut, and she herself now a walnut. The old woman answered, "The bread is to throw to the beasts before the house, that they may not eat you; and, when you find yourself in the greatest danger, ask counsel, first from the nut, and then from the walnut."

Then the king's son continued his wandering, till he came at last to a thick forest, in the midst of which he saw a house with only a single window. When he came near it, he was attacked by a multitude of beasts of all kinds, and, following the advice of the old woman, he threw the bit of bread towards them. Then the beasts came and smelt at the bread one after the other, and, upon doing so, each drew his tail between his legs and lay down quietly.

The house had no door and but one window, which was very high above the ground, so high that, do what he could, he was not able to reach it. Suddenly he saw a girl letting down her golden hair, so he rushed and caught hold of it, and she drew him up thereby into the house. Then he saw that the girl was she for whose sake he had come to this place. The prince and the girl were equally pleased to see each other, and she said, "Thank God that my mother happened to be away from home. She is gone into the forest to gather the plants by the aid of which she transforms into beasts all the young men who venture here to ask me to be their wife. Those are the beasts who would have killed you, if God had not helped you. But let us fly away from this place." So they fled away through the forest as quickly as they could. As they happened to look back, however, they saw that the girl's mother was pursuing them, and they became frightened. The old woman was already very near them before the prince remembered his nut. He took it out quickly and asked, "For God's sake! Tell me what we must do now!" The nut replied, "Open me." The prince opened it, and from the little nut flowed out a large river, which stopped the way, so that for a time the girl's mother could not pass.

However, she touched the waters with her staff, and they immediately divided and left her a dry path, so that she could run on quickly after the prince and the girl.

When the prince saw she would soon catch up with them, he took out the walnut and asked, "Tell me, what must we do now?" And the walnut replied, "Break me." The king's son broke the walnut, and a great fire flamed out from it – so great a fire that the whole forest barely escaped being consumed by it. But the girl's mother spat on the fire, and it extinguished itself in a moment. Then the king's son saw that these were nothing but the jugglings of the devil, so he turned eastward, made the sign of the cross, and called on the mighty God to help him. Then it suddenly thundered and lightened, and from heaven flashed a thunderbolt which struck the mother of the girl, and she fell dead upon the ground.

Thus at length the king's son arrived safely at home, and when the girl had been made a Christian, he married her.

Sir Peppercorn

THREE BROTHERS once upon a time went out into the neighbouring forest to choose some trees fit for building. Before going, however, they told their mother not to forget to send their sister into the wood after them with their dinners. The mother sent the girl as she had been told to do; but as the girl was on her way, a giant met her in the wood and carried her off to a cave, where he lived.

All day long the brothers waited, expecting their sister, and wondering why their mother had forgotten to send them food. At length, after remaining two days in the forest, and becoming anxious and angry at the delay, they went home. When they arrived there, they asked their mother why she had not sent their sister with their food, as she had promised to do; she replied that she had sent the girl three days ago, and had been wondering greatly why she had not come back.

When the three brothers heard this, they were exceedingly troubled, and the eldest said, "I will go back into the forest and look for my sister." Accordingly he went. After wandering about some time, he came to a shepherdess, who was minding a flock of sheep. He asked her anxiously if she had seen his sister in the wood, or whether she could tell him anything about her. The shepherdess replied that she had indeed seen a girl carrying food, but a giant had met her and carried her off to his cave. Then the young man asked her to tell him the way to the giant's cave, which she did. The cave was hidden in a deep ravine. The brother at once went down, and called aloud on his sister by name. In a short time, the girl came to the mouth of the cave, and, seeing her eldest brother, invited him to come in. This he did, and was exceedingly surprised to see that the seeming cave was in reality a magnificent palace. Whilst he stood there talking to his sister and inquiring how she liked her new home, he heard a loud whirring in the air overhead, and immediately afterwards saw a heavy mace fall on the ground just in front of the cave. Greatly terrified and astonished, he asked his sister what this meant, and she told him not to be afraid, for it was only the way the giant let her know of his return three hours before he came, that she might begin to prepare his supper.

When it grew dark, the giant came home, and was at once aware that a stranger was in his place. In reply to his angry questions, his wife told him it was only her brother, who had come to visit them. When the giant heard this, he went to the mouth of the cave, and, calling a shepherd, ordered him to kill the largest sheep in his flock and roast it.

When the meat was ready, the giant called his brother-in-law and said, as he cut the sheep in two equal parts, "My dear brother-in-law, listen well to what I say; if you eat your half of the meat sooner than I eat mine, I will give you leave to kill me; but if I eat my half quicker than you eat yours, I shall certainly kill you."

Thereupon the poor brother-in-law began to shake all over with fright; and, fearing the worst, tried to eat as fast as he could. But he had hardly swallowed three mouthfuls before the giant finished his share of the sheep, and killed him, according to his threat.

For some time the other two brothers and their old mother waited impatiently to see if the elder brother would come back. At last, hearing nothing either of the brother or of the sister, the second son said, "I will go and look after them." So he went into the same forest where his brother had gone, and, meeting there the same shepherdess minding her sheep, he inquired if she had seen his brother or sister. The shepherdess answered him as she had answered the elder brother, and he, too, asked the way to the giant's cave, and, on being told, went down the ravine until he reached the place. There he called on his sister by name, and she came out and invited him to enter the cave. This he did, and shared the fate of his brother; for, being unable to eat his part of the sheep as quickly as the giant ate his, he also was killed.

Not long after, the third brother went forth on the same road to look for his two elder brothers and sister, and, having found the giant's cave, was likewise invited to eat half a sheep, or be put to death. He, however, failed like his brothers had done before him, and, being unable to eat his part of the sheep as quickly as the giant ate his, he was also killed.

Now the parents, being alone in their house, prayed that God would give them another son, even were he no bigger than a peppercorn. As they prayed so it came to pass, and not very long after, a little boy was born to them, who was so extremely small that they christened him "Peppercorn."

When the boy was old enough, he went out to play with other boys; and one day, in a quarrel, one of these said to him, "May you share the fate of your elder brothers." Hearing this, Peppercorn ran off home at once, and asked his mother what these words meant. So the mother was forced to tell him how his three brothers had gone into the forest to look for their lost sister, and had never come back again. As soon as he heard this, Peppercorn began to search the house for pieces of old iron, and, having found some scraps, carried them off in the evening to a blacksmith, that with them he might make him a mace.

Next morning Peppercorn went to the smith to ask for his mace, which the man gave him, saying at the same time, "Now pay me for making it." To this Peppercorn replied, "First let me see if it is strong enough"; and he threw it up in the air and held his head so that the mace might fall upon it. As soon as the mace struck his head, it broke into pieces; and Peppercorn, seeing how badly it was made, fell into a passion and killed the smith. Then he gathered up the pieces of iron and went off to look for a better workman.

He soon found another blacksmith who was willing to make him a mace, but demanded a ducat for the work. Peppercorn said he would willingly pay the ducat if the smith made him a really strong, serviceable mace. So next morning he went to ask if it was ready, and the smith said, "Yes, but you must first pay me the ducat, and then I will give it you." Peppercorn, however, answered, "The ducat is ready in my pocket, but I must first see if the mace is good before I pay for it." Thereupon he caught it, flung it up in the air, and held his head under it as it fell. As soon as the mace struck his head, it broke into pieces; and he, again falling into a great passion, killed this smith also.

Gathering up the pieces of iron, he now carried them to a third smith, who undertook to make him a good strong mace, and demanded a ducat for doing so. Next morning Peppercorn went for the mace and, after trying it three times, each time throwing it up higher in the air and letting it fall on his head, where it raised great bumps, he owned that he was satisfied with it, and accordingly paid the smith the ducat as he had promised.

Having now a good strong mace, Peppercorn started off at once for the forest, in which his three elder brothers and his sister had been lost. After wandering about for some time, he came to the place where the shepherdess sat watching her sheep, and, in reply to his questions, she told him that she had seen his three brothers go down the ravine in search of their sister, but had never seen them come up again.

Notwithstanding this, Peppercorn went resolutely down the ravine, calling aloud upon his sister by name. When she heard this, she was exceedingly surprised, and said to herself, "Who can this be calling me by name, now that all my brothers are killed? I have no other relations to come and look for me." Then she went to the entrance of the cave and called out, "Who is it that calls me? I have no longer any brothers."

Peppercorn said to her, "I am your brother who was born after you left home, and my name is Peppercorn."

On hearing this, his sister led him into the palace, but he had hardly had time to say a few words to her before a loud whirring was heard in the air, and the giant's mace fell to the ground. For a moment Peppercorn was terrified at this, but he recovered himself quickly, and, pulling the mace out of the ground, flung it back to the giant, who, in astonishment, said to himself, "Who is this who throws my mace back to me? Methinks I have at last found someone able to fight with me."

When the giant came home, he immediately asked his wife who had been in the cave, and she answered him, "It is my youngest brother." Thereupon the giant ordered the shepherd to bring the largest sheep in his flock. When this was brought, the giant killed it himself, and, whilst preparing it for roasting, said to Peppercorn, "Will you turn the meat, or will you take care of the fire?" Peppercorn said he would rather gather wood and make the fire; so he went out and tumbled down some large trees with his mace. These he carried to the mouth of the cave and made a large fire ready for the meat.

When the sheep was roasted, the giant cut it in two parts, and gave one half to Peppercorn, saying, "Take this half, and if you eat it before I eat my half, you are free to kill me; but if you don't, I shall surely kill you." So Peppercorn and the giant began to eat as fast as they could, swallowing down large pieces of meat, and, in their haste, almost choking themselves. At last Peppercorn, by trickery, managed to get rid of his share of the sheep, and, according to the arrangement, killed the giant. This done, with the help of his sister, he collected all the treasures the giant had heaped up in his palace, and, taking them with him, returned home with his sister, to the great joy of their parents.

Peppercorn remained some time after this with his father, mother, and sister, and they lived very merrily on the treasures he had brought from the giant's cave. At length, however, he saw that the riches were coming to an end, so he resolved to go into the world to seek his fortune.

After travelling about a good while, he came one day to a large city, where he saw a great crowd gathered about a man who held an iron pike in his hand, and every now and then squeezed drops of water out of the iron. Whilst the people watched, wondering and admiring his great strength, Peppercorn went up and asked him, "Do you think there is any man in the world stronger than yourself?"

"There is only one man alive who is stronger than myself, and that one is a certain person called Peppercorn," answered he. "Peppercorn can receive a mace on his head without being hurt."

Thereupon Peppercorn told the man who he was, and proposed to him that they should travel about the world together.

"That will I right gladly," said the Pikeman. "How can I help being glad to go with a trusty fellow like you!"

Travelling together, they came one day to a certain city, and, finding a concourse of people assembled, they went to see what was the matter. They found a man sitting on the bank of a river turning the wheels of nine mills with his little finger. So they said to him, "Is there anyone stronger than you in the world?"

And he answered them, "There are only two men stronger than I am – a certain person named Peppercorn and a certain Pikeman." Hearing this, Peppercorn and the Pikeman told him who they were, and proposed that he should join them in their travels about the world.

The Mill-turner very gladly accepted the offer, and so all three continued their journey together.

After travelling some time, they came to a city where they found all the people greatly excited because someone had stolen the three daughters of the king, and, notwithstanding the immense rewards His Majesty had offered, no one had as yet dared to go out to look for the princesses. As soon as Peppercorn and his two comrades heard this, they went to the king and offered to search for his three daughters. But in order to accomplish the task, they demanded that the king should give them a hundred thousand loads of wood. The king gave them what they wanted, and they made a fence all around the city with the timber. This done, they began to watch.

The first morning they prepared a whole ox for their dinners, and discussed the question of which of the three should stay behind to mind the meat whilst the other two watched the fence. The Pikeman said, "I think I will stay here and take care of the meat, and I will have dinner ready for you when you come back from looking after the fence." So it was thus settled. Just, however, as the Pikeman thought the ox was well roasted, he was frightened by the sudden approach of a man with a forehead a yard high and a beard a span long. This man said to the Pikeman, "Good morning!" but the latter ran away instead of answering, he was so shocked by the strange appearance of the man.

Yard-high-forehead-and-span-long-beard was quite content at this, and, sitting down, soon finished the whole ox. When he had ended his dinner, he got up and went away.

Shortly afterwards, Sir Peppercorn and the Mill-turner came for their dinners, and, being very hungry, shouted from afar to the Pikeman, "Let us dine at once!" But the Pikeman, keeping himself hidden among the bushes, called out to them, "There is nothing left for us to eat! A little while ago Yard-high-forehead-and-span-long-beard came up and ate up the whole ox to the very last morsel! I was afraid of him, and so I did not say one word against it."

Peppercorn and the Mill-turner reproached their companion bitterly for allowing all their dinner to be stolen without once trying to prevent it, and the Mill-turner said scornfully, "Well, I will stop tomorrow and look after the meat, and Yard-high-forehead-and-span-long-beard may come if he likes!"

So the next day the Mill-turner stayed to roast the ox, and his two comrades went to look after the fence they had built round about the city.

Just before dinnertime, Yard-high-forehead-and-span-long-beard came out of the forest and walked straight up to the ox, and stretched his hands out greedily to grasp it. The Mill-turner was so frightened by his strange appearance that he ran off as hard as he could to look for a place to hide in.

By-and-by Peppercorn and the Pikeman came for their dinners and asked angrily where the meat was. Whereupon the Mill-turner answered, "There is no meat! It has all been eaten by that horrible Yard-high-forehead-and-span-long-beard, and his looks frightened me so that I dared not say a single word to him."

It was no use complaining, so Peppercorn only said, "Tomorrow I will stay to mind the ox, and you two shall go and look after the fence. I will see if we are to remain the third day without dinner."

The next morning, the Pikeman and the Mill-turner went to see if all was right round about the city, and Peppercorn remained to roast the ox. Exactly as on the two former days, just before dinner was ready, Yard-high-forehead-and-span-long-beard made his appearance and went up to seize the meat. But Peppercorn pushed him roughly back, saying, "Two days I have been dinnerless on your account, but the third day I will not be so, as long as my head stands on my shoulders!"

Much astonished at his boldness, Yard-high-forehead-and-span-long-beard exclaimed, "Take care you don't begin to quarrel with me. There is no one in all the world who can conquer me, except a fellow called Peppercorn!"

Peppercorn was very pleased to hear this, and, without more hesitation, sprang at once on Yard-high-forehead-and-span-long-beard, and, after some struggling, pulled him down to the earth and bound him. This done, he tied him fast to a tall pine tree. Now the Pikeman and Mill-turner came up and were exceedingly glad to find their dinners safe. Just as they were in the middle of their dinners, however, Yard-high-forehead-and-span-long-beard, with a sudden jerk, pulled up the pine tree by the roots and ran off with tree and all, making furrows in the earth with it just as if three ploughs had been passing over the ground.

Seeing him run off, the Pikeman and Mill-turner jumped up quickly and ran after him, but Peppercorn called them back and told them to finish their dinners first, for there would be plenty of time to catch him after they had dined! So they all three went on eating, and when they had done, they followed the furrows which Yard-high-forehead-and-span-long-beard had made in the ground. After a while they came to a deep dark hole in the earth, and when they had examined it all round and tried in vain on account of the darkness to look down into it, they returned to the king and asked him to give them a thousand miles of strong rope so that they could go down into the pit.

The king at once ordered his servants to give them what they required, and when they had got the great cable, they went back to the hole. On the way, as they were going, they discussed which of the three should venture down first, and it was at last settled that the Pikeman should be let down. However, he made them solemnly promise him that they should pull him up again the instant he shook the rope.

He had been let down but a very little way before he shook the rope, and so they pulled him up as they had promised.

Then the Mill-turner said, "Let *me* go down." And so the other two lowered him, but in a moment or two he shook the rope violently; and so he, too, was pulled up.

Now Peppercorn grew angry and exclaimed, "I did not think you were such cowards as to be afraid of a dark hole! Now let *me* down!" So they let him down and down until his foot touched solid ground. Finding that he had reached the bottom, he looked round him and saw that he stood just in the very middle of a most beautiful green plain – a plain so beautiful that it was a real pleasure to look on it.

At one end of the plain stood a large handsome palace, and Peppercorn went nearer to look at it. There, in the gardens, walking, he met two young girls, and asked them if they were not the daughters of the king. When they said that they were, he inquired what had become of the other sister; and the princesses told him that their youngest sister was in the palace very busy binding up the wounds that Yard-high-forehead-and-span-long-beard had lately received from a certain knight called Peppercorn.

Then Peppercorn told them who he was, and that he had come down on purpose to release them, and to take them back to the king, their father. On hearing this good news, the two princesses rejoiced greatly, and told Peppercorn where he would find Yard-high-forehead-and-span-long-beard and their youngest sister. But they warned him not to rush in on the giant, but rather to go softly, and first try to get hold of the sabre which hung on the wall over his bed, for this sabre possessed the wonderful power of killing a man when he was a whole day's journey from it.

Peppercorn took care to do as the princesses had told him. He stole very quietly into the room where Yard-high-forehead-and-span-long-beard was lying, and when he was near the bed, he sprang up suddenly and seized the sword. The moment the wounded giant saw his sabre in the hands of Peppercorn, he jumped up quickly and ran out of the palace.

Peppercorn followed him some time before he remembered what the two princesses had told him of the wonderful properties of the sword, but as soon as he recollected this, he made a sharp cut with it in the air, as if he were cutting off a man's head, and the moment he did so, Yard-high-forehead-and-span-long-beard fell down dead.

Then Peppercorn went back to the palace, and, taking with him the three princesses, prepared to return to the upper world.

When he came to the place where the rope was hanging, he took a large basket, and, placing the eldest princess in it, fastened it to the rope, then, giving her a note, in which he said that he sent her for the Pikeman, he made the signal agreed upon for the rope to be drawn up. So his comrades pulled up the rope, and when it came down again with the empty basket, Peppercorn sent up the second princess, after giving her a paper, in which he had written, "This one is for the Mill-turner."

When the rope descended the third time, he sent up the youngest princess, who was by far the most beautiful of the three. He gave her a paper which said that this one he meant to keep for himself. Just as the Pikeman and the Mill-turner began to pull up the rope, the princess gave Peppercorn a little box, saying, "Open it when you have need of anything!"

Now, when the Pikeman and Mill-turner drew up the youngest princess, and saw how very beautiful she was, they determined to leave Peppercorn down in the pit and go back without delay to the king's palace, and there to see which of them could get the youngest princess for his wife.

Peppercorn waited patiently some time for the rope to be let down that he might be drawn up, but no rope appeared. At last he was obliged to own to himself that his two comrades had deceived and deserted him, and, seeing how useless it was to remain standing still any longer, he walked off without knowing where the road would take him. Walking on, after a long time he came to the shore of a large lake, and heard a great noise of crying and shouting. Very soon a multitude of people, looking like a wedding party, made their appearance. After placing a young girl in bridal attire on the shore of the lake, the people left her there alone and went away.

Peppercorn, seeing the girl left by herself, and noticing how sad she looked, went up to her, and asked her why her friends had left her there, and why she was so sad. The girl answered, "In this lake is a dragon who, every year, swallows up a young girl. It is now my turn; and our people have brought me as a bride to the dragon, and left me to be swallowed up."

Peppercorn, on hearing this, asked her to let him rest near her a little, because he was very tired, but she answered, "You had far better fly away, my good knight; if it is necessary that I should die, it is not needful that you should die also."

But Peppercorn said to her, "Don't trouble yourself about me, only let me rest near you a little, for I am very tired. It will be time enough for me to run away when the dragon comes." Having said this, he sat down near the girl, and in a little while fell asleep. He had not slept long before the surface of the lake became agitated, and the water rose up in large waves; presently the dragon lifted its head, and swam straight to the shore where the girl sat, evidently intending to swallow her at once. The maiden cried bitterly and, a tear falling on Peppercorn's face, awakened him. He sprang up quickly, grasped his sword, and, smiting fiercely, with one stroke cut off the dragon's head.

Then he took the girl by the hand and led her back to the city, where he found that she was the only daughter of the king of that country. The king was overjoyed at hearing that the dragon was killed, and also at seeing his daughter brought back to him safe and sound. So he insisted that Peppercorn should marry the princess, which he did, and they all lived together very happily for a long time.

After a while, however, Peppercorn began to long greatly for the other world, and grew sadder and sadder every day. When his wife noticed this change in his appearance, she asked him very often what ailed him, but he would not tell her for a long time, because he did not wish to trouble her. At last, however, he could keep his secret no longer, and confessed to the princess how much he longed to go back to the upper world. Though she was very sorry to hear this, she promised him that she herself would beg the king to let him go, since he so greatly wished it. This she did; and when the king objected, not wishing to lose so good a son-in-law, the princess said, "Let him go; he has saved my life, and why should we keep him against his will? My three sons will still remain to comfort us!"

Then the king consented, saying, "Very well; let it be as he wishes, since you have nothing to say against it. Tell your benefactor to go to the lake shore, and to say to the giant-bird he will find there that the king sends her his greetings and desires her to take the bearer of them up to the other world."

The princess returned to her husband and told him what her father had said, and then began to prepare some provisions for the journey. When these were ready and the king had sent the letter for the bird, Peppercorn took a kind leave of his wife, and went down to the lake shore, where he soon found the nest of the giant-bird and her little ones in it, though she herself was not there. So he sat down to wait under the tree where the nest was. As he sat there, he heard the little birds chirping very restlessly and anxiously. Then he saw that the lake was beginning to throw up high waves, and soon a monster came out of the water and made straight for the nest to swallow the young birds.

Peppercorn, however, did not stop long to think about the matter, but quickly drew his wonderful sword and killed the monster. It happened that the giant-bird was just coming back, and when she saw Peppercorn under the tree, she shrieked as she ran up to kill him, "Now I have caught you – you who have been killing all my little ones for so many years! Now you shall pay me for it, for I will kill you!" But the little birds from their nest high in the tree cried out to her, "Don't do him any harm! he has saved us from being swallowed by a monster who came out of the lake to kill us."

Meanwhile, Peppercorn went to her and presented the king's letter. The giant-bird read it through carefully and then said to him, "Go home and kill twelve sheep. Fill their skins with water, and bring them here, together with the flesh of the sheep."

Peppercorn went back to the king, who at once ordered that he should be supplied with the flesh of twelve sheep, as well as with twelve sheep-skins full of fresh water. With this provision Peppercorn returned to the shore of the lake.

Then the giant-bird placed the twelve skins full of water under her left wing, and the flesh of the twelve sheep under her right, and took

Peppercorn on her back. This done, she told him that he must watch well her movements, and when she turned her beak to the left side, he must give her water, and when she turned it to the right he must give her meat. After impressing these directions upon Peppercorn, the giant-bird rose with her triple load in the air, and flew straight up towards the other world. As she flew, she turned from time to time her beak, now to the left and then to the right, and Peppercorn gave her water or meat, as she had directed him to do. At last, however, all the meat disappeared. So, when the giant-bird turned her beak once more to the right, Sir Peppercorn, having no more meat to give her, and fearing some evil might happen if he did not satisfy her, took out his knife, and, cutting a piece of flesh from the sole of his right foot, gave it to her.

But the bird knew by the taste that he had cut it from his own foot, so she did not swallow it, but hid it under her tongue, and held it there until she reached the other world.

Then she set Peppercorn down on the earth and told him to walk, and when he tried to do so he was forced to limp, because of the loss of part of his foot. When the giant-bird noticed this, she asked him, "Why do you limp so?" To this Peppercorn answered, "Oh, it is nothing! Do not trouble yourself about it!" But the bird told him to lift his right foot, and when he did so, she took the piece of flesh she had kept hidden under her tongue and laid it on the place where he had cut it from. Then she tapped it two or three times with her beak to make it grow to the rest of the foot.

Peppercorn walked on some time before he remembered the little box which the youngest of the three daughters of the king had given him. Now, however, he opened it, and a bee and a fly flew out and asked him what he desired. He said, "I want a good horse to carry me to the king's residence, and a decent suit of clothes to wear." Next moment a suit of good clothes lay before him, and a handsome horse stood ready saddled for him to mount. Then he took the clothes, and, mounting the horse, rode off to the city where the king dwelt. Before entering the city, however, he opened his little box and said to the fly and the bee, "I do not want the horse anymore at present." Accordingly they took it with them into their little box.

Peppercorn went to live in the house of an old woman in the city. Next morning he heard the public crier shouting in the street, "Is there anyone bold enough to fight with the mighty Pikeman, the king's son-in-law?"

Peppercorn was very pleased to hear this challenge, and, opening his box without delay, told the bee and fly, who flew out to receive his orders, that he wanted at once a fine suit of clothes and a strong charger, so that he might go to fight with the Pikeman. The bee and fly instantly gave him what he required, and he dressed himself and rode off to the field, where he found the Pikeman proudly awaiting anyone who might presume to accept his challenge.

So Peppercorn and the Pikeman fought, and before very long the first son-in-law of the king was slain. Then Peppercorn returned home quickly, and, opening his box, bade the bee and fly take away the horse and the fine clothes.

The king sought everywhere for the stranger who had killed his son-in-law, but no one knew anything about him. So, after some days, the city crier went round again, proclaiming that the Mill-turner, the second son-in-law of the king, would fight anyone who dared to meet him.

Peppercorn again let out his bee and his fly, and asked for a finer horse and handsomer clothes than the last. So they brought him a very gorgeous suit and a most beautiful coal-black charger, and with these he went on the field to meet the Mill-turner. They fought, but Peppercorn soon killed the king's second son-in-law, and again went to his lodgings, where he ordered the bee and fly to take the horse and clothes with them into their little box.

Now, not only the king but all his people were very much puzzled as to who the powerful knight could be who had killed the two valiant sons-in-law of the king. So a strict search was made, and he was sought everywhere. But no one could tell anything about him, while such horses as he rode and such clothes as he wore were not to be found in the whole kingdom.

Some time had passed since the king's sons-in-law had been killed, and people had begun to be a little quieter and had given up all hope of finding out who the strange knight might be. Then Peppercorn wrote a letter to the king's youngest daughter, and sent it to her by the old woman in whose house he lived. In the letter he told the princess everything that had happened to him since he had sent her up in the basket to his false comrades, and told her also that he himself had slain both of the traitors in fair fight.

The young princess, as soon as she had read the letter, quickly ran to her father and begged him to pardon Peppercorn. The king saw he could not justly deny her this favour, since the two men who had been killed had deceived and deserted their friend, without whose superior courage they would never have been themselves his sons-in-law, seeing that all the three princesses, but for Peppercorn, must have remained in the other world where Yard-high-forehead-and-span-long-beard had carried them.

So, after thinking all this over in his mind, the king told his daughter that he willingly forgave Peppercorn, and that she might invite him to the palace. This the princess did at once, and very soon after, Peppercorn made his appearance before the king in splendid attire and was received very kindly.

Not long afterwards, the marriage of Peppercorn with the beautiful princess, the king's youngest daughter, was celebrated with great rejoicings, and the king built them a fine house near his palace to live in.

There Peppercorn and his princess lived long and happily, and he never had any wish to wander again about the world.

The Trade that No One Knows

A LONG WHILE AGO there lived a poor old couple, who had an only son. The old man and his wife worked very hard to nourish their child well and bring him up properly, hoping that he, in return, would take care of them in their old age.

When, however, the boy had grown up, he said to his parents, "I am a man now, and I intend to marry, so I wish you to go at once to the king and ask him to give me his daughter for wife." The astonished parents rebuked him, saying, "What can you be thinking of? We have only this poor hut to shelter us, and hardly bread enough to eat, and we dare not presume to go into the king's presence, much less can we venture to ask for his daughter to be your wife."

The son, however, insisted that they should do as he said, threatening that if they did not comply with his wishes, he would leave them and go away into the world. Seeing that he was really in earnest in what he said, the unhappy parents promised him they would go and ask for the king's daughter. Then the old mother made a wedding cake in her son's presence, and, when it was ready, she put it in a bag, took her staff in her hand, and went straight to the palace where the king lived. There the king's servants bade her come in, and led her into the hall where His Majesty was accustomed to receive the poor people who came to ask alms or to present petitions.

The poor old woman stood in the hall, confused and ashamed at her worn-out, shabby clothes, and looking as if she were made of stone, until the king said to her kindly, "What do *you* want from me, old mother?"

She dared not, however, tell His Majesty why she had come, so she stammered out in her confusion, "Nothing, Your Majesty."

Then the king smiled a little and said, "Perhaps you come to ask alms?"

Then the old woman, much abashed, replied, "Yes, Your Majesty, if you please!"

Thereupon the king called his servants and ordered them to give the old woman ten crowns, which they did. Having received this money, she thanked His Majesty, and returned home, saying to herself, "I dare say when my son sees all this money he will not think anymore of going away from us."

In this thought, however, she was quite mistaken, for no sooner had she entered the hut than the son came to her and asked impatiently, "Well, mother, have you done as I asked you?"

At this she exclaimed, "Do give up, once and for all, this silly fancy, my son. How could you expect me to ask the king for his daughter to be your wife? That would be a bold thing for a rich nobleman to do, how then can *we* think of such a thing? Anyhow, *I* dared not say one word to the king about it. But only look what a lot of money I have brought back. Now you can look for a wife suitable for you, and then you will forget the king's daughter."

When the young man heard his mother speak thus, he grew very angry, and said to her, "What do I want with the king's money? I don't want his money, but I *do* want his daughter! I see you are only playing with me, so I shall leave you. I will go away somewhere – anywhere – wherever my eyes lead me."

Then the poor old parents prayed and begged him not to go away from them and leave them alone in their old age; but they could only quiet him by promising faithfully that the mother should go again next day to the king, and this time really ask him to give his daughter to her son for a wife.

In the morning, therefore, the old woman went again to the palace, and the servants showed her into the same hall she had been in before. The king, seeing her stand there, inquired, "What want you, my old woman, now?"

She was, however, so ashamed that she could hardly stammer, "Nothing, please, Your Majesty."

The king, supposing that she came again to beg, ordered his servants to give her this time also ten crowns.

With this money the poor woman returned to her hut, where her son met her, asking, "Well, mother, *this* time I hope you have done what I asked you?" But she replied, "Now, my dear son, do leave the king's daughter in peace. How can you really think of such a thing? Even if she would marry you, where is the house to bring her to? So be quiet, and take this money which I have brought you."

At these words the son was angrier than before, and said sharply, "As I see you will not let me marry the king's daughter, I will leave you this moment and never come back again"; and, rushing out of the hut, he ran away.

His parents hurried after him, and at length prevailed on him to return, by swearing to him that his mother should go again to the king next morning and really and in truth ask His Majesty this time for his daughter.

So the young man agreed to go back home and wait until the next day.

On the morrow the old woman, with a heavy heart, went to the palace, and was shown as before into the king's presence. Seeing her there for the third time, His Majesty asked her impatiently, "What do you want this time, old woman?" And she, trembling all over, said, "Please, Your Majesty – nothing." Then the king exclaimed, "But it cannot be nothing. Something you must want, so tell me the truth at once, if you value your life!" Thereupon the old woman was forced to tell all the story to the king; how her son had a great desire to marry the princess, and so had forced her to come and ask the king to give her to him for wife.

When the king had heard everything, he said, "Well, after all, *I* shall say nothing against it if my daughter will consent to it." He then told his servants to lead the princess into his presence. When she came, he told her all about the affair, and asked her, "Are you willing to marry the son of this old woman?"

The princess answered, "Why not? If only he learns first the trade that no one knows!" Thereupon the king bade his attendants give money to the poor woman, who now went back to her hut with a light heart.

The moment she entered, her son asked her, "Have you engaged her?" And she returned, "Do let me get my breath a little! Well, *now* I have really asked the king; but it is of no use, for the princess declares she will not marry you until you have learnt the trade that no one knows!"

"Oh, that matters nothing!" exclaimed the son. "Now I only know the condition, it's all right!" The next morning the young man set out on his travels through the world in search of a man who could teach him the trade that no one knows. He wandered about a long time without being able to find out where he could learn such a trade. At length one day, being quite tired out with walking and very sad, he sat down on a fallen log by the wayside. After he had sat thus a little while, an old woman came up to him and asked, "Why art thou so sad, my son?" And he answered, "What is the use of your asking, when you cannot help me?" But she continued, "Only tell me what is the matter, and perhaps I can help you." Then he said, "Well, if you must know, the matter is this: I have been travelling about the world a long time to find a master who can teach me the trade which no one knows." "Oh, if it is only that," cried the old woman, "just listen to me! Don't be afraid, but go straight into the forest which lies before you, and there you will find what you want."

The young man was very glad to hear this, and got up at once and went to the forest. When he had gone pretty far in the wood, he saw a large castle, and, whilst he stood looking at it and wondering what it was, four giants came out of it and ran up to him, shouting, "Do you wish to learn the trade that no one knows?" He said, "Yes, that is just the reason why I came here." Whereupon they took him into the castle.

Next morning the giants prepared to go out hunting, and, before leaving, they said to him, "You must on no account go into the first room by the dining hall." Hardly, however, were the giants well out of sight before the young man began to reason thus with himself: "I see very well that I have come into a place from which I shall never go out alive with my head, so I may as well see what is in the room, come what may afterwards." So he went and opened the door a little and peeped in. There stood a golden ass, bound to a golden manger. He looked at it a little, and was just going to shut the door when the ass said, "Come and take the halter from my head, and keep it hidden about you. It will serve you well if you only understand how to use it." So he took the halter, and, after fastening the room door, quickly concealed it under his clothes.

He had not sat very long before the giants came home. They asked him at once if he had been in the first room, and he, much frightened, replied, "No, I have not been in." "But we know that you have been!" said the giants in great anger, and, seizing some large sticks, they beat him so severely that he could hardly stand on his feet. It was very lucky for him that he had the halter wound round his body under his clothes, or else he would certainly have been killed.

The next day the giants again prepared to go out hunting, but before leaving him they ordered him on no account to enter the second room.

Almost as soon as the giants had gone away, he became so very curious to see what might be in the second room, that he could not resist going to the door. He stood there a little, thinking within himself, "Well, I am already more dead than alive, much worse cannot happen to me!" And so he opened the door and looked in. There he was surprised to see a very beautiful girl, dressed all in gold and silver, who sat combing her hair, and setting in every tress a large diamond. He stood admiring her a little while, and was just going to shut the door again, when she spoke, "Wait a minute, young man. Come and take this key, and mind you keep it safely. It will serve you some time, if you only know how to use it." So he went in and took the key from the girl, and then, going out, fastened the door and went and sat down in the same place he had sat before.

He had not remained there very long before the giants came home from hunting. The moment they entered the house they took up their large sticks to beat him, asking, at the same time, whether he had been in the second room.

Shaking all over with fear, he answered them, "No, I have not!"

"But we know that you have been," shouted the giants in great anger, and they then beat him worse than on the first day.

The next morning, as the giants went out as usual to hunt, they said to him, "Do not go into the third room, for anything in the world; for if you do go in, we shall not forgive you as we did yesterday and the day before! We shall kill you outright!" No sooner, however, had the giants gone out of sight, than the young man began to say to himself, "Most likely they will kill me, whether I go into the room or not. Besides, if they do not kill me, they have beaten me so badly already that I am sure I cannot live long, so, anyhow, I will go and see what is in the third room." Then he got up and went and opened the door.

He was quite shocked, however, when he saw that the room was full of human heads! These heads belonged to young men who had come, like himself, to learn the trade that no one knows, and who, not having obeyed faithfully and strictly the orders of the giants, had been killed by them.

The young man was turning quickly to go away, when one of the heads called out, "Don't be afraid, but come in!" Thereupon he went into the room. Then the head gave him an iron chain, and said, "Take care of this chain, for it will serve you some time if you know how to use it!" So he took the chain, and, going out, fastened the door.

He went and sat down in the usual place to wait for the coming home of the giants, and, as he waited, he grew quite frightened, for he fully expected that they would really kill him this time.

The instant the giants came home they took up their thick sticks and began to beat him without stopping to ask anything. They beat him so terribly that he was all but dead; then they threw him out of the house, saying to him, "Go away now, since you have learnt the trade that no one knows!" When he had lain a long time on the ground where they had thrown him, feeling very sore and miserable, at length he tried to move away, saying to himself, "Well, if they really have taught me the trade that no one knows, for the sake of the king's daughter I can suffer gladly all this pain, if I can only win her!"

After travelling for a long time, the young man came at last to the palace of the king whose daughter he wished to marry. When he saw the palace, he was exceedingly sad, and remembered the words of the princess; for, after all his wanderings and sufferings, he had learnt no trade, and had never been able to find what trade it was "that no one knows."

Whilst considering what he had better do, he suddenly recollected the halter, the key, and the iron chain, which he had carried concealed about him ever since he left the castle of the four giants. He then said to himself, "Let me see what these things can do!" So he took the halter and struck the earth with it, and immediately a handsome horse, beautifully caparisoned, stood before him. Then he struck the ground with the iron chain, and instantly a hare and a greyhound appeared, and the hare began to run quickly and the greyhound to follow her. In a moment the young man hardly knew himself, for he found himself in a fine hunting-dress, riding on the horse after the hare, which took a path that passed immediately under the windows of the king's palace.

Now, it happened that the king stood at a window looking out, and noticed at once the beautiful greyhound which was chasing the hare, and the very handsome horse which a huntsman in a splendid dress was mounted on. The king was so pleased with the appearance of the horse and the greyhound that he called instantly some of his servants, and, sending them after the strange rider, bade them invite him to come to the palace. The young man, however, hearing some people coming behind him calling and shouting, rode quickly behind a thick bush, and shook a little the halter and the iron chain. In a moment the horse, the greyhound, and the hare had vanished, and he found himself sitting on the ground under the trees dressed in his old shabby clothes. By this time the king's servants had come up, and, seeing him sitting there, they asked him whether he had seen a fine huntsman on a beautiful horse pass that way. But he answered them rudely, "No! I have not seen anyone pass, neither do I care to look to see who passes!"

Then the king's servants went on and searched the forest, calling and shouting as loudly as they could, but it was all in vain; they could neither see nor hear anything of the hunter. At length they went back to the king, and told him that the horse the huntsman rode was so exceedingly quick that they could not hear anything of him in the forest.

The young man now resolved to go to the hut where his old parents lived; and they were glad to see that he had come back to them once more.

Next morning, the son said to his father, "Now, father, I will show you what I have learned. I will change myself into a beautiful horse, and you must lead me into the city and sell me, but be very careful not to give away the halter, or else I shall remain always a horse!" Accordingly, in a moment he changed himself into a horse of extraordinary beauty, and the father took him to the marketplace to sell him. Very soon a great number of people gathered round the horses wondering at his unusual beauty, and very high prices were offered for him; the old man, however, raised the price higher and higher at every offer.

The news spread quickly about the city that a wonderfully handsome horse was for sale in the marketplace, and at length the king himself heard of it, and sent some servants to bring the horse, that he might see it. The old man led the horse at once before the palace, and the king, after looking at it for some time with great admiration, could not help exclaiming, "By my word, though I am a king, I never yet saw, much less rode, so handsome a horse!" Then he asked the old man if he would sell it him. "I will sell it to Your Majesty, very willingly," said the old man, "but I will sell only the horse, and not the halter." Thereupon the king laughed, saying, "What should I want with your dirty halter? For such a horse I will have a halter of gold made!" So the horse was sold to the king for a very high price, and the old man returned home with the money.

Next morning, however, there was a great stir and much consternation in the royal stables, for the beautiful horse had vanished somehow during the night. And at the time when the horse disappeared, the young man returned to his parents' hut.

A day or two afterwards the young man said to his father, "Now I will turn myself into a fine church not far from the king's palace, and if the king wishes to buy it, you may sell it to him, only be sure not to part with the key, or else I must remain always a church!"

When the king got up that morning and went to his window to look out, he saw a beautiful church which he had never noticed before. Then he sent his servants out to see what it was, and soon after they came back saying that the church belonged to an old pilgrim, who told them that he was willing to sell it if the king wished to buy it. Then the king sent to ask what price he would sell it for, and the pilgrim replied, "It is worth a great deal of money."

Whilst the servants were bargaining with the father, an old woman came up. Now, this was the same old woman who had sent the young man to the castle of the four giants, and she herself had been there and had learnt the trade that no one knew. As she understood at once all about the church and had no mind to have a rival in the trade, she resolved to put an end to the young man. For this purpose she began to outbid the king, and offered, at last, so very large a sum of ready money that the old man was quite astonished and confused at seeing the money which she showed him. He accordingly accepted her offer, but whilst he was counting the money, quite forgot about the key.

Before long, however, he recollected what his son had said, and then, fearing some mischief, he ran after the old woman and demanded the key back. But the old woman could not be persuaded to give back the key, and said it belonged to the church which she had bought and paid for. Seeing she would not give up the key, the old man grew more and more alarmed, lest some ill should befall his son, so he took hold of the old woman by the neck and forced her to drop the key. She struggled very hard to get it back again, and, whilst the old man and she wrestled together, the key changed itself suddenly into a dove and flew away high in the air over the palace gardens.

When the old woman saw this, she changed herself into a hawk and chased the dove. Just, however, as the hawk was about to pounce upon it, the dove turned itself into a beautiful bouquet and dropped down into the hand of the king's daughter, who happened to be walking in the garden. Then the hawk changed again into the old woman, who went to the gate of the palace and begged very hard that the princess would give her that bouquet, or, at least, one single flower from it.

But the princess said, "No! not for anything in the world. These flowers fell to me from heaven!" The old woman, however, was determined to get one flower from the bouquet, so, seeing the princess would not hear her, she went straight to the king, and begged piteously that he would order his daughter to give her one of the flowers from her bouquet. The king, thinking the old woman wanted one of the flowers to cure some disease, called his daughter to him, and told her to give one to the beggar.

But just as the king said this, the bouquet changed itself into a heap of millet seed and scattered itself all over the ground. Then the old woman quickly changed herself into a hen and chickens, and began greedily to pick up the seeds. Suddenly, however, the millet vanished, and in its place appeared a fox, which sprang on the hen and killed her.

Then the fox changed into the young man, who explained to the astonished king and princess that he it was who had demanded the hand of the princess, and that, in order to obtain it, he had wandered all over the world in search of someone who could teach him "the trade that no one knows."

When the king and his daughter heard this, they gladly fulfilled their part of the bargain, seeing how well the young man had fulfilled his.

Then, shortly afterwards, the king's daughter married the son of the poor old couple; and the king built for the princess and her husband a palace close to his own. There they lived long and had plenty of children, and people say that some of their descendants are living at present, and that these go constantly to pray in the church, which is always open because the key of it turned itself into a young man who married the king's daughter after he had shown to her that he had done as she wished, and learnt, for her sake, "the trade that no one knows."

About the Maiden Swifter than a Horse

ONCE UPON A TIME there lived a maiden. She had not been begotten by a father and a mother, but the Vile had shaped her out of snow, which they had fetched up on St. Elias's Day in the height of summer from out of a bottomless pit. The wind had breathed life into the form; dew had nourished it; the forest had clothed it with leaves; and the meadow had adorned it with most beautiful flowers. She was whiter than the snow, rosier than the prettiest rose, more brilliant than the sun. She was so beautiful that there never was a girl like her, nor ever will be.

This maiden announced on a certain day that on a fixed date a race would be held in such and such a place, and that she would marry the youth who on horseback would be able to overtake her, relying on her own fleetness. Within a few days the news had spread throughout the world, and thousands of suitors at once gathered together, all mounted on the most magnificent steeds, each one appearing still more splendid than the other. Even the Tsar's son came into the racecourse. The suitors, all seated on horseback, now took their places side by side in a row; the maiden, however, without a horse, stood in their midst and said, "There, near the goal, I have set up a golden apple. Whoever arrives there first and takes the apple may claim me as his wife. But if I reach the goal before you and get the apple, all of you will then drop dead. So now you know the risk, therefore consider well what you are going to do."

The horsemen, however, were all infatuated; each hoped to win the maiden, and they said to one another, "We are absolutely certain that the maiden on foot cannot escape any one of us, and someone whom God and Fortune favour must and will lead her home!" Then, on a given signal, they all raced along the course. When they had covered half the distance, the girl was already far ahead, for she spread out tiny wings under her shoulders. Then the horsemen swore at one another, and spurred and whipped their horses, and they were just coming close up to the maiden when she, perceiving it, pulled a hair from the top of her head and threw it away. At once a large wood arose, and the suitors lost all sense of direction. Only after some time they succeeded in tracking the maiden, who, of course, was now far ahead.

But again the horsemen spurred and whipped their horses, and again overtook her. And the maiden saw herself to be in danger of defeat; she wept a tear, and the tear grew into a rapid and roaring river, in which nearly all the suitors got drowned; and only the Tsar's son, swimming with his horse through the river, pursued the maiden. And when he saw that the maiden had passed quickly ahead, he threw a spell over her, mentioning the name of God and asking her to stand still. This she did. He picked her up, put her behind him on his horse, swam back through the river, and returned home through a chain of mountains; but when he had reached the highest mountain peak and turned round, the maiden had vanished.

Clothes Made of Dew and Sunrays

ONCE UPON A TIME there was an emperor, the father of an only daughter, whose beauty was great beyond all belief. The emperor caused an announcement to be made that would give her in marriage to a youth who could guess what kind of birthmark she had and where it was. In addition, the fortunate young man was to have half his empire. But anyone who failed to guess the truth would either be turned into a black lamb or have his head chopped off. The news soon spread throughout the world, and thousands of suitors came, but all

in vain. An incredibly large number of youths were turned into black lambs; the others had their heads chopped off.

The rumour about the beautiful princess also reached a youth, who, though poor, was thoughtful and wise. He was seized with a great longing to possess both the maiden and the half share in the empire. So he set out, and went not to woo the girl, but just to see her and ask her something.

When he came to the Imperial Court, he beheld most remarkable things. The palace simply swarmed with lambs of all kinds, and gambolling about him, they began to bleat as though they wanted to induce him to desist from his plan lest he too might be turned into a black lamb. At the same time, all the chopped-off heads, stuck on poles in a long row, began to shed tears. When he saw this, the horror of it overwhelmed him so that he was just on the point of retracing his steps. But a man clad in a blood-soaked garment, with wings and with only one eye in the middle of his forehead, stopped him and said, "Where are you going? Back, else you are lost!"

Then he turned back again and betook himself to the princess, who was already waiting for him, and asked, "Are you, too, come to marry me?" "No, happy princess, but since I have heard that you intend getting married, I have come to inquire whether you might not be in need of really beautiful bridal clothes?" "And what kind of garments are they which you could offer me?" she asked. And he replied, "I have ever such pretty hose made of marble; a dainty skirt made of dew; a shawl into which are woven golden sunrays, the stars, and the moon; I have also wonderful shoes made of purest gold, and they are neither a shoemaker's nor a goldsmith's work. If you desire to buy all these nice things, command me and I will fetch them. But you must know this, if you want to try on these grand garments one after another, no one but myself must be permitted to be present. If the clothes should fit you, I am sure we shall come to terms; if they do not fit you, I undertake not to show them to anybody else, but will keep them for my own future bride." The princess was allured by his description, and ordered him to fetch the things. He went and brought everything, and God only knows how he came by these garments.

Both now locked themselves in a room, and she began by first putting on the hose. He, however, paid the greatest attention whether he might not behold the mole somewhere, and, lo! fortunately he noticed it near her right knee, and it looked like a golden star. Of course, he did not betray that he had seen the mole, and only thought to himself, "Well, I have made my fortune for the remainder of my life." Then the princess tried on the dainty skirt and all the other things, but he paid no longer any heed whether there might be another mark. Everything fitted her as though it had been specially made for her. They then concluded the bargain, and she paid him what he asked. He took his money, and procured for himself the most magnificent and splendid raiments that could be found anywhere. And some days afterwards he went to the emperor to seek the princess in marriage.

When he stepped before the emperor, he commenced speaking: "Most gracious emperor! I have come to ask for your daughter's hand; do not refuse her to me!" "Very well," said the emperor to him, "but do you know in what manner men have to woo my daughter? Beware! If you do not guess the mark she has, you are lost; but if you can guess its place, my daughter shall be yours and with her half the empire." Then he bowed to the emperor and said, "Praise be unto you, emperor and father-in-law of mine! If that is so, she belongs to me, for I know she has a golden star on her right knee." The emperor was amazed that he knew this, and since he saw no other way out of it, he gave him his daughter in marriage, and the wedding was duly celebrated.

When the question arose of sharing the empire with him, the son-in-law said, "Willingly I shall renounce half of your empire if you will give back their true shape to these unfortunate men who either have been turned into lambs or had their heads chopped off." Then the emperor said, "To do that is not within my power; only my daughter can restore their true form to these men." Then he appealed to his daughter, and she said, "Very well, let the physicians bleed me underneath this star on my knee. Let every lamb lick up a little of the blood which will well forth, and let the lower lip of each head upon the poles be touched with it, and at once the lambs will resume their natural human shape, and the heads will be restored to life and become human beings as before."

This was accordingly done, and when all had resumed their original shape, the bridegroom invited them all to be his guests at the wedding. And with much singing and beating of drums, he took the maiden home. After he had entertained his guests there too with food and drink, everybody went to his own home, but his newlywed wife stayed with him. And God knows what else befell them after this, of which nowadays one no longer troubles to think.

The Gypsies and the Nobleman

A VERY RICH and powerful nobleman was one day driving through his vast estates. From afar four *Tzigans* noted that he was alone, and greedily coveting his fine carriage horses, determined to deprive him of them.

As the carriage approached, they rushed onto the road, respectfully took off their hats, knelt before him, and one of them began to speak, saying, "O how happy we are to have an opportunity of manifesting to you, O most gracious lord, our deep gratitude for the noble deeds and many acts of kindness with which your late and generous father used to overwhelm us! As we have no valuable presents to offer you, allow us to harness ourselves to your carriage and draw you home."

The haughty nobleman, proud of his father's good deeds, was pleased to assent to this unusual form of courtesy. Two gypsies thereupon detached the horses, harnessed themselves to the carriage, and drew it for some distance. Suddenly, however, they cut themselves loose and ran back to the two other rascals who by this time had got clear away with the horses.

The Era from the Other World

A TURK AND HIS WIFE halted in the shadow of a tree. The Turk went to the river to water his horse, and his wife remained to await his return. Just then an Era passed by and saluted the Turkish woman. "Allah help you, noble lady."

"May God aid you," she returned; "whence do you come?" "I come from the Other World, noble lady." "As you have been in the Other World, have you not, perchance, seen there my son Mouyo, who died a few months ago?" "Oh, how could I help seeing him? He is my immediate neighbour." "Happy me! How is he, then?" "He is well, may God be praised! But he could stand just a little more tobacco and some more pocket-money to pay for black coffee." "Are you going back again? And if so, would you be so kind as to deliver to him this purse with his parent's greetings?" The Era took the money, protesting that he would be only too glad to convey so pleasant a surprise to the youth, and hurried away.

Soon the Turk came back, and his wife told him what had transpired. He perceived at once that she had been victimized, and without stopping to reproach her, he mounted his horse and galloped after the Era, who, observing the pursuit and guessing at once that the horseman was the husband of the credulous woman, made all the speed that he could. There was a mill nearby, and making for it, the Era rushed in and addressed the miller with: "For Goodness' sake, brother, fly! There is a Turkish horseman coming with drawn sword; he will kill you. I heard him say so and have hurried to warn you in time." The miller had no time to ask for particulars. He knew how cruel the Turks were, and without a word he dashed out of the mill and fled up the adjacent rocks.

Meantime the Era placed the miller's hat upon his own head and sprinkled flour copiously over his clothes, that he might look like a miller. No sooner was this done than the Turk came up. Alighting from his horse, he rushed into the mill and hurriedly asked the Era where he had hidden the thief. The Era pointed indifferently to the flying miller on the rock, whereupon the Turk requested him to take care of his horse while he ran and caught the swindler. When the Turk was gone some distance up the hill, our Era brushed his clothes, swiftly mounted the horse, and galloped away. The Turk caught the real miller, and demanded, "Where is the money you took from my wife, swindler?" The poor miller made the sign of the cross and said, "God forbid! I never saw your noble lady, still less did I take her money."

After about half an hour of futile discussion, the Turk was convinced of the miller's innocence, and returned to where he had left his horse. But lo! there was no sign of a horse! He walked sadly back to his wife, and she, seeing that her husband had no horse, asked in surprise, "Where did you go, and what became of your horse?" The Turk replied, "You sent money to our darling son, so I thought I had better send him the horse that he need not go on foot in the Other World!"

Lying for a Wager

ONE DAY A FATHER sent his boy to the mill with corn to be ground, and, at the moment of his departure, he warned him not to grind it in any mill where he should happen to find a beardless man.

When the boy came to a mill, he was therefore disappointed to find that the miller was beardless.

"God bless you, Beardless!" saluted the boy.

"May God help you!" returned the miller.

"May I grind my corn here?" asked the boy.

"Yes, why not?" responded the beardless one. "My corn will be soon ground; you can then grind yours as long as you please."

But the boy, remembering his father's warning, left this mill and went to another up the brook. But Beardless took some grain and, hurrying by a shorter way, reached the second mill first and put some of his corn there to be ground. When the boy arrived and saw that the miller was again a beardless man, he hastened to a third mill; but again Beardless hurried by a shortcut, and reached it before the boy. He did the same at a fourth mill, so that the boy concluded that all millers are beardless men. He therefore put down his sack, and when the corn of Beardless was ground, he took his turn at the mill. When all of his grain had been ground, Beardless proposed, "Listen, my boy! Let us make a loaf of your flour."

The boy had not forgotten his father's injunction to have nothing to do with beardless millers, but as he saw no way out of it, he accepted the proposal. So Beardless now took all the flour, mixed it with water, which the boy brought him, and thus made a very large loaf. Then they fired the oven and baked the loaf, which, when finished, they placed against the wall.

Then the miller proposed, "Listen, my boy! If we were now to divide this loaf between us, there would be little enough for either of us, let us therefore tell each other stories, and whoever tells the greatest lie shall have the whole loaf for himself."

The boy reflected a little and, seeing no way of helping himself, said, "Very well, but you must begin."

Then Beardless told various stories till he got quite tired. Then the boy said, "Eh, my dear Beardless, it is a pity if you do not know any more, for what you have said is really nothing. Only listen, and I shall tell you now the real truth."

The Boy's Story

"In my young days, when I was an old man, we possessed many beehives, and I used to count the bees every morning; I counted them easily enough, but I could never contrive to count the beehives. Well, one morning, as I was counting the bees, I was greatly surprised to find that the best bee was missing, so I saddled a cock, mounted it, and started in search of my bee. I traced it to the seashore, and saw that it had gone over the sea, so I decided to follow it. When I had crossed the water, I discovered that a peasant had caught my bee; he was ploughing his fields with it and was about to sow millet. So I exclaimed, 'That is my bee! How did you get it?' And the ploughman answered, 'Brother, if this is really your bee, come here and take it!' So I went to him and he gave me back my bee, and a sack full of millet on account of the services my bee had rendered him. Then I put the sack on my back, and moved the saddle from the cock to the bee.

"Then I mounted, and led the cock behind me that it might rest a little. As I was crossing the sea, one of the strings of my sack burst, and all the millet poured into the water. When I had got across, it was already night, so I alighted and let the bee loose to graze. As to the cock, I fastened him near me, and gave him some hay. After that, I laid myself down to sleep. When I rose next morning, great was my surprise to see that during the night, the wolves had slaughtered and devoured my bee; and the honey was spread about the valley, knee-deep and ankle-deep on the hills. Then I was puzzled to know in what vessel I could gather up all the honey. Meantime I remembered I had a little axe with me, so I went into the woods to catch a beast, in order to make a bag of its skin. When I reached the forest, I saw two deer dancing on one leg. So I threw my axe, broke their only leg, and caught them both. From those two deer I drew three skins and made a bag of each, and in them gathered up all the honey. Then I loaded the cock with the bags and hurried homeward.

"When I arrived home, I found that my father had just been born, and I was told to go to heaven to fetch some holy water. I did not know how to get there, but as I pondered the matter, I remembered the millet which had fallen into the sea. I went back to that place and found that the grain had grown up quite to heaven, for the place where it had fallen was rather damp, so I climbed up by one of the stems. Upon reaching heaven, I found that the millet had ripened, and an angel had harvested the grain and had made a loaf of it, and was eating it with some warm milk. I greeted him, saying, 'God bless you!' The angel responded, 'May God help you!' and gave me some holy water.

"On my way back I found that there had been a great rain, so that the sea had risen so high that my millet was carried away! I was frightened as to how I should descend again to earth, but at length I remembered that I had long hair – it is so long that when I am standing upright it reaches down to the ground, and when I sit it reaches to my ears. Well, I took out my knife and cut off one hair after another, tying them end to end as I descended on them. Meantime darkness overtook me before I got to the bottom, and so I decided to make a large knot and to pass the night on it. But what was I to do without a fire! The tinderbox I had with me, but I had no wood. Suddenly I remembered that I had in my vest a sewing needle, so I found it, split it and made a big fire, which warmed me nicely. Then I laid myself down to sleep.

When I fell asleep, unfortunately a flame burnt the hair through, and, head over heels, I fell to the ground, and sank into the earth up to my girdle. I moved about to see how I could get out, and, when I found that I was tightly interred, I hurried home for a spade and came back and dug myself out. As soon as I was freed, I took the holy water and started for home.

"When I arrived, reapers were working in the field. It was such a hot day, that I feared the poor men would burn to death, and called to them, 'Why do you not bring here our mare which is two days' journey long and half a day broad, and on whose back large willows are growing? She could make some shade where you are working.' My father, hearing this, quickly brought the mare, and the reapers continued working in the shade. Then I took a jug in which to fetch some water. When I came to the well, I found the water was quite frozen, so I took my head off and broke the ice with it. Then I filled the jug and carried the water to the reapers. When they saw me, they asked me, 'Where is your head?' I lifted my hand, and, to my great surprise, my head was not upon my shoulders, and then I remembered having left it by the well. I went back at once, but found that a fox was there before me, and was busy devouring my head. I approached slowly and struck the beast fiercely with my foot, so that in great fear it dropped a little book. This I picked up and, on opening it, found written in it these words: 'The whole loaf is for thee, and Beardless is to get nothing!'"

Saying this, the boy took hold of the loaf and made off. As for Beardless, he was speechless, and remained gazing after the boy in astonishment.

The Maiden Wiser than the Tsar

LONG AGO there lived an old man, who dwelt in a poor cottage. He possessed one thing only in the world, and that was a daughter who was so wise that she could teach even her old father.

One day the man went to the tsar to beg, and the tsar, astonished at his cultivated speech, asked him whence he came and who had taught him to converse so well. He told the tsar where he lived, and that it was his daughter who had taught him to speak with eloquence.

"And where was your daughter taught?" asked the tsar.

"God and our poverty have made her wise," answered the poor man.

Thereupon the tsar gave him thirty eggs and said, "Take these to your daughter, and command her in my name to bring forth chickens from them. If she does this successfully, I will give her rich presents, but if she fails you shall be tortured."

The poor man, weeping, returned to his cottage and told all this to his daughter. The maiden saw at once that the eggs which the tsar had sent were boiled, and bade her father rest while she considered what was to be done. Then while the old man was sleeping, the girl filled a pot with water and boiled some beans.

Next morning she woke her father and begged him to take a plough and oxen and plough near the road where the tsar would pass. "When you see him coming," said she, "take a handful of beans, and while you are sowing them you must shout, 'Go on, my oxen, and may God grant that the boiled beans may bear fruit!' Then," she went on, "when the tsar asks you, 'How can you expect boiled beans to bear fruit?' answer him: 'just as from boiled eggs one can produce chicks!'"

The old man did as his daughter told him, and went forth to plough. When he saw the tsar, he took out a handful of beans, and exclaimed, "Go on, my oxen! And may God grant that the boiled beans may bear fruit!" Upon hearing these words, the tsar stopped his carriage and said to the man, "My poor fellow, how can you expect boiled beans to bear fruit?"

"Just as from boiled eggs one can produce chicks!" answered the apparently simple old man.

The tsar laughed and passed on, but he had recognized the old man, and guessed that his daughter had instructed him to say this. He therefore sent officers to bring the peasant into his presence. When the old man came, the tsar gave him a bunch of flax, saying, "Take this, and make out of it all the sails necessary for a ship. If you do not, you shall lose your life."

The poor man took the flax with great fear, and went home in tears to tell his daughter of his new task. The wise maiden soothed him, and said that if he would rest she would contrive some plan. Next morning she gave her father a small piece of wood, and bade him take it to the tsar with the demand that from it should be made all the necessary tools for spinning and weaving, that he should thereby be enabled to execute His Majesty's order. The old man obeyed, and when the tsar heard the extraordinary request, he was greatly astounded at the astuteness of the girl, and, not to be outdone, he took a small glass, saying, "Take this little glass to your daughter, and tell her she must empty the sea with it, so that dry land shall be where the ocean now is."

The old man went home heavily to tell this to his daughter. But the girl again reassured him, and next morning she gave him a pound of tow, saying, "Take this to the tsar and say that when with this tow he dams the sources of all rivers and streams, I will dry up the sea."

The Tsar Sends for the Girl

The father went back to the tsar and told him what his daughter had said, and the tsar, seeing that the girl was wiser than himself, ordered that she should be brought before him. When she appeared, the tsar asked her, "Can you guess what it is that can be heard at the greatest distance?" And the girl answered, "Your Majesty, there are two things: the thunder and the lie can be heard at the greatest distance!"

The astonished tsar grasped his beard, and, turning to his attendants, exclaimed, "Guess what my beard is worth?" Some said so much, others again so much; but the maiden observed to the tsar that none of his courtiers had guessed right. "His Majesty's beard is worth as much as three summer rains," she said. The tsar, more astonished than ever, said, "The maiden has guessed rightly!"

Then he asked her to become his wife, for "I love you," said he. The girl had become enamoured of the tsar, and she bowed low before him and said, "Your glorious Majesty! Let it be as you wish! But I pray that Your Majesty may be graciously pleased to write with your own hand on a piece of parchment that, should you or any of your courtiers ever be displeased with me, and in consequence banish me from the palace, I shall be allowed to take with me any one thing which I like best."

The tsar gladly consented, wrote out this declaration, and affixed his signature.

Some years passed by happily, but there came at last a day when the tsar was offended with the tsarina, and he said angrily, "You shall be no longer my wife. I command you to leave my palace!"

The tsarina answered dutifully, "O most glorious tsar, I will obey; permit me to pass but one night in the palace, and tomorrow I will depart."

To this the tsar assented.

That evening at supper, the tsarina mixed certain herbs in wine and gave the cup to the tsar, saying, "Drink, O most glorious tsar! And be of good cheer! I am to go away, but, believe me, I shall be happier than when I first met you!"

The tsar, having drunk the potion, fell asleep. Then the tsarina, who had a coach in readiness, placed the tsar in it and carried him off to her father's cottage.

When His Majesty awoke next morning and saw that he was in a cottage, he exclaimed, "Who brought me here?"

"I did," answered the tsarina.

The tsar protested, saying, "How have you dared do so? Did I not tell you that you are no longer my wife?"

Instead of answering, the tsarina produced the parchment containing the tsar's promise, and he could not find a word to say.

Then the tsarina said, "As you see, you promised that, should I be banished from your palace, I should be at liberty to take with me that which I liked best!"

Hearing this, the tsar's love for his spouse returned, he took her in his arms, and they returned to the palace together.

He Whom God Helps No One Can Harm

ONCE UPON A TIME there lived a man and his wife, and they were blessed with three sons. The youngest son was the most handsome, and he possessed a better heart than his brothers, who thought him a fool. When the three brothers had arrived at the man's estate, they came together to their father, each of them asking permission to marry. The father was embarrassed with this sudden wish of his sons, and said he would first take counsel with his wife as to his answer.

The First Quest

A few days later the man called his sons together and told them to go to the neighbouring town and seek for employment. "He who brings me the finest rug will obtain my permission to marry first," he said.

The brothers started off to the neighbouring town together. On the way, the two elder brothers began to make fun of the youngest, mocking his simplicity, and finally they forced him to take a different road.

Abandoned by his malicious brothers, the young man prayed for God to grant him good fortune. At length he came to a lake, on the further shore of which was a magnificent castle. The castle belonged to the daughter of a tyrannous and cruel prince who had died long ago. The young princess was uncommonly beautiful, and many a suitor had come there to ask for her hand. The suitors were always made very welcome, but when they went to their rooms at night, the late master of the castle would invariably come as a vampire and suffocate them.

As the youngest brother stood upon the shore wondering how to cross the lake, the princess noticed him from her window and at once gave an order to the servants to take a boat and bring the young man before her. When he appeared, he was a little confused, but the noble maiden reassured him with some kind words – for he had, indeed, made a good impression upon her, and she liked him at first sight. She asked him whence he came and where he intended to go, and the young man told her all about his father's command.

When the princess heard that, she said to the young man, "You will remain here for the night, and tomorrow morning we will see what we can do about your rug."

After they had supped, the princess conducted her guest to a green room, and, bidding him goodnight, said, "This is your room. Do not be alarmed if during the night anything unusual should appear to disturb you."

Being a simple youth, he could not even close his eyes, so deep was the impression made by the beautiful things which surrounded him, when suddenly, toward midnight, there was a great noise. In the midst of the commotion, he heard distinctly a mysterious voice whisper, "This youth will inherit the princely crown; no one can do him harm!" The young man took refuge in earnest prayer, and, when day dawned, he arose safe and sound.

When the princess awoke, she sent a servant to summon the young man to her presence, and he was greatly astonished to find the young man alive; so also was the princess and everyone in the castle.

After breakfast the princess gave her guest a rich rug, saying, "Take this rug to your father, and if he desires aught else, you have only to come back." The young man thanked his fair hostess and with a deep bow took his leave of her.

When he arrived home, he found his two brothers already there; they were showing their father the rugs they had brought. When the youngest exhibited his, they were astounded, and exclaimed, "How did you get hold of such a costly rug? You must have stolen it!"

The Second Quest

At length the father, in order to quieten them, said, "Go once more into the world, and he who brings back a chain long enough to encircle our house nine times shall have my permission to marry first!" Thus the father succeeded in pacifying his sons. The two elder brothers went their way, and the youngest hurried back to the princess. When he appeared, she asked him, "What has your father ordered you to do now?" And he answered, "That each of us should bring a chain long enough to encircle our house nine times." The princess again made him welcome and, after supper, she showed him into a yellow room, saying, "Somebody will come again to frighten you during the night, but you must not pay any attention to him, and tomorrow we will see what we can do about your chain."

And sure enough, about midnight there came many ghosts dancing round his bed and making fearful noises, but he followed the advice of the princess and remained calm and quiet. Next morning a servant came once more to conduct him to the princess, and, after breakfast, she gave him a fine box, saying, "Take this to your father, and if he should desire anything more, you have but to come to me." The young man thanked her and took his leave.

Again he found that his brothers had reached home first with their chains, but these were not long enough to encircle the house even once, and they were greatly astonished when their youngest brother produced from the box the princess had given an enormous gold chain of the required length. Filled with envy, they exclaimed, "You will ruin the reputation of our house, for you must have stolen this chain!"

The Third Quest

At length the father, tired of their jangling, sent them away, saying, "Go, bring each of you his sweetheart, and I will give you permission to marry." Thereupon the two elder brothers went joyfully to fetch the girls they loved, and the youngest hurried away to the princess to tell her what was now his father's desire. When she heard, the princess said, "You must pass a third night here, and then we shall see what we can do."

So, after supping together, she took him into a red room. During the night he heard again a blood-curdling noise, and from the darkness a mysterious voice said, "This young man is about to take possession of my estates and crown!" He was assaulted by ghosts and vampires, and was dragged from his bed. But through all the young man strove earnestly in prayer, and God saved him.

Next morning when he appeared before the princess, she congratulated him on his bravery, and declared that he had won her love. The young man was overwhelmed with happiness, for although he would never have dared to reveal the secret of his heart, he also loved the princess. A barber was now summoned to attend upon the young man, and a tailor to dress him like a prince. This done, the couple went together to the castle chapel and were wedded.

A few days later they drove to the young man's village, and as they stopped outside his home, they heard great rejoicing and music, whereat they understood that his two elder brothers were celebrating their marriage feasts. The youngest brother knocked on the gate, and when his father came, he did not recognize his son in the richly attired prince who stood before him. He was surprised that such distinguished guests should pay him a visit, and still more so when the prince said, "Good man, will you give us your hospitality for tonight?" The father answered, "Most gladly, but we are having festivities in our house, and I fear that these common people will disturb you with their singing and music." To this the young prince said, "Oh, no, it would please me to see the peasants feasting, and my wife would like it even more than I."

They now entered the house, and as the hostess curtsied deeply before them, the prince congratulated her, saying, "How happy you must be to see your two sons wedded on the same day!" The woman sighed. "Ah," said she, "on one hand I have joy and on the other mourning; I had a third son, who went out in the world, and who knows what ill fate may have befallen him?"

After a time the young prince found an opportunity to step into his old room, and put on one of his old suits over his costly attire. He then returned to the room where the feast was spread and stood behind the door. Soon his two brothers saw him, and they called out, "Come here, father, and see your much-praised son, who went and stole like a thief!" The father turned, and seeing the young man, he exclaimed, "Where have you been for so long, and where is your sweetheart?"

Then the youngest son said, "Do not reproach me. All is well with me and with you!" As he spake, he took off his old garments and stood revealed in his princely dress. Then he told his story and introduced his wife to his parents.

The brothers now expressed contrition for their conduct, and received the prince's pardon, after which they all embraced; the feasting was renewed, and the festivities went on for several days. Finally, the young prince distributed amongst his father and brothers large portions of his new lands, and they all lived long and happily together.

The Ram with the Golden Fleece

ONCE UPON A TIME when a certain hunter went to the mountains to hunt, there came toward him a ram with golden fleece. The hunter took his rifle to shoot it, but the ram rushed at him and, before he could fire, pierced him with its horns, and he fell dead. A few days later some of his friends found his body; they knew not who had killed him, and they took the body home and interred it. The hunter's wife hung up the rifle on the wall in her cottage, and when her son grew up he begged his mother to let him take it and go hunting. She, however, would not consent, saying, "You must never ask me again to give you that rifle! It did not save your father's life, and do you wish that it should be the cause of your death?"

One day, however, the youth took the rifle secretly and went out into the forest to hunt. Very soon the same ram rushed out of a thicket and said, "I killed your father; now it is your turn!" This frightened the youth, and he exclaimed, "God help me!" He pressed the trigger of his rifle and, lo! the ram fell dead.

The youth was exceedingly glad to have killed the golden-fleeced ram, for there was not another like it throughout the land. He took off its skin and carried the fleece home, feeling very proud of his prowess. By and by the news spread over the country till it reached the Court, and the king ordered the young hunter to bring him the ram's skin, so that he might see what kind of beasts were to be found in his forests. When the youth brought the skin to the king, the latter said to him, "Ask whatever you like for this skin, and I will give you what you ask!" But the youth answered, "I would not sell it for anything."

It happened that the prime minister was an uncle of the young hunter, but he was not his friend; on the contrary, he was his greatest enemy. So he said to the king, "As he does not wish to sell you the skin, set him something to do which is surely impossible!" The king called the youth back and ordered him to plant a vineyard and to bring him, in seven days' time, some new wine from it. The youth began to weep, and implored that he might be excused from such an impossible task. But the king insisted, saying, "If you do not obey me within seven days, your head shall be cut off!"

The Youth Finds a Friend

Still weeping, the youth went home and told his mother all about his audience with the king, and she answered, "Did I not tell you, my son, that that rifle would cost you your life?" In deep sorrow and bewilderment, the youth went out of the village and walked a long way into the wood. Suddenly a girl appeared before him and asked, "Why do you weep, my brother?" And he answered, somewhat angrily, "Go your way! You cannot help me!" He then went on, but the maiden followed him, and again begged him to tell her the reason of his tears. "For perhaps," she added, "I may, after all, be able to help you." Then he stopped and said, "I will tell you, but I know that God alone can help me." And then he told her all that had happened to him, and about the task he had been set to do.

When she heard the story, she said, "Do not fear, my brother, but go and ask the king to say exactly where he would like the vineyard planted, and then have it dug in perfectly straight lines. Next you must go and take a bag with a sprig of basil in it, and lie down to sleep in the place where the vineyard is to be, and in seven days you will see that there are ripe grapes."

He returned home and told his mother how he had met a maiden who had told him to do a ridiculous thing. His mother, however, said earnestly, "Go, go, my son, do as the maiden bade; you cannot be in a worse case anyhow." So he went to the king as the girl had directed him, and the king gratified his wish. However, he was still very sad when he went to lie down in the indicated place with his sprig of basil.

When he awoke next morning, he saw that the vines were already planted, on the second morning they were clothed with leaves, and by the seventh day they bore ripe grapes. Notwithstanding the girl's promise, the youth was surprised to find ripe grapes at a time of year when they were nowhere to be found. But he gathered them, made wine, and, taking a basketful of the ripe fruit with him, went to the king.

The Second Task

When he reached the palace, the king and the whole court were amazed. The prime minister said, "We must order him to do something absolutely impossible!" And he advised the king to command the youth to build a castle of elephants' tusks.

Upon hearing this cruel order, the youth went home weeping and told his mother what had transpired, adding, "This, my mother, is utterly impossible!" But the mother again advised him, and said, "Go, my son, beyond the village. Maybe you will again meet that maiden!"

The youth obeyed, and, indeed, as soon as he came to the place where he had found the girl before, she appeared before him and said, "You are again sad and tearful, my brother!" And he began to complain of the second impossible task which the king had set him to perform. Hearing this, the girl said, "This will also be easy. But first go to the king and ask him to give you a ship with three hundred barrels of wine and as many kegs of brandy, and also twenty carpenters. Then, when you arrive at such and such a place, which you will find between two mountains, dam the water there, and pour into it all the wine and brandy. Elephants will come down to that spot to drink the water, and will get drunk and fall on the ground. Then your carpenters must at once cut off their tusks and carry them to the place where the king wishes his castle to be built. There you may all lie down to sleep, and within seven days the castle will be ready."

When the youth heard this, he hurried home, and told his mother all about the plan of the maiden. The mother was quite confident, and counselled her son to do everything as directed by the maiden. So he went to the king and asked him for the ship, the three hundred barrels of wine and brandy, as well as the twenty carpenters; and the king gave him all he wanted. Next he went where the girl had told him, and did everything she had advised. Indeed, the elephants came as was expected, drank, and then duly fell down intoxicated. The carpenters cut off the innumerable tusks, took them to the chosen place, and began building, and in seven days the castle was ready. When the king saw this, he was again amazed, and said to his prime minister, "Now what shall I do with him? He is not an ordinary youth! God alone knows who he is!" Thereupon the officer answered, "Give him one more order, and if he executes it successfully, he will prove that he is a supernatural being."

The Third Task

Thus he again advised the king, who called the youth and said to him, "I command you to go and bring me the princess of a certain kingdom, who is living in such and such a castle. If you do not bring her to me, you will surely lose your life!" When the youth heard this, he went straight to his mother and told her of this new task, whereupon the mother advised him to seek his friend once more. He hurried to where beyond the village he had met the girl before, and as he came to the spot, she reappeared.

She listened intently to the youth's account of his last visit to the court, and then said, "Go and ask the king to give you a galley; in the galley there must be made twenty shops with different merchandise in each; in each shop there must, also, be a handsome youth to sell the wares. On your voyage you will meet a man who carries an eagle; you must buy his eagle and pay for it whatever price he may ask. Then you will meet a second man, in a boat carrying in his net a carp with golden scales; you must buy the carp at any cost. The third man whom you will meet, will be carrying a dove, which you must also buy. Then you must take a feather from the eagle's tail, a scale from the carp, and a feather from the left wing of the dove, and give the creatures their freedom.

"When you reach that distant kingdom and are near the castle in which the princess resides, you must open all shops and order each youth to stand at his door. And the girls who come down to the shore to fetch water are sure to say that no one ever saw a ship loaded with such wonderful and beautiful things in their town before; and then they will go and spread the news all over the place. The news will reach the ears of the princess, who will at once ask her father's permission to go and visit the galley. When she comes on board with her ladies-in-waiting, you must lead the party from one shop to another, and bring out and exhibit before her all the finest merchandise you have; thus divert her and keep her on board your galley until evening, then you must suddenly set sail; for by that time it will be so dark that your departure will be unnoticed.

"The princess will have a favourite bird on her shoulder, and, when she perceives that the galley is sailing off, she will turn the bird loose, and it will fly to the palace with a message to her father of what has befallen her. When you see that the bird has flown, you must burn the eagle's feather; the eagle will appear, and, when you command it to catch the bird, it will instantly do so. Next, the princess will throw a pebble into the sea, and the galley will immediately be still. Upon this you must burn the scale of the carp at once; the carp will come to you and you must instruct it to find the pebble and swallow it. As soon as this is done, the galley will sail on again.

"Then you will proceed in peace for a while; but, when you reach a certain spot between two mountains, your galley will be suddenly petrified, and you will be greatly alarmed. The princess will then order you to bring her some water of life, whereupon you must burn the feather of the dove, and when the bird appears, you must give it a small flask in which it will bring you the elixir, after which your galley will sail on again and you will arrive home with the princess without further adventure."

The youth returned to his mother, and she advised him to do as the girl counselled him. So he went to the king and asked for all that was necessary for his undertaking, and the king again gave him all he asked for.

On his voyage everything was accomplished as the girl had foretold, and he succeeded in bringing home the princess in triumph. The king and his prime minister from the balcony of the palace saw the galley returning, and the prime minister said, "Now you really must have him killed as soon as he lands, otherwise you will never be able to get rid of him!"

When the galley reached the port, the princess first came ashore with her ladies-in-waiting, then the handsome young men who had sold the wares, and finally the youth himself. The king had ordered an executioner to be in readiness, and as soon as the youth stepped on shore, he was seized by the king's servants and his head was chopped off.

It was the king's intention to espouse the beautiful princess, and, as soon as he saw her, he approached her with compliments and flattery. But the princess would not listen to his honeyed words; she turned away and asked, "Where is my captor who did so much for me?" And, when she saw that his head had been cut off, she immediately took the small flask and poured some of its contents over the body and, lo! the youth arose in perfect health. When the king and his minister saw this marvellous thing, the latter said, "This young man must now be wiser than ever, for was he not dead, and has he not returned to life?" Whereupon the king, desirous of knowing if it were true that one who has been dead knows all things when he returns to life, ordered the executioner to chop off his head, that the princess might bring him to life again by the power of her wonderful water of life.

But, when the king's head was off, the princess would not hear of restoring him to life, but immediately wrote to her father, telling him of her love for the youth and declaring her wish to marry him, and she described to her father all that had happened. Her father replied, saying that he approved of his daughter's choice, and he issued a proclamation which stated that, unless the people would elect the youth to be their ruler, he would declare war against them. The men of that country immediately recognized that this would be only just, and so the youth became king, wedded the fair princess, and gave large estates and titles to all the handsome youths who had helped him on his expedition.

A Trade Before Everything

ONCE UPON A TIME a king set out in his luxurious pleasure-galley, accompanied by his queen and a daughter. They had proceeded a very little way from the shore when a powerful wind drove the galley far out to sea, where at last it was dashed upon a barren rock. Fortunately there was a small boat upon the galley, and the king, being a good sailor, was able to launch this frail bark, and he rescued his wife and daughter from the waves. After long tossing and drifting, good fortune smiled upon the wanderers; they began to see birds and floating leaves, which indicated that they were approaching dry land. And, indeed, they soon came in sight of shore, and, as the sea was now calm, were able to land without further adventure. But, alas, the king knew no trade, and had no money upon his person. Consequently he was forced to offer his services as a shepherd to a rich landowner, who gave him a hut and a flock of sheep to tend. In these idyllic and simple conditions they lived contentedly for several years, undisturbed by regrets for the magnificence of their past circumstances.

One day the only son of the ruler of that strange country lost his way while riding in the neighbourhood after a fox, and presently he beheld the beautiful daughter of our shepherd. No sooner did his eyes fall upon the maiden than he fell violently in love with her, and she was not unwilling to receive the protestations of undying affection which he poured into her ears. They met again and again, and the maiden consented to marry the prince, provided her parents would approve the match.

The prince first declared his wish to his own parents, who, of course, were greatly astonished at their son's apparently foolish selection, and would not give their consent. But the prince protested solemnly that his resolution was unshakable; he would either marry the girl he loved or remain single all his days. Finally his royal father took pity on him, and sent his first adjutant to the shepherd secretly to ask the hand of his daughter for the prince.

The Condition

When the adjutant came and communicated the royal message, the shepherd asked him, "Is there any trade with which the royal prince is familiar?" The adjutant was amazed at such a question. "Lord forbid, foolish man!" he exclaimed. "How could you expect the heir-apparent to know a trade? People learn trades in order to earn their daily bread; princes possess lands and cities, and so do not need to work."

But the shepherd persisted, saying, "If the prince knows no trade, he cannot become my son-in-law."

The royal courier returned to the palace and reported to the king his conversation with the shepherd, and great was the astonishment throughout the palace when the news became known, for all expected that the shepherd would be highly flattered that the king had chosen his daughter's hand for the prince in preference to the many royal and imperial princesses who would have been willing to marry him for the asking.

The king sent again to the shepherd, but the man remained firm in his resolution. "As long as the prince," said he, "does not know any trade, I shall not grant him the hand of my daughter."

When this second official brought back to the palace the same answer, the king informed his son of the shepherd's condition, and the royal prince resolved to put himself in the way of complying with it.

His first step was to go through the city from door to door in order to select some simple and easy trade. As he walked through the streets, he beheld various craftsmen at their work, but he did not stay until he came to the workshop of a carpet-maker, and this trade appeared to him both easy and lucrative. He therefore offered his services to the master, who gladly undertook to teach him the trade. In due time the prince obtained a certificate of efficiency, and he went to the shepherd and showed it to him, together with samples of his handiwork.

The shepherd examined these and asked the prince, "How much could you get for this carpet?" The prince replied, "If it is made of grass, I could sell it for threepence." "Why, that is a splendid trade," answered the shepherd, "threepence today and another threepence tomorrow would make sixpence, and in two other days you would have earned a shilling! If I only had known this trade a few years ago I would not have been a shepherd." Thereupon he related to the prince and his suite the story of his past life, and what ill fate had befallen him, to the greatest surprise of all. You may be sure that the prince rejoiced to learn that his beloved was highly born and the worthy mate of a king's son. As for his father, he was especially glad that his son had fallen in love, not with the daughter of a simple shepherd, but with a royal princess.

The marriage was now celebrated with great magnificence, and when the festivities came to an end, the king gave the shepherd a fine ship, together with a powerful escort, that he might go back to his country and reassume possession of his royal throne.

The Biter Bit

ONCE UPON A TIME there was an old man who, whenever he heard anyone complain how many sons he had to care for, always laughed and said, "I wish that it would please God to give me a hundred sons!"

This he said in jest; as time went on, however, he had, in reality, neither more nor less than a hundred sons.

He had trouble enough to find different trades for his sons, but when they were once all started in life they worked diligently and gained plenty of money. Now, however, came a fresh difficulty. One day the eldest son came in to his father and said, "My dear father, I think it is quite time that I should marry."

Hardly had he said these words before the second son came in, saying, "Dear father, I think it is already time that you were looking out for a wife for me."

A moment later came in the third son, asking, "Dear father, don't you think it is high time that you should find me a wife?" In like manner came the fourth and fifth, until the whole hundred had made a similar request. All of them wished to marry, and desired their father to find wives for them as soon as he could.

The old man was not a little troubled at these requests. He said, however, to his sons, "Very well, my sons, *I* have nothing to say against your marrying; there is, however, I foresee, one great difficulty in the way. There are one hundred of you asking for wives, and I hardly think we can find one hundred marriageable girls in all the fifteen villages which are in our neighbourhood."

To this the sons, however, answered, "Don't be anxious about that, but mount your horse and take in your sack sufficient engagement-cakes. You must take, also, a stick in your hand so that you can cut a notch in it for every girl you see. It does not signify whether she be handsome or ugly, or lame or blind, just cut a notch in your stick for every one you meet with."

The old man said, "Very wisely spoken, my sons! I will do exactly as you tell me."

Accordingly he mounted his horse, took a sack full of cakes on his shoulder and a long stick in his hand, and started off at once to beat up the neighbourhood for girls to marry his sons.

The old man had travelled from village to village during a whole month, and whenever he had seen a girl he cut a notch in his stick. But he was getting pretty well tired, and he began to count how many notches he had already made. When he had counted them carefully over and over again, to be certain that he had counted all, he could only make out seventy-four, so that still twenty-six were wanting to complete the number required. He was, however, so weary with his month's ride that he determined to return home. As he rode along, he saw a priest driving oxen yoked to a plough, and seemingly very deep in anxious thought about something. Now the old man wondered a little to see the priest ploughing his own cornfields without even a boy to help him; he therefore shouted to ask him why he drove his oxen himself. The priest, however, did not even turn his head to see who called to him, so intent was he in urging on his oxen and in guiding his plough.

The old man thought he had not spoken loud enough, so he shouted out again as loud as he could: "Stop your oxen a little, and tell me why you are ploughing yourself without even a lad to help you, and this, too, on a holy day!"

Now the priest – who was in a perspiration with his hard work – answered testily, "I conjure you by your old age leave me in peace! I cannot tell you my ill-luck."

The Hundred Daughters

At this answer, however, the old man was only the more curious, and persisted all the more earnestly in asking questions to find out why the priest ploughed on a saint's day. At last the priest, tired with his importunity, sighed deeply and said, "Well, if you *will* know, I am the only man in my household, and God has blessed me with a hundred daughters!"

The old man was overjoyed at hearing this, and exclaimed cheerfully, "That's very good! It is just what I want, for *I* have a hundred sons, and so, as you have a hundred daughters, we can be friends!"

The moment the priest heard this he became pleasant and talkative, and invited the old man to pass the night in his house. Then, leaving his plough in the field, he drove the oxen back to the village. Just before reaching his house, however, he said to the old man, "Go yourself into the house whilst I tie up my oxen."

No sooner, however, had the old man entered the yard than the wife of the priest rushed at him with a big stick, crying out, "We have not bread enough for our hundred daughters, and we want neither beggars nor visitors," and with these words she drove him away.

Shortly afterwards the priest came out of the barn, and, finding the old man sitting on the road before the gate, asked him why he had not gone into the house as he had told him to do. Whereupon the old man replied, "I went in, but your wife drove me away!"

Then the priest said, "Only wait here a moment till I come back to fetch you." He then went quickly into his house and scolded his wife right well, saying, "What have you done? What a fine chance you have spoiled! The man who came in was going to be our friend, for he has a hundred sons who would gladly have married our hundred daughters!"

When the wife heard this, she changed her dress hastily, and arranged her hair and headdress in a different fashion. Then she smiled very sweetly, and welcomed with the greatest possible politeness the old man, when her husband led him into the house. In fact, she pretended that she knew nothing at all of anyone having been driven away from their door. And as the old man wanted much to find wives for his sons, he also pretended that he did not know that the smiling housemistress and the woman who drove him away with a stick were one and the self-same person.

So the old man passed the night in the house, and next morning asked the priest formally to give him his hundred daughters for wives for his hundred sons. Thereupon the priest answered that he was quite willing, and had already spoken to his daughters about the matter, and that they, too, were all quite willing. Then the old man took out his "engagement-cakes," and put them on the table beside him, and gave each of the girls a piece of money to *mark*. Then each of the engaged girls sent a small present by him to that one of his sons to whom she was thus betrothed. These gifts the old man put in the bag wherein he had carried the engagement-cakes. He then mounted his horse, and rode off merrily homewards. There were great rejoicings in his household when he told how successful he had been in his search, and that he really had found a hundred girls ready and willing to be married – and these hundred, too, a priest's daughters.

The sons insisted that they should begin to make the wedding preparations without delay, and commenced at once to invite the guests who were to form part of the wedding procession to go to the priest's house and bring home the brides.

Here, however, another difficulty occurred. The old father must find two hundred bride-leaders (two for each bride); one hundred kooms; one hundred starisvats; one hundred chaious (running footmen who go before the processions); and three hundred vojvodes (standard-bearers); and, besides these, a respectable number of other non-official guests. To find all these persons the father had to hunt throughout the neighbourhood for three years; at last, however, they were all found, and a day was appointed when they were to meet at his house, and go thence in procession to the house of the priest.

The Wedding Procession

On the appointed day all the invited guests gathered at the old man's house. With great noise and confusion, after a fair amount of feasting, the wedding procession was formed properly, and set out for the house of the priest, where the hundred brides were already prepared for their departure for their new home.

So great was the confusion, indeed, that the old man quite forgot to take with him one of the hundred sons, and never missed him in the greeting and talking and drinking he was obliged, as father of the bridegrooms, to go through. Now the young man had worked so long and so hard in preparing for the wedding day that he never woke up till long after the procession had started. And everyone had had, like his father, too much to do and too many things to think of to miss him.

The wedding procession arrived in good order at the priest's house, where a feast was already spread out for them. Having done honour to the various good things, and having gone through all the ceremonies usual on such occasions, the hundred brides were given over to their "leaders," and the procession started on its return to the old man's house. But, as they did not set off until pretty late in the afternoon, it was decided that the night should be spent somewhere on the road. When they came, therefore, to a certain river named Luckless, as it was already dark, some of the men proposed that the party should pass the night by the side of the water without crossing over. However, some others of the chief of the party so warmly advised the crossing the river and encamping on the other bank that this course was at length, after a very lively discussion, determined on; accordingly the procession began to move over the bridge.

Just, however, as the wedding party were halfway across the bridge, its two sides began to draw nearer each other, and pressed the people so close together that they had hardly room to breathe – much less could they move forwards or backwards.

The Black Giant

They were kept for some time in this position, some shouting and scolding, others quiet because they were frightened, until at length a black giant appeared, and shouted to them in a terribly loud voice, "Who are you all? Where do you come from? Where are you going?"

Some of the bolder among them answered, "We are going to our old friend's house, taking home the hundred brides for his hundred sons. But unluckily we ventured on this bridge after nightfall, and it has pressed us so tightly together that we cannot move one way or the other."

"And where is your old friend?" inquired the black giant.

Now all the wedding guests turned their eyes towards the old man. Thereupon he turned towards the giant, who instantly said to him, "Listen, old man! Will you give me what you have forgotten at home, if I let your friends pass over the bridge?"

The old man considered some time what it might be that he had forgotten at home, but, at last, not being able to recollect anything in particular that he had left, and hearing on all sides the groans and moans of his guests, he replied, "Well, I will give it you, if you will only let the procession pass over."

Then the black giant said to the party, "You all hear what he has promised, and are all my witnesses to the bargain. In three days I shall come to fetch what I have bargained for."

Having said this, the black giant widened the bridge and the whole procession passed on to the other bank in safety. The people, however, no longer wished to spend the night on the way, so they moved on as fast as they could, and early in the morning reached the old man's house.

As everybody talked of the strange adventure they had met with, the eldest son, who had been left at home, soon began to understand how the matter stood, and went to his father saying, "O my father! you have sold *me* to the black giant!"

Then the old man was very sorry, and troubled. But his friends comforted him, saying, "Don't be frightened! nothing will come of it."

The marriage ceremonies were celebrated with great rejoicings. Just, however, as the festivities were at their height, on the third day, the black giant appeared at the gate and shouted, "Now, give me at once what you have promised."

The old man, trembling all over, went forward and asked him, "What do you want?"

"Nothing but what you have promised me!" returned the black giant.

As he could not break his promise, the old man, very distressed, was then obliged to deliver up his eldest son to the giant, who thereupon said, "Now I shall take your son with me, but after three years have passed, you can come to the Luckless River and take him away."

Having said this, the black giant disappeared, taking with him the young man, whom he carried off to his workshop as an apprentice to the trade of witchcraft.

From that time, the poor old man had not a single moment of happiness. He was always sad and anxious, and counted every year, and month, and week, and even every day, until the dawn of the last day of the three years. Then he took a staff in his hand and hurried off to the bank of the river Luckless. As soon as he reached the river, he was met by the black giant, who asked him, "Why are you come?" The old man answered that he had come to take home his son, according to his agreement.

Thereupon the giant brought out a tray on which stood a sparrow, a turtledove, and a quail, and said to the old man, "Now, if you can tell which of these is your son, you may take him away."

The poor old father looked intently at the three birds, one after the other, and over and over again, but at last he was forced to own that he could not tell which of them was his son. So he was obliged to go away by himself, and was far more miserable than before. He had hardly, however, got halfway home when he thought he would go back to the river and take one of the birds which remembered and looked at him intently.

When he reached the river Luckless, he was again met by the black giant, who brought out the tray again, and placed on it this time a partridge, a titmouse, and a thrush, saying, "Now, my old man, find out which is your son!"

The anxious father again looked at one bird after the other, but he felt more uncertain than before, and so, crying bitterly, again went away.

The Old Woman

Just as the old man was going through a forest, which was between the river Luckless and his house, an old woman met him, and said, "Stop a moment! Where are you hurrying to? And why are you in such trouble?" Now, the old man was so deeply musing over his great unhappiness that he did not at first attend to the old woman. But she followed him, calling after him, and repeating her questions with more earnestness. So he stopped at last, and told her what a terrible misfortune had fallen upon him. When the old woman had listened to the whole story, she said cheerfully, "Don't be cast down! Don't be afraid! Go back again to the river, and, when the giant brings out the three birds, look into their eyes sharply. When you see that one of the birds has a tear in one of its eyes, seize that bird and hold it fast, for it has a human soul."

The old man thanked her heartily for her advice, and turned back, for the third time, towards the Luckless River. Again the black giant appeared, and looked very merry whilst he brought out his tray and put upon it a sparrow, a dove, and a woodpecker, saying, "My old man! find out which is your son!" Then the father looked sharply into the eyes of the birds, and saw that from the right eye of the dove a tear dropped slowly down. In a moment he grasped the bird tightly, saying, "This is my son!" The next moment he found himself holding fast his eldest son by the shoulder, and so, singing and shouting in his great joy, took him quickly home, and gave him over to his eldest daughter-in-law, the wife of his son.

Now, for some time they all lived together very happily. One day, however, the young man said to his father, "Whilst I was apprentice in the workshop of the black giant, I learned a great many tricks of witchcraft. Now I intend to change myself into a fine horse, and you shall take me to market and sell me for a good sum of money. But be sure not to give up the halter."

The father did as the son had said. Next market day he went to the city with a fine horse, which he offered for sale. Many buyers came round him, admiring the horse, and bidding some sums for it, so that at last the old man was able to sell it for two thousand ducats. When he received the money, he took good care not to let go of the halter, and he returned home far richer than he ever dreamt of being.

A few days later, the man who had bought the horse sent his servant with it to the river to bathe, and, whilst in the water, the horse got loose from the servant and galloped off into the neighbouring forest. There he changed himself back into his real shape, and returned to his father's house.

After some time had passed, the young man said one day to his father, "Now I will change myself into an ox, and you can take me to market to sell me. But take care not to give up the rope with which you lead me."

So next market day the old man went to the city leading a very fine ox, and soon found a buyer, who offered ten times the usual price paid for an ox. The buyer asked also for the rope to lead the animal home, but the old man said, "What do you want with such an old thing? You had better buy a new one!" and he went off taking with him the rope.

That evening, whilst the servants of the buyer were driving the ox to the field, he ran away into a wood near, and, having taken there his human shape, returned home to his father's house.

On the eve of the next market day, the young man said to his father, "Now I will change myself into a cow with golden horns, and you can sell me as before, only take care not to give up the string."

Accordingly he changed himself next morning into a cow, and the old man took it to the marketplace, and asked for it three hundred crowns.

But the black giant had learnt that his former apprentice was making a great deal of money by practising the trade he had taught him, and, being jealous at this, he determined to put an end to the young man's gains.

The Giant Buys the Cow

Therefore, on the third day he came to the market himself as a buyer, and the moment he saw the beautiful cow with golden horns, he knew that it could be no other than his former apprentice.

So he came up to the old man, and, having outbid all the other would-be purchasers, paid at once the price he had agreed on. Having done this, he caught the string in his hand, and tried to wrench it from the terrified old man, who called out, "I have not sold you the string, but the cow!" and held the string as fast as he could with both hands.

"Oh, no!" said the buyer, "I have the law and custom on my side! Whoever buys a cow, buys also the string with which it is led!" Some of the amused and astonished lookers-on said that this was quite true, therefore the old man was obliged to give up the string.

The black giant, well satisfied with his purchase, took the cow with him to his castle, and, after having put iron chains on her legs, fastened her in a cellar. Every morning the giant gave the cow some water and hay, but he never unchained her.

One evening, however, the cow, with incessant struggles, managed to get free from the chains, and immediately opened the cellar door with her horns and ran away.

Next morning the black giant went as usual into the cellar, carrying the hay and water for the cow. But seeing she had got free and run away, he threw the hay down, and started off at once to pursue her.

When he came within sight of her, he turned himself into a wolf and ran at her with great fury; but his clever apprentice changed himself instantly from a cow into a bear, whereupon the giant turned himself from a wolf into a lion; the bear then turned into a tiger, and the lion changed into a crocodile, whereupon the tiger turned into a sparrow. Upon this the giant changed from the form of a crocodile into a hawk, and the apprentice immediately changed into a hare; on seeing which the hawk became a greyhound.

Then the apprentice changed from a hare into a falcon, and the greyhound into an eagle; whereupon the apprentice changed into a fish; the giant then turned from an eagle into a mouse, and immediately the apprentice, as a cat, ran after him; then the giant turned himself into a heap of millet, and the apprentice transformed himself into a hen and chickens, which very greedily picked up all the millet except one single seed, in which the master was, who changed himself into a squirrel; instantly, however, the apprentice became a hawk, and, pouncing on the squirrel, killed it.

In this way the apprentice beat his master, the black giant, and revenged himself for all the sufferings he had endured whilst learning the trade of witchcraft. Having killed the squirrel, the hawk took his proper shape again, and the young man returned joyfully to his father, whom he made immensely rich.

The Two Brothers
(A Serbian story from Bosnia)

THERE WAS A MAN who had a wife but no sons, a female hound but no puppies, and a mare but no foal. "What in the world shall I do?" said he to himself. "Come, let me go away from home to seek my fortune in the world, as I haven't any at home." As he thought, so he did, and went out by himself into the white world as a bee from flower to flower.

One day, when it was about dinnertime, he came to a spring, took down his knapsack, took out his provisions for the journey, and began to eat his dinner. Just then a traveller appeared in front of him, and sat down beside the spring to rest. He invited him to sit down by him that they might eat together. When they had inquired after each other's health and shaken hands, then the second corner asked the first on what business he was travelling about the world. He said to him, "I have no luck at home, therefore I am going from home. My wife has no children, my hound has no puppies, and my mare has never had a foal. I am going about the white world as a bee from flower to flower."

When they had had a good dinner and got up to travel further, then the one who had arrived last thanked the first for his dinner, and offered him an apple, saying, "Here is this apple for you," – if I am not mistaken it was a Frederic pippin – "and return home at once; peel the apple and give the peel to your hound and mare; cut the apple in two, give half to your wife to eat, and eat the other half yourself.

What has hitherto been unproductive will henceforth be productive. And as for the two pips which you will find in the apple, plant them on the top of your house." The man thanked him for the apple. They rose up and parted, the one going onwards and the other back to his house. He peeled the apple and did everything as the other had instructed him.

As time went on his wife became the mother of two sons, his hound of two puppies, and his mare of two foals, and, moreover, out of the house grew two apple trees. While the two brothers were growing up, the young horses grew up, and the hounds became fit for hunting. After a short time the father and mother died, and the two sons, being now left alone like a tree cut down on a hill, agreed to go out into the world to seek their fortune. Each brother took a horse and a hound, they cut down the two apple trees and made themselves a spear apiece, and went out into the wide world.

I can't tell you for certain how many days they travelled together; this I do know, that at the first parting of the road they separated. Here they saw it written up: "If you go by the upper road, you will not see the world for five years; if you go by the lower road, you will not see the world for three years." Here they parted, one going by the upper and the other by the lower road. The one that went by the lower road, after three years of travelling through another world, came to a lake, beside which there was written on a post: "If you go in, you will repent it; if you don't go in, you will repent it." "If it is so," thought he to himself, "let me take whatever God gives," and swam across the lake. And lo! a wonder! He, his horse, and his hound were all gilded with gold. After this he speedily arrived at a very large and spacious city. He went up to the emperor's palace and inquired for an inn where he might pass the night. They told him, up there, yon large tower, that was an inn.

In front of this tower he dismounted. Servants came out and welcomed him, and conducted him into the presence of their master in the courtyard. But it was not an innkeeper, but the king of the province himself. The king welcomed and entertained him handsomely. The next day he began to prepare to set forth on his journey.

The evening before, the king's only daughter, when she saw him go in front of her apartments, had observed him well, and fixed her eyes upon him. This she did because such a golden traveller had never before arrived, and consequently she was unable to close her eyes the whole night. Her heart thumped, as it were, and it was fortunate that the summer night was brief, for if it had been a winter one, she could hardly have waited for the dawn. It all seemed to her and whirled in her brain as if the king was calling her to receive a ring and an apple. The poor thing would fly to the door, but it was shut and there was nobody at hand. Although the night was a short one, it seemed to her that three had passed one after another.

When she observed in the morning that the traveller was getting ready to go, she flew to her father, implored him not to let that traveller quit his court, but to detain him and to give her to him in marriage. The king was good-natured, and could easily be won over by entreaties. What his daughter begged for, she also obtained. The traveller was detained and offered marriage with the king's daughter. The traveller did not hesitate long, kissed the king's hand, presented a ring to the maiden, and she a handkerchief to him, and thus they were betrothed. Methinks they did not wait for publication of banns. Erelong they were wedded. The wedding feast and festival were very prolonged, but came to an end in due course.

One morning after all this, the bridegroom was looking in somewhat melancholy fashion down on the country through a window in the tower. His young wife asked him what ailed him. He told her that he was longing for a hunt, and she told him to take three servants and go while the dew was still on the grass. Her husband would not take a single servant, but, mounting his gilded horse and calling his gilded hound, went down into the country to hunt. The hound soon found scent, and put up a stag with gilded horns. The stag began to run straight for a tower, the hound after him, and the hunter after the hound, and he overtook the stag in the gate of the courtyard, and was going to cut off its head.

He had drawn his sword, when a damsel cried through the window, "Don't kill my stag, but come upstairs. Let us play at draughts for a wager. If you win, take the stag; if I win, you shall give me the hound." He was as ready for this as an old woman for a scolding match. He went up into the tower and onto the balcony, staked the hound against the stag, and they began to play. The hunter was on the point of beating her, when some damsels began to sing, "A king, a king, I've gained a king!" He looked round, and she altered the position of the draughtsmen, beat him, and took the hound. Again they began to play a second time, she staking the hound and he his horse. She cheated him the second time also. The third time they began to play, she wagered the horse, and he himself. When the game was nearly over, and he was already on the point of beating her, the damsels began to sing this time too, just as they had done the first and second times. He looked round, she cheated and beat him, took a cord, bound him, and put him in a dungeon.

The brother, who went by the upper road, came to the lake, forded it, and came out all golden – himself, his horse, and his hound. He went for a night's lodging to the king's tower. The servants came out and welcomed him. His father-in-law asked him whether he was tired, and whether he had had any success in hunting. But the king's daughter paid special attention to him, frequently kissing and embracing him. He couldn't wonder enough how it was that everybody recognised him. Finally, he felt satisfied that it was his brother, who was very like him, that had been there and got married. The king's daughter could not wonder enough, and it was very distressing to her, that her newly married husband was so soon tired of her, for the more affectionate she was to him, the more did he repulse her.

When the morrow came, he got ready to go out to look for his brother. The king, his daughter, and all the courtiers begged him to take a rest. "Why," said they to him, "you only returned yesterday from hunting, and do you want to go again so soon?" All was in vain; he refused to take the thirty servants whom they offered him, but went down into the country by himself. When he was in the midst of the country, his hound put up a stag, and he went after them on his horse, and drove it up to a tower. He raised his sword to kill the stag, but a damsel cried through a window, "Don't meddle with my stag, but come upstairs that we may have a game at draughts, then let the one that wins take off the stakes, either you my hound, or I yours." When he went into the basement. In it was a hound and a horse – the hounds and horses recognised each other – and he felt sure that his brother had fallen into prison there.

They began the game at draughts, and when the damsel saw that he was going to beat her, some damsels began to sing behind them, "A king! a king! I've gained a king!" He took no notice, but kept his eye on the draughtsmen. Then the damsel, like a she-devil, began to make eyes and wink at the young man. He gave her a flip with his coat behind the ears. "Play now!" he said, and thus beat her. The second game they both staked a horse. She couldn't cheat him. He took both the hound and the horse from her. The third and last time they played, he staked himself and she herself. And after giving her a slap in her face for her winking and making of eyes, he won the third game. He took possession of her, brought his brother out of the dungeon, and they went to the town.

Now the brother, who had been in prison, began to think within himself, "He was yesterday with my wife, and who knows whether she does not prefer him to me?" He drew his sword to kill him, but the draught-player defended him.

He darted before his brother into the courtyard, and as he stepped onto the passage from the tower, his wife threw her arms round his neck and began to scold him affectionately for having driven her from him overnight, and conversed so coldly with her. Then he repented of having so foolishly suspected his brother, who had, moreover, released him from prison, and of having wanted to kill him. But his brother was a considerate person and forgave him. They kissed each other and were reconciled. He retained his wife and her kingdom with her, and his brother took the draught-player and her kingdom with her. And thus they attained to greater fortune than they could ever have even hoped for.

Uncanny Creatures

ANY NUMBER OF STRANGE creatures are encountered in this chapter, which is composed entirely of magic tales. 'The Bear's Son' is a well-known narrative that features one of the strangest figures in oral traditional narrative: a creature who is half human and half bear. He has had a special birth and a precocious childhood; he also possesses superhuman strength and is able to perform astonishing deeds.

Other magic tales include the helpful talking vixen who appears in 'Animals as Friends and as Enemies; and 'The Lame Fox'. As a female fox, the vixen provides a type of female-helper in animal form. Finally, the dragon is a frightening creature of remarkable size and fury. It is clear that unusual creatures can be the male protagonist (such as the bear's son, who is human plus beast), a female helper, or a destructive dragon.

The Wonderful Hair

THERE ONCE LIVED a man who was very poor, and who had many children – so many that he was unable to support them. As he could not endure the idea of their perishing of hunger, he was often tempted to destroy them; his wife alone prevented him. One night, as he lay asleep, there appeared to him a lovely child in a vision. The child said, "Oh, man! I see your soul is in danger, in the thought of killing your helpless children. But I know you are poor, and am come here to help you. You will find under your pillow in the morning a looking-glass, a red handkerchief, and an embroidered scarf. Take these three things, but show them to no one, and go to the forest. In that forest you will find a rivulet. Walk by the side of this rivulet until you come to its source. There you will see a girl, as bright as the sun, with long hair streaming down her shoulders. Take care that she does you no harm. Say not a word to her, for if you utter a single syllable, she will change you into a fish or some other creature, and eat you. Should she ask you to comb her hair, obey her. As you comb it, you will find one hair as red as blood. Pull it out, and run away with it. Be swift, for she will follow you. Then throw on the ground first the embroidered scarf, then the red handkerchief, and last of all the looking-glass; they will delay her pursuit of you. Sell the hair to some rich man, but see that you do not allow yourself to be cheated, for it is of boundless worth. Its produce will make you rich and thus you will be able to feed your children."

Next morning, when the poor man awoke, he found under his pillow exactly the things the child had told him of in his dream. He went immediately into the forest, and when he had discovered the rivulet, he walked by the side of it, on and on, until he reached its source. There he saw a girl sitting on the bank, threading a needle with the rays of the sun. She was embroidering a net made of the hair of heroes, spread on a frame before her. He approached and bowed to her.

The girl got up and demanded, "Where did you come from, strange knight?" The man remained silent. Again she asked him, "Who are you, and why do you come here?" And many other questions. But he remained silent as a stone, indicating with his hands only that he was dumb and in need of help. She told him to sit at her feet, and when he had gladly done so, she inclined her head toward him, that he might comb her hair. He began to arrange her hair as if to comb it, but as soon as he had found the red one, he separated it from the rest, plucked it out, leaped up, and ran from her with his utmost speed.

The girl sprang after him, and was soon at his heels. The man, turning round as he ran, and seeing that his pursuer would soon overtake him, threw the embroidered scarf on the ground as he had been told. When the girl saw it, she stopped and began to examine it, turning it over on both sides, and admiring the embroidery. Meanwhile the man gained a considerable distance in advance. The girl tied the scarf round her bosom and recommenced the pursuit. When the man saw that she was again about to overtake him, he threw down the red handkerchief. At the sight of it, the girl again stopped, examined, and wondered at it; the peasant, in the meantime, was again enabled to increase the distance between them. When the girl perceived this, she became furious, and, throwing away both scarf and handkerchief, began to run with increased speed after him. She was just upon the point of catching the poor peasant, when he threw the looking-glass at her feet.

At the sight of the looking-glass, the like of which she had never seen before, the girl checked herself, picked it up, and looked in it. Seeing her own face, she fancied there was another girl looking at her. While she was thus occupied, the man ran so far that she could not possibly overtake him. When the girl saw that further pursuit was useless, she turned back, and the peasant, joyful and unhurt, reached his home. Once within doors, he showed the hair to his wife and children, and told them all that had happened to him. But his wife only laughed at the story. The peasant, however, took no heed of her ridicule, but went to a neighbouring town to sell the hair. He was soon surrounded by a crowd of people, and some merchants began to bid for his prize. One merchant offered him one gold piece, another two, for the single hair, and so on, until the price rose to a hundred gold pieces. Meanwhile the king, hearing of the wonderful red hair, ordered the peasant to be called in, and offered him a thousand gold pieces for it. The man joyfully sold it for that sum.

What wonderful kind of hair was this after all? The king split it carefully open from end to end, and in it was found the story of many marvellous secrets of nature, and of things that had happened since the creation of the world.

Thus the peasant became rich, and henceforth lived happily with his wife and children. The child he had seen in his dream was an angel sent down from heaven to succour him, and to reveal to mankind the knowledge of many wonderful things which had hitherto remained unexplained.

The Bear's Son

ONCE UPON A TIME a bear married a woman, and they had one son. When the boy was yet a little fellow, he begged very hard to be allowed to leave the bear's cave, and to go out into the world to see what was in it. His father, the Bear, however, would not consent to this, saying, "You are too young yet, and not strong enough. In the world there are multitudes of wicked beasts called men, who will kill you." So the boy was quieted for a while, and remained in the cave.

But, after some time, the boy prayed so earnestly for the Bear, his father, to let him go into the world, that the Bear brought him into the wood, and showed him a beech tree, saying, "If you can pull up that beech by the roots, I will let you go; but if you cannot, then this is a proof that you are still too weak, and must remain with me." The boy tried to pull up the tree, but, after long trying, had to give it up and go home again to the cave.

Again some time passed, and he then begged again to be allowed to go into the world, and his father told him, as before, if he could pull up the beech tree he might go out into the world. This time the boy pulled up the tree, so the Bear consented to let him go, first, however, making him cut away the branches from the beech, so that he might use the trunk for a club. The boy now started on his journey, carrying the trunk of the beech over his shoulder.

One day as the Bear's son was journeying, he came to a field, where he found hundreds of ploughmen working for their master. He asked them to give him something to eat, and they told him to wait a bit till their dinner was brought them, when he should have some – for, they said, "Where so many are dining one mouth more or less matters but little." Whilst they were speaking, there came carts, horses, mules, and asses, all carrying the dinner. But when the meats were spread out, the Bear's son declared he could eat all that up himself. The workmen wondered greatly at his words, not believing it possible that one man could consume as great a quantity of victuals as would satisfy several hundred men. This, however, the Bear's son persisted in affirming he could do, and offered to bet with them that he would do this. He proposed that the stakes should be all the iron of their ploughshares and other agricultural implements.

To this they assented. No sooner had they made the wager than he fell upon the provisions, and in a short time consumed the whole. Not a fragment was left. Hereupon the labourers, in accordance with their wager, gave him all the iron which they possessed.

When the Bear's son had collected all the iron, he tore up a young birch tree, twisted it into a band, and tied up the iron into a bundle, which he hung at the end of his staff, and, throwing it across his shoulder, trudged off from the astonished and affrighted labourers.

Going on a short distance, he arrived at a forge, in which a smith was employed making a ploughshare. This man he requested to make him a mace with the iron which he was carrying. This the smith undertook to do; but, putting aside half the iron, he made of the rest a small, coarsely finished mace.

The Bear's son saw at a glance that he had been cheated by the smith. Moreover, he was disgusted at the roughness of the workmanship. He however took it, and declared his intention of testing it. Then, fastening it to the end of his club and throwing it into the air high above the clouds, he stood still and allowed it to fall on his shoulder. It had no sooner struck him than the mace shivered into fragments, some of which fell on and destroyed the forge. Taking up his staff, the Bear's son reproached the smith for his dishonesty, and killed him on the spot.

Having collected the whole of the iron, the Bear's son went to another smithy, and desired the smith whom he found there to make him a mace, saying to him, "Please play no tricks on me. I bring you these fragments of iron for you to use in making a mace. Beware that you do not attempt to cheat me as I was cheated before!" As the smith had heard what had happened to the other one, he collected his workpeople, threw all the iron on his fire, and welded the whole together and made a large mace of perfect workmanship.

When it was fastened on the head of his club, the Bear's son, to prove it, threw it up high and caught it on his back. This time the mace did not break, but rebounded. Then the Bear's son got up and said, "This work is well done!" and, putting it on his shoulder, walked away. A little farther on, he came to a field wherein a man was ploughing with two oxen, and he went up to him and asked for something to eat. The man said, "I expect every moment my daughter to come with my dinner, then we shall see what God has given us!" The Bear's son told him how he had eaten up all the dinner prepared for many hundreds of ploughmen, and asked, "From a dinner prepared for one person, how much can come to me or to you?"

Meanwhile the girl brought the dinner. The moment she put it down, the Bear's son stretched out his hand to begin to eat, but the man stopped him. "No," said he, "you must first say grace, as I do!" The Bear's son, hungry as he was, obeyed, and, having said grace, they both began to eat. The Bear's son, looking at the girl who brought the dinner (she was a tall, strong, beautiful girl), became very fond of her, and said to the father, "Will you give me your daughter for a wife?" The man answered, "I would give her to you very gladly, but I have promised her already to the Moustached." The Bear's son exclaimed, "What do I care for Moustachio? I have my mace for him!" But the man answered, "Hush! hush! Moustachio is also somebody! You will see him here soon." Shortly after a noise was heard afar off, and lo! behind a hill a moustache showed itself, and in it were three hundred and sixty-five birds' nests. Shortly after appeared the other moustache, and then came Moustachio himself.

Having reached them, he lay down on the ground immediately to rest. He put his head on the girl's knee, and told her to scratch his head a little. The girl obeyed him, and the Bear's son, getting up, struck him with his club over the head. Whereupon Moustachio, pointing to the place with his finger, said, "Something bit me here." The Bear's son struck him with his mace on another spot, and Moustachio again pointed to the place, saying to the girl, "Something has bitten me here!" When he was struck a third time he said to the girl angrily, "Look, you! Something bites me here!" Then the girl said, "Nothing has bitten you; a man struck you."

When Moustachio heard that, he jumped up, but the Bear's son had thrown away his mace and run away. Moustachio pursued him, and though the Bear's son was lighter than he, and had gained the start of him a considerable distance, he would not give up pursuing him.

At length the Bear's son, in the course of his flight, came to a wide river, and found, near it, some men threshing corn. "Help me, my brothers, help – for God's sake!" he cried. "Help! Moustachio is pursuing me! What shall I do? How can I get across the river?" One of the men stretched out his shovel, saying, "Here, sit down on it, and I will throw you over the river." The Bear's son sat on the shovel, and the man threw him over the water to the other shore. Soon after, Moustachio came up, and asked, "Has anyone passed here?" The threshers replied that a man had passed. Moustachio demanded, "How did he cross the river?" They answered, "He sprang over." Then Moustachio went back a little to take a start, and with a hop he sprang to the other side, and continued to pursue the Bear's son.

Meanwhile this last, running hastily up a hill, got very tired. At the top of the hill he found a man sowing, and the sack with seeds was hanging on his neck. After every handful of seed sown in the ground, the man put a handful in his mouth and ate them. The Bear's son shouted to him, "Help, brother, help – for God's sake! Moustachio is following me, and will soon catch me! Hide me somewhere!" Then the man said, "Indeed, it is no joke to have Moustachio pursuing you. But I have nowhere to hide you, unless in this sack among the seeds." So he put him in the sack. When Moustachio came up to the sower, he asked him if he had seen the Bear's son anywhere. The man replied, "Yes, he passed by long ago, and God knows where he has got to before this!"

Then Moustachio went back again. By-and-by the sower forgot that Bear's son was in the sack, and he took him out with a handful of seeds, and put him in his mouth. Then Bear's son was afraid of being swallowed, so he looked round the mouth quickly, and, seeing a hollow tooth, hid himself in it.

When the sower returned home in the evening, he called to his sisters-in-law, "Children, give me my toothpick! There is something in my broken tooth." The sisters-in-law brought him two iron picks, and, standing one on each side, they poked about with the two picks in his tooth till the Bear's son jumped out. Then the man remembered him, and said, "What bad luck you have! I had nearly swallowed you."

After they had taken supper, they talked about many different things, till at last the Bear's son asked what had happened to break that one tooth, whilst the others were all strong and healthy. Then the man told him in these words: "Once upon a time, ten of us started with thirty horses to the seashore to buy some salt. We found a girl in a field watching sheep, and she asked us where we were going. We said we were going to the seashore to buy salt. She said, 'Why go so far? I have in the bag in my hand here some salt which remained over after feeding the sheep. I think it will be enough for you.' So we settled about the price, and then she took the salt from her bag, whilst we took the sacks from the thirty horses, and we weighed the salt and filled the sacks with it till all the thirty sacks were full. We then paid the girl and returned home. It was a very fine autumn day, but as we were crossing a high mountain, the sky became very cloudy and it began to snow, and there was a cold north wind, so that we could not see our path, and wandered about here and there. At last, by good luck, one of us shouted, 'Here, brothers! Here is a dry place!' So we went in one after the other till we were all, with the thirty horses, under shelter. Then we took the sacks from the horses, made a good fire, and passed the night there as if it were a house. Next morning, just think what we saw! We were all in one man's head, which lay in the midst of some vineyards. And whilst we were yet wondering and loading our horses, the keeper of the vineyards came and picked the head up. He put it in a sling and, slinging it about several times, threw it over his head, and cast it far away over the vines to frighten the starlings away from his grapes. So we rolled down a hill, and it was then that I broke my tooth."

The Golden Apple Tree and the Nine Peahens

ONCE UPON A TIME there lived a king who had three sons. Now, before the king's palace grew a golden apple tree, which in one and the same night blossomed, bore fruit, and lost all its fruit, though no one could tell who took the apples. One day the king, speaking to his eldest son, said, "I should like to know who takes the fruit from our apple tree." And the son said, "I will keep guard tonight, and will see who gathers the apples." So, when the evening came, he went and laid himself down under the apple tree upon the ground to watch. Just as the apples ripened, however, he fell asleep, and when he awoke in the morning there was not a single one left on the tree. Whereupon he went and told his father what had happened. Then the second son offered to keep watch by the tree, but he had no better success than his eldest brother.

94

So the turn came to the king's youngest son to keep guard. He made his preparations, brought his bed under the tree, and immediately went to sleep. Before midnight he awoke and looked up at the tree, and saw how the apples ripened, and how the whole palace was lit up by their shining. At that minute nine peahens flew towards the tree, and eight of them settled on its branches, but the ninth alighted near him and turned instantly into a beautiful girl – so beautiful, indeed, that the whole kingdom could not produce one who could in any way compare with her. She stayed, conversing kindly with him, till after midnight, then, thanking him for the golden apples, she prepared to depart; but, as he begged she would leave him one, she gave him two, one for himself and one for the king, his father. Then the girl turned again into a peahen and flew away with the other eight. Next morning, the king's son took the two apples to his father, and the king was much pleased, and praised his son.

When the evening came, the king's youngest son took his place again under the apple tree to keep guard over it. He again conversed as he had done the night before with the beautiful girl, and brought to his father, the next morning, two apples as before. But, after he had succeeded so well several nights, his two elder brothers grew envious because he had been able to do what they could not. At length they found an old woman, who promised to discover how the youngest brother had succeeded in saving the two apples. So, as the evening came, the old woman stole softly under the bed which stood under the apple tree and hid herself. And after a while came also the king's son, who laid himself down as usual to sleep. When it was near midnight the nine peahens flew up as before, and eight of them settled on the branches and the ninth stood by his bed, and turned into a most beautiful girl.

Then the old woman slowly took hold of one of the girl's curls and cut it off, and the girl immediately rose up, changed again into a peahen and flew away, and the other peahens followed her, and so they all disappeared. Then the king's son jumped up and cried out, "What is that?" And, looking under the bed, he saw the old woman, and drew her out. Next morning he ordered her to be tied to a horse's tail, and so torn to pieces. But the peahens never came back, so the king's son was very sad for a long time, and wept at his loss. At length he resolved to go and look after his peahen, and never to come back again unless he should find her. When he told the king, his father, of his intention, the king begged him not to go away, and said that he would find him another beautiful girl, and that he might choose out of the whole kingdom.

But all the king's persuasions were useless. His son went into the world to search everywhere for his peahen, taking only one servant to serve him. After many travels he came one day to a lake. Now, by the lake stood a large and beautiful palace. In the palace lived an old woman as queen, and with the queen lived a girl, her daughter. He said to the old woman, "For heaven's sake, grandmother, do you know anything about nine golden peahens?" and the old woman answered, "Oh, my son, I know all about them; they come every midday to bathe in the lake. But what do you want with them? Let them be, think nothing about them. Here is my daughter. Such a beautiful girl! and such an heiress! All my wealth will remain to you if you marry her." But he, burning with desire to see the peahens, would not listen to what the old woman spoke about her daughter.

Next morning, when day dawned, the prince prepared to go down to the lake to wait for the peahens. Then the old queen bribed the servant and gave him a little pair of bellows, and said, "Do you see these bellows? When you come to the lake you must blow secretly with them behind his neck, and then he will fall asleep, and not be able to speak to the peahens." The mischievous servant did as the old woman told him; when he went with his master down to the lake, he took occasion to blow with the bellows behind his neck, and the poor prince fell asleep just as though he were dead. Shortly after, the nine peahens came flying, and eight of them alighted by the lake, but the ninth flew towards him, as he sat on horseback, and caressed him, and tried to awaken him. "Awake, my darling! Awake, my heart! Awake, my soul!" But for all that he knew nothing, just as if he were dead. After they had bathed, all the peahens flew away together, and after they were gone, the prince woke up and said to his servant, "What has happened? Did they not come?" The servant told him they had been there, and that eight of them had bathed, but the ninth had sat by him on his horse, and caressed and tried to awaken him. Then the king's son was so angry that he almost killed himself in his rage.

Next morning he went down again to the shore to wait for the peahens, and rode about a long time till the servant again found an opportunity of blowing with the bellows behind his neck, so that he again fell asleep as though dead. Hardly had he fallen asleep when the nine peahens came flying, and eight of them alighted by the water, but the ninth settled down by the side of his horse and caressed him, and cried out to awaken him, "Arise, my darling! Arise, my heart! Arise, my soul!"

But it was of no use; the prince slept on as if he were dead. Then she said to the servant, "Tell your master tomorrow he can see us here again, but never more." With these words the peahens flew away. Immediately after, the king's son woke up, and asked his servant, "Have they not been here?" And the man answered, "Yes, they have been, and say that you can see them again tomorrow, at this place, but after that they will not return again." When the unhappy prince heard that, he knew not what to do with himself, and in his great trouble and misery he tore the hair from his head.

The third day he went down again to the shore, but, fearing to fall asleep, instead of riding slowly, galloped along the shore. His servant, however, found an opportunity of blowing with the bellows behind his neck, and again the prince fell asleep. A moment after came the nine peahens, and the eight alighted on the lake and the ninth by him, on his horse, and sought to awaken him, caressing him. "Arise, my darling! Arise, my heart! Arise, my soul!" But it was of no use; he slept on as if dead. Then the peahen said to the servant, "When your master awakens, tell him he ought to strike off the head of the nail from the lower part, and then he will find me." Thereupon all the peahens fled away. Immediately the king's son awoke, and said to his servant, "Have they been here?" And the servant answered, "They have been, and the one which alighted on your horse ordered me to tell you to strike off the head of the nail from the lower part, and then you will find her." When the prince heard that, he drew his sword and cut off his servant's head.

After that he travelled alone about the world, and, after long travelling, came to a mountain and remained all night there with a hermit, whom he asked if he knew anything about nine golden peahens. The hermit said, "Eh, my son, you are lucky; God has led you in the right path. From this place it is only half a day's walk. But you must go straight on, then you will come to a large gate, which you must pass through. And, after that, you must keep always to the right hand, and so you will come to the peahens' city, and there find their palace." So next morning the king's son arose and prepared to go. He thanked the hermit and went as he had told him. After a while he came to the great gate, and, having passed it, turned to the right, so that at midday he saw the city, and, beholding how white it shone, rejoiced very much. When he came into the city, he found the palace where lived the nine golden peahens. But at the gate he was stopped by the guard, who demanded who he was, and whence he came. After he had answered these questions, the guards went to announce him to the queen. When the queen heard who he was, she came running out to the gate and took him by the hand to lead him into the palace. She was a young and beautiful maiden, and so there was a great rejoicing when, after a few days, he married her and remained there with her.

One day, some time after their marriage, the queen went out to walk, and the king's son remained in the palace. Before going out, however, the queen gave him the keys of twelve cellars, telling him, "You may go down into all the cellars except the twelfth – that you must on no account open, or it will cost you your head." She then went away. The king's son, whilst remaining in the palace, began to wonder what there could be in the twelfth cellar, and soon commenced opening one cellar after the other. When he came to the twelfth, he would not at first open it, but again began to wonder very much why he was forbidden to go into it. "What *can* be in this cellar?" he exclaimed to himself. At last he opened it.

In the middle of the cellar lay a big barrel with an open bunghole, but bound fast round with three iron hoops. Out of the barrel came a voice, saying, "For God's sake, my brother – I am dying with thirst – please give me a cup of water." Then the king's son took a cup and filled it with water, and emptied it into the barrel. Immediately after he had done so, one of the hoops burst asunder. Again came the voice from the barrel: "For God's sake, my brother, I am dying of thirst. Please give me a cup of water." The king's son again took the cup and filled it, and poured the water into the barrel, and the third hoop burst. Then the barrel fell to pieces, and a dragon flew out of the cellar, and caught the queen on the road and carried her away.

Then the servant, who went out with the queen, came back quickly, and told the king's son what had happened, and the poor prince knew not what to do with himself, so desperate was he, and full of self-reproaches. At length, however, he resolved to set out and travel through the world in search of her. After long journeying, one day he came to a lake, and near it, in a little hole, he saw a little fish jumping about. When the fish saw the king's son, she began to beg pitifully, "For God's sake, be my brother, and throw me into the water. Some day I may be of use to you, so take now a little scale from me, and when you need me, rub it gently." Then the king's son lifted the little fish from the hole and threw her into the water, after he had taken one small scale, which he wrapped up carefully in a handkerchief. Some time afterwards, as he travelled about the world, he came upon a fox caught in an iron trap. When the fox saw the prince, he spoke, "In God's name, be a brother to me and help me to get out of this trap. One day you will need me, so take just one hair from my tail, and when you want me, rub it gently." Then the king's son took a hair from the tail of the fox and set him free.

Again, as he crossed a mountain, he found a wolf fast in a trap; and when the wolf saw him it spoke, "Be a brother to me; in God's name set me free, and one day I will help you. Only take a hair from me, and when you need me, rub it gently." So he took a hair and set the wolf free. After that the king's son travelled about a very long time, till one day he met a man, to whom he said, "For God's sake, brother, have you ever heard anyone say where is the palace of the dragon king?" The man gave him very particular directions which way to take, and in what length of time he could get there. Then the king's son thanked him and continued his journey until he came to the city where the dragon lived.

When there, he went into the palace and found therein his wife, and both of them were exceedingly pleased to meet each other, and began to take counsel how they could escape. They resolved to run away, and prepared hastily for the journey. When all was ready, they mounted on horseback and galloped away. As soon as they were gone, the dragon came home, also on horseback, and, entering his palace, found that the queen had gone away. Then he said to his horse, "What shall we do now? Shall we eat and drink, or go at once after them?" The horse answered, "Let us eat and drink first, we shall anyway catch them; do not be anxious."

After the dragon had dined, he mounted his horse, and in a few moments came up with the runaways. Then he took the queen from the king's son and said to him, "Go now, in God's name! This time I forgive you, because you gave me water in the cellar; but if your life is dear to you, do not come back here anymore." The unhappy young prince went on his way a little, but could not long resist, so he came back next day to the dragon's palace and found the queen sitting alone and weeping. Then they began again to consult how they could get away. And the prince said, "When the dragon comes, ask him where he got that horse, and then you will tell me so that I can look for such another one; perhaps in this way we can escape." He then went away, lest the dragon should come and find him with the queen.

By-and-by the dragon came home, and the queen began to pet him and speak lovingly to him about many things, till at last she said, "Ah, what a fine horse you have! Where did you get such a splendid horse?" And he answered, "Eh, where I got it everyone cannot get one! In such and such a mountain lives an old woman who has twelve horses in her stable, and no one can say which is the finest, they are all so beautiful. But in one corner of the stable stands a horse which looks as if he were leprous, but, in truth he is the very best horse in the whole world. He is the brother of my horse, and whoever gets him may ride to the sky. But whoever wishes to get a horse from that old woman must serve her three days and three nights. She has a mare with a foal, and whoever during three nights guards and keeps for her this mare and this foal has a right to claim the best horse from the old woman's stable. But whoever engages to keep watch over the mare and does not must lose his head."

Next day, when the dragon went out, the king's son came, and the queen told him all she had learned from the dragon. Then the king's son went away to the mountain and found the old woman, and entered her house with the greeting, "God help you, grandmother!" And she answered, "God help you, too, my son! What do you wish?" "I should like to serve you," said the king's son. Then the old woman said, "Well, my son, if you keep my mare safe for three days and three nights, I will give you the best horse, and you can choose him yourself. But if you do not keep the mare safe, you shall lose your head."

Then she led him into the courtyard, where all around stakes were ranged. Each of them had on it a man's head, except one stake, which had no head on it, and shouted incessantly, "Oh, grandmother, give me a head." The old woman showed all this to the prince, and said, "Look here, all these are the heads of those who tried to keep my mare, and they have lost their heads for their pains."

But the prince was not a bit afraid, so he stayed to serve the old woman. When the evening came, he mounted the mare and rode her into the field, and the foal followed. He sat still on her back, having made up his mind not to dismount, that he might be sure of her. But before midnight he slumbered a little, and when he awoke he found himself sitting on a rail and holding the bridle in his hand. Then he was greatly alarmed, and went instantly to look about to find the mare, and whilst looking for her he came to a piece of water. When he saw the water he remembered the little fish, and took the scale from the handkerchief and rubbed it a little.

Then immediately the little fish appeared and said, "What is the matter, my half-brother?" And he replied, "The mare of the old woman ran away whilst under my charge, and now I do not know where she is." And the fish answered, "Here she is, turned to a fish, and the foal to a smaller one. But strike once upon the water with the bridle and cry out 'Heigh! mare of the old woman!'"

The prince did as he was told, and immediately the mare came, with the foal, out of the water to the shore. Then he put on her the bridle and mounted and rode away to the old woman's house, and the foal followed. When he got there, the old woman gave him his breakfast. She, however, took the mare into the stable and beat her with a poker, saying, "Why did you not go down among the fishes, you cursed mare?" And the mare answered, "I have been down to the fishes, but the fish are his friends, and they told him about me." Then the old woman said, "Then go among the foxes."

When evening came, the king's son mounted the mare and rode to the field, and the foal followed the mare. Again he sat on the mare's back until near midnight, when he fell asleep as before. When he awoke, he found himself riding on the rail and holding the bridle in his hand. So he was much frightened, and went to look after the mare.

As he went, he remembered the words the old woman had said to the mare, and he took from the handkerchief the fox's hair and rubbed it a little between his fingers. All at once the fox stood before him and asked, "What is the matter, half-brother?" And he said, "The old woman's mare has run away, and I do not know where she can be." Then the fox answered, "Here she is with us; she has turned into a fox, and the foal into a cub; but strike once with the bridle on the earth and cry out, 'Heigh! you old woman's mare!'"

So the king's son struck with the bridle on the earth and cried, "Heigh! you old woman's mare!" And the mare came and stood, with her foal, near him. He put on the bridle, and mounted and rode off home, and the foal followed the mare.

When he arrived, the old woman gave him his breakfast, but took the mare into the stable and beat her with the poker, crying, "To the foxes, cursed one! to the foxes!" And the mare answered, "I have been with the foxes, but they are his friends, and told him I was there!" Then the old woman cried, "If that is so, you must go among the wolves."

When it grew dark again, the king's son mounted the mare and rode out to the field, and the foal galloped by the side of the mare. Again he sat still on the mare's back till about midnight, when he grew very sleepy and fell into a slumber, as on the former evenings, and when he awoke he found himself riding on the rail, holding the bridle in his hand, just as before. Then, as before, he went in a hurry to look after the mare.

As he went, he remembered the words the old woman had said to the mare, and took the wolf's hair from the handkerchief and rubbed it a little. Then the wolf came up to him and asked, "What is the matter, half-brother?" And he answered, "The old woman's mare has run away, and I cannot tell where she is." The wolf said, "Here she is with us; she has turned herself into a wolf, and the foal into a wolf's cub. Strike once with the bridle on the earth and cry out, 'Heigh! old woman's mare!'" And the king's son did so, and instantly the mare came again and stood with the foal beside him. So he bridled her, and galloped home, and the foal followed.

When he arrived, the old woman gave him his breakfast, but she led the mare into the stable and beat her with the poker, crying, "To the wolves, I said, miserable one." Then the mare answered, "I have been to the wolves; but they are his friends, and told him all about me."

Then the old woman came out of the stable, and the king's son said to her, "Eh, grandmother, I have served you honestly; now give me what you promised me." And the old woman answered, "My son, what is promised must be fulfilled. So look here: here are the twelve horses; choose which you like." And the prince said, "Why should I be too particular? Give me only that leprous horse in the corner; fine horses are not fitting for me." But the old woman tried to persuade him to choose another horse, saying, "How can you be so foolish as to choose that leprous thing whilst there are such very fine horses here?" But he remained firm by his first choice, and said to the old woman, "You ought to give me that which I choose, for so you promised." So, when the old woman found she could not make him change his mind, she gave him the scabby horse, and he took leave of her, and went away, leading the horse by the halter.

When he came to a forest, he curried and rubbed down the horse, when it shone as bright as gold. He then mounted, and the horse flew as quickly as a bird, and in a few seconds brought him to the dragon's palace.

The king's son went in and said to the queen, "Get ready as soon as possible." She was soon ready, when they both mounted the horse, and began their journey home. Soon after, the dragon came home, and when he saw the queen had disappeared, said to his horse, "What shall we do? Shall we eat and drink first, or shall we pursue them at once?" The horse answered, "Whether we eat and drink or not, it is all one; we shall never reach them."

When the dragon heard that, he got quickly on his horse and galloped after them. When they saw the dragon following them, they pushed on quicker, but their horse said, "Do not be afraid; there is no need to run away." In a very few moments the dragon came very near to them, and his horse said to their horse, "For God's sake, my brother, wait a moment! I shall kill myself running after you."

Their horse answered, "Why are you so stupid as to carry that monster? Fling your heels up and throw him off, and come along with me." When the dragon's horse heard that, he shook his head angrily and flung his feet high in the air, so that the dragon fell off and brake in pieces, and his horse came up to them. Then the queen mounted him and returned with the king's son happily to her kingdom, where they reigned together in great prosperity until the day of their death.

Bird Girl

ONCE UPON A TIME lived a king, who had only one son; and when this son grew up, his father sent him to travel about the world, in order that he might find a maiden who would make him a suitable wife.

The king's son started on his journey, and travelled through the whole world without finding anywhere a maiden whom he loved well enough to marry. Seeing then that he had taken so much trouble, and had spent so much time and money, and all to no purpose, he resolved to kill himself. With this intention he climbed to the top of a high mountain, that he might throw himself from its summit; for he wished that even his bones might never be found. Having arrived at the top of the mountain, he saw a sharp rock jutting out from one side of it, and was climbing up to throw himself from it, when he heard a voice behind him calling, "Stop! stop! O, man! Stop for the sake of three hundred and sixty-five which are in the year!" He looked back, and seeing no one, asked, "Who are you that speaks to me? Let me see you. When you know how miserable I am, you will not prevent my killing myself."

He had scarcely said these words when there appeared to him an old man, with hair as white as wool, who said, "I know all about you. But listen! Do you see that high hill?" "Yes, I do," said the prince. "And do you see the multitude of marble blocks which are on it?" said the old man. "Yes, I do," rejoined the prince. "Well, then," continued the old man, "on the summit of that hill there is an old woman with golden hair, who sits night and day on that very spot, and holds a bird in her bosom. Whoever can get this bird into his hands will be the happiest man in the world. But be careful. If you are willing to try to get the bird, you must take the old woman by her hair before she sees you. If she sees you before you catch her by her hair, you will be changed into a stone on the spot. Thus it happened to all those young men you see standing there, as if they were blocks of marble."

When the king's son heard this, he thought, "It is all one to me whether I die here or there. If I succeed, so much the better for me; if I fail, I can but die as I had resolved." So he went up the hill. When he arrived near the old woman, he walked very cautiously towards her, hoping to reach her unseen; for, luckily, the old woman was lying with her back towards him, sunning herself, and playing with the bird.

When near enough, he sprang suddenly and caught her by the hair. Then the old woman cried out, so that the whole hill shook as with a great earthquake; but the king's son held fast by her hair, and when she found that she could not escape, she said, "What do you desire from me?" He replied, "That you should give me the bird in your bosom, and that you call back to life all these Christian souls." The old woman consented, and gave him the bird. Then from her mouth she breathed a blue wind towards the men of stone, and immediately they again became alive. The king's son, having the bird in his hands, was so rejoiced that he began to kiss it; and as he kissed it, the bird was transformed into a most beautiful maiden.

This girl the enchantress had turned into a bird, in order that she might allure the young men to her. The girl pleased the king's son exceedingly, and he took her with him, and prepared to return home. As he was going down the hill, the girl gave him a stick, and told him the stick would do everything that he desired of it. So the king's son struck with it once upon the rock, and in a moment there came out a mass of golden coin, of which they took plenty for use on their journey.

As they were travelling, they came to a great river, and could find no place by which they could pass over; so the king's son touched the surface of the river with his stick, and the water divided, so that a dry path lay before them, and they were able to cross over the river dry-shod. A little farther, they came to a pack of wolves, and the wolves attacked them, and seemed about to tear them to pieces; but the prince struck at them with his stick, and one by one the wolves were turned into ants. Thus, at length, the king's son reached home safely with his beloved, and they were shortly after married, and lived long and happily together.

Bash-Chalek, or, True Steel

ONCE UPON A TIME there was a king who had three sons and three daughters. At length old age overtook him, and the hour came for him to die. While dying, he called to him his three sons and three daughters, and told his sons to let their sisters marry the very first men who came to ask them in marriage. "Do this or dread my curse!" said he, and soon after expired.

Some time after his death, there came one night a great knocking at the gate; the whole palace shook, and outside was heard a great noise of squeaking, singing, and shouting, whilst lightnings played round the whole court of the palace. The people in the palace were very much frightened, so that they shook for fear, when all at once someone shouted from the outside, "O princes! open the door!" Thereupon the king's eldest son said, "Do not open!" The second son added, "Do not open, for anything in the world!" But the youngest son said, "I will open the door!" and he jumped up and opened it.

The moment he had opened the door, something came in, but the brother could see nothing except a bright light in one part of the room. Out of this light came these words: "I have come to demand your eldest sister for wife, and I shall take her away this moment, without any delay; for I wait for nothing, neither will I come a second time to ask for her! Therefore answer me quickly: will you give her or not?"

The eldest brother said, "I will not give her. How can I give her when I cannot see you, and do not know who you are, nor whence you come? You come tonight for the first time, and wish to take her away instantly! Should I not know where I can visit my sister sometimes?"

The second said, "I will not give my sister tonight to be taken away!"

But the youngest said, "I will give her if you will not. Have you forgotten what our father commanded us?" And, with these words, taking his sister by the hand, he gave her away, saying, "May she be to you a happy and honest wife!"

As the sister passed over the threshold, everyone in the palace fell to the ground from fear, so vivid was the lightning and loud the claps of thunder. The heavens seemed to be on fire and the whole sky rumbled, so that the whole palace shook as if about to fall. All this, however, passed over, and soon after the day dawned. When it grew light enough, the brothers went to see if any trace was left of the mighty power to whom they had given their sister, so that they might be able to trace the road by which it had gone. There was, however, nothing which they could either see or hear.

The second night, about the same time, there was heard again round the whole palace a great noise, as if an army was whistling and hissing, and at length someone at the door cried out, "Open the door, O princes!" They were afraid to disobey, and opened the door, and some dreadful power began to speak, "Give here the girl, your second sister! I am come to demand her!" The eldest brother answered, "I will not give her away!" The second brother said, "I will not give you my sister!" But the youngest said, "I will give her! Have you forgotten what our father told us to do?" So he took his sister by the hand and gave her over, saying, "Take her! May she be honest and bring you happiness!" Then the unseen noises departed with the girl. Next day, as soon as it dawned, all three brothers walked round the palace and for some distance beyond, looking everywhere for some trace where the power had gone, but nothing could be seen or heard.

The third night, at the same hour as before, again the palace rocked from its very foundations, and there was a mighty uproar outside. Then a voice shouted, "Open the door!" The sons of the king arose and opened the door, and a great power passed by them and said, "I am come to demand your youngest sister!" The eldest and the second son shouted, "No! We will not give our sister this third night! At any rate, we will know before our youngest sister goes away from our house to whom we are giving her, and where she is going, so that we can come to visit her whenever we wish to do so!" Thereupon the youngest brother said, "Then I will give her! Have you forgotten what our father on his deathbed recommended us? It is not so very long ago!" Then he took the girl by the hand and said, "Here she is! Take her! And may she bring you happiness and be happy herself!" Then instantly the power went away with a great noise. When the day dawned, the brothers were very anxious about the fate of their sister, but could find no trace of the way in which she had gone.

Some time after the brothers, speaking together, said, "It is really very wonderful what has happened to our sisters! We have no news – no trace of them! We do not know where they are gone, nor whom they have married!" At last they said to each other, "Let us go and try to find our sisters!" So they prepared immediately for their journey, took money for their travelling expenses, and went away in search of their three sisters.

They had travelled some time when they lost their way in a forest, and wandered about a whole day. When it grew dark, they thought they would stop for the night at some place where they could find water. So, having come to a lake, they decided to sleep near it, and sat down to take some supper. When the time for sleep came, the eldest brother said, "I will keep watch while you sleep!" And so the two younger brothers went to sleep and the eldest watched. In the middle of the night, the lake began to be greatly agitated, and the brother who was watching grew quite frightened, especially when he saw something was coming towards him from the middle of the lake. When it came near, he saw that it was a terrific alligator with two ears, and it ran at him; but he drew his knife and struck it, and cut off its head. When he had done this, he cut off the ears also, and put them in his pocket, the body and the head, however, he threw back into the lake. Meanwhile the day began to dawn, but the two brothers slept on and knew nothing of what their eldest brother had done. At length he awakened them, but told them nothing, so they went on their travels together. When the next day was closing, and it began again to grow dark, they took counsel with each other where they should rest for the night, and where they should find water. They felt also afraid, because they were approaching some dangerous mountains.

Coming to a small lake, they resolved to rest there that night; and having made a fire they placed their things near it, and prepared to sleep. Then the second brother said, "This night I will keep guard whilst you sleep!" So the two others fell asleep, and the second brother remained watching.

All at once the lake began to move, and lo! an alligator, with two heads, came running to swallow up the three. But the brother who watched grasped his knife, felled the alligator to the ground with one blow, and cut off both the heads. Having done this, he cut off the two pairs of ears, put them in his pocket, and threw the body into the water, and the two heads after it. The other brothers, however, knew nothing about the danger which they had escaped, and continued to sleep very soundly till the morning dawned.

Then the second brother awoke them, saying, "Arise, my brothers! It is day!" and they instantly jumped up, and prepared to continue their journey. But they knew not in what country they now were, and as they had eaten up nearly all their food, they feared greatly lest they should die of hunger in that unknown land. So they prayed for God to give them sight of some city or village or, at least, that they might meet someone to guide them, for they had already been wandering three days up and down in a wilderness, and could see no end to it. Pretty early in the morning they came to a large lake and resolved to go no further, but to remain there all the day, and also to spend the night there. "For if we go on," said they, "we are not sure that we shall find any more water near which we can rest." So they remained there.

When evening came, they made a great fire, took their frugal supper, and prepared to sleep. Then the youngest brother said, "This night I will keep guard whilst you sleep." And so the other two went to sleep, and the youngest brother kept awake, looking sharply about him, his eyes being turned often towards the lake. Part of the night had already passed, when suddenly the whole lake began to move; the waves dashed over the fire and half quenched it. Then he drew his sword and placed himself near the fire, as there appeared a great alligator with three heads, which rushed upon the brothers as if about to swallow them all three.

But the youngest brother had a brave heart, and would not awaken his brothers, so he met the alligator, and gave him three blows in succession, and at each blow he cut off one of the three heads. Then he cut off the six ears and put them in his pocket, and threw the body and the three heads into the lake. Whilst he was thus busy, the fire had quite gone out, so he – having nothing there with which he could light the fire, and not wishing to awaken his brothers from their deep slumbers – stepped a little way into the forest, with the hope of seeing something with which he might rekindle the fire.

There was, however, no trace of any fire anywhere. At last, in his search, he climbed up a very high tree, and, having reached the top, looked about on all sides. After much looking, he thought he saw the glare of a fire not very far off. So he came down from the tree and went in the direction in which he had seen the fire, in order to get some brand with which he might again light the fire. He walked very far on this errand, and though the glare seemed always near him, it was a very long time before he reached it. Suddenly, however, he came upon a cave, and in the cave a great fire was burning. Round it sat nine giants, and two men were being roasted, one on each side of the fire. Besides that, there stood upon the fire a great kettle full of the limbs of men ready to be cooked. When the king's son saw that, he was terrified and would gladly have gone back, but it was no longer possible.

Then he shouted as loud and cheerfully as he could, "Good evening, my dear comrades! I have been a very long time in search of you!"

They received him well, saying, "Welcome! if thou art of our company!"

He answered, "I shall remain yours for ever, and would give my life for your sake!"

"Eh!" said they, "if you intend to be one of us, you know, you must also eat man's flesh, and go out with us in search of prey."

The king's son answered, "Certainly, I shall do everything that you do!"

"Then come and sit with us!" cried the giants; and the whole company, sitting round the fire, took meat out of the kettle and began to eat. The king's son pretended to eat, also, but instead of eating, he always threw the meat behind him, and thus deceived them.

When they had eaten up the whole of the roasted meat, the giants got up and said, "Let us now go to hunt, that we may have meat for tomorrow." So they went away, all nine of them, the king's son making the tenth. "Come along!" they said to him, "there is a city near in which a great king lives. We have been supplying ourselves with food from that city a great many years." As they came near the city, they pulled two tall pine trees up by the roots, and carried them along with them. Having come to the city wall, they reared one pine tree up against it, and said to the king's son, "Go up, now, to the top of the wall, so that we may be able to give you the other pine tree, which you must take by the top and throw down into the city. Take care, however," they said, "to keep the top of the tree in your hands, so that we can go down the stem of it into the city." Thereupon the king's son climbed up on the wall and then cried out to them, "I don't know what to do; I am not acquainted with this place, and I don't understand how to throw the tree over the wall; please, one of you come up and show me what I must do." Then one of the giants climbed up the tree placed against the wall, caught the top of the other pine tree, and threw it over the wall, keeping the top all the time safe in his hand.

Whilst he was thus standing, the king's son drew his sword, struck him on the neck, and cut his head off, so that the giant fell down into the city.

Then he called to the other eight giants, "Your brother is in the city; come, one after the other, so that I can let you also down into the city!" And the giants, not knowing what had happened to the first one, climbed up one after the other, and thus the king's son cut off their heads till he had killed all the nine.

After that, he himself slowly descended the pine tree and went into the city, walking through all the streets, but there was not one living creature to be seen. The city seemed quite deserted. Then he said to himself, "Surely those giants have made this great devastation and carried all the people away."

After walking about a very long time, he came to a tall tower, and, looking up, he saw a light in one of the rooms. So he opened the door and went up the steps into the room. And what a beautiful room it was in which he had entered! It was decorated with gold and silk and velvet, and there was no one there except a girl lying on a couch sleeping. As soon as the king's son entered, his eyes fell upon the girl, who was exceedingly beautiful. Just then he saw a large serpent coming down the wall, and it had stretched out its head and was ready to strike the girl on the forehead, between the eyes. So he drew his dagger very quickly, and nailed the snake's head to the wall, exclaiming, "God grant that my dagger may not be taken out of the wall by any hand but my own!" and thereupon he hurried away, and passed over the city wall, climbing up and going down the pine trees. When he got back to the cavern where the giants had been, he plucked a brand from the fire, and ran away very quickly to the spot where he had left his brothers, and found them still sleeping.

He soon lighted the fire again, and meanwhile, the sun having arisen, he awoke his brothers, and they arose, and all three continued their journey. The same day they came to the road leading to the city. In that city lived a mighty king, who used to walk about the streets every morning, weeping over the great destruction of his people by the giants. The king feared greatly that one day his own daughter might also be eaten up by one of them. That morning he rose very early, and went to look about the city; the streets were all empty, because most of the people of the city had been eaten up by the giants. Walking about, at last he observed a tall pine tree, pulled up quite by the roots, and leaning against the city wall. He drew near and saw a great wonder. Nine giants, the frightful enemies of his people, were lying there with their heads off. When the king saw that, he rejoiced exceedingly, and all the people who were left gathered round and praised God, and prayed for good health and good luck to those who had killed the giants. At that moment a servant came running to tell the king that a serpent had very nearly killed his daughter. So the king hurried back to the palace, and went quickly to the room wherein his daughter was, and there he saw the snake pinned to the wall, with a dagger through its head. He tried to draw the knife out, but he was not able to do so.

Then the king sent a proclamation to all the corners of the kingdom, announcing that whoever had killed the nine giants and nailed the snake to the wall should come to the king, who would make him great presents and give him his daughter for a wife. This was proclaimed throughout the whole kingdom. The king ordered, moreover, that large inns should be built on all the principal roads, and that every traveller who passed by should be asked if he had ever heard of the man who had killed the nine giants, and any traveller who knew anything about the matter should come and tell what he knew to the king, when he should be well rewarded.

After some time the three brothers, travelling in search of their sisters, came one night to sleep at one of those inns. After supper the master of the inn came in to speak to them, and, after boasting very much what great things he had himself done, he asked them if they themselves had ever done any great thing?

Then the eldest brother began to speak, and said, "After I started with my brothers on this journey, one night we stopped to sleep by a lake in the midst of a great forest; whilst my two brothers slept, I watched, and, suddenly, an alligator came out of the lake to swallow us, but I took my knife and cut off its head; if you don't believe me, see! here are the two ears from his head!" And he took the ears from his pocket and threw them on the table.

When the second brother heard that, he said, "I kept guard the second night, and I killed an alligator with two heads; if you do not believe me, look! here are its four ears!" And he took the ears out of his pocket and showed them.

But the youngest brother kept silent. The master of the inn began then to speak to him, saying, "Well, my boy, your brothers are brave men; let us hear if you have not done some bold deed."

Then the youngest brother began, "I have also done something, though it may not be a great thing. When we stayed to rest the third night in the great wilderness on the shore of the lake, my brothers lay down to sleep, for it was my turn to keep guard. In the middle of the night the water stirred mightily, and a three-headed alligator came out and wished to swallow us, but I drew my sword and cut off all the three heads; if you do not believe, see! here are the six ears of the alligator!" The brothers themselves were greatly surprised, and he continued, "Meanwhile the fire had gone out, and I went in search of fire. Wandering about the mountain, I met nine giants in one cave." And so he went on, telling all that had happened and what he had done.

When the innkeeper heard that, he hurried off and told everything to the king. The king gave him plenty of money, and sent some of his men to bring the three brothers to him. When they came to the king, he asked the youngest, "Have you really done all these wonders in this city – killed the giants and saved my daughter from death?" "Yes, Your Majesty," answered the king's son. Then the king gave him his daughter to wife, and allowed him to take the first place after him in the kingdom.

After that he said to the two elder brothers, "If you like, I will also find wives for you two and build palaces for you." But they thanked him, saying they were already married, and so told him how they had left home to search for their sisters. When the king heard that, he kept by him only the youngest brother, his son-in-law, and gave the other two each a mule loaded with sacks full of money; and so the two elder brothers went back to their kingdom. All the time, however, the youngest brother was thinking of his three sisters, and many a time he wished to go in search of them again, though he was also sorry to leave his wife. The king would never consent to his going, so the prince wasted away slowly without speaking about his grief.

One day the king went out hunting, and said to his son-in-law, "Remain here in the palace, and take these nine keys, and keep them carefully. If you wish, however," added he, "you can open three or four rooms, wherein you will see plenty of gold and silver, and other precious things. Indeed, if you much wish to do so, you can open eight of the rooms, but let nothing in the world tempt you to open the ninth. If you open that, woe to you!"

The king went away, leaving his son-in-law in the palace, who immediately began to open one room after another, till he had opened the whole eight, and he saw in all masses of all sorts of precious things. When he stood before the door of the ninth room, he said to himself, "I have passed luckily through all kinds of adventures, and now I must not dare to open this door!" Thereupon he opened it. And what did he see? In the room was a man, whose legs were bound in iron up to the knees, and his arms to the elbows; in the four corners of the chamber there were four columns, and from each an iron chain, and all the chains met in a ring round the man's neck. So fast was he bound that he could not move at all any way.

In the front of him was a reservoir, and from it water was streaming through a golden pipe into a golden basin just before him. Near him stood, also, a golden mug, all covered with precious stones. The man looked at the water and longed to drink, but he could not move to reach the cup. When the king's son saw that, he was greatly surprised, and stepped back; but the man cried, "Come in, I conjure you in the name of the living God!" Then the prince again approached, and the man said, "Do a good deed for the sake of the life hereafter. Give me a cup of water to drink, and be assured you will receive, as a recompense from me, another life." The king's son thought, "It is well, after all, to have two lives," so he took the mug and filled it, and gave it to the man, who emptied it at once. Then the prince asked him, "Now tell me, what is your name?" And the man answered, "My name is True Steel." The king's son moved to go away, but the man begged again, "Give me yet one cup of water, and I will give you in addition a second life." The prince said to himself, "One life is mine already, and he offers to give me another

– that is indeed wonderful!" So he took the mug and gave it to him, and the man drank it up.

The prince began already to fasten the door, while the man called to him, "Oh, my brave one, come back a moment! You have done two good deeds; do yet a third one and I will give you a third life. Take the mug, fill it with water, and pour the water on my head, and for that I will give you a third life." When the king's son heard that, he turned, filled the beaker with water, and poured it over the man's head. The moment the water met his head, all the fastenings around the man's neck broke, and all the iron chains burst asunder. True Steel jumped up like lightning, spread his wings, and started to fly, taking with him the king's daughter, the wife of his deliverer, with whom he disappeared. What was to be done now? The prince was afraid of the king's anger.

When the king returned from the chase, his son-in-law told him all that had happened, and the king was very sorry, and said to him, "Why did you do this? I told you not to open the ninth room!" The king's son answered, "Don't be angry with me! I will go and find True Steel and bring my wife back!" Then the king attempted to persuade him not to go away. "Do not go, for anything in the world!" he said. "You do not know True Steel. It cost me very many soldiers and much money to catch him! Better remain here, and I will find you some other maiden for a wife; do not fear, for I love you as my own son, notwithstanding all that has happened!" The prince, however, would not hear of remaining there, so taking some money for his journey, he saddled and bridled his horse, and started on his travels in search of True Steel.

After travelling a long time, he one day entered a strange city, and, as he was looking about, a girl called to him from a kiosk, "O son of the king, dismount from your horse and come into the forecourt." When he entered the courtyard, the girl met him, and on looking at her he recognized his eldest sister. They greeted each other, and the sister said to him, "Come, my brother – come with me into the kiosk."

When they came into the kiosk, he asked her who her husband was, and she answered, "I am married to the King of Dragons, who is also a dragon. I must hide you well, my dear brother, for my husband has often said that he would kill his brothers-in-law if he could only meet them. I will try him first, and if he will promise not to injure you, I will tell him you are here." So she hid her brother and his horse as well as she could. At night, supper was prepared in readiness for her husband, and at last he came. When he came flying into the courtyard, the whole palace shone. The moment he came in, he called his wife and said, "Wife, there is a smell of human bones here! Tell me directly what it is!"

"There is no one here!" said she. But he exclaimed, "That is not true!"

Then his wife said, "My dear, will you answer me truly what I am going to ask you? Would you do any harm to my brothers, if one of them came here to see me?" And the dragon answered, "Your eldest and your second brother I would kill and roast, but I would do no harm to the youngest." Then his wife said, "Well, then, I will tell you that my youngest brother, and your brother-in-law, is here." When the Dragon King heard that, he said, "Let him come to me!" So the sister led the brother before the king, her husband, and he embraced him. They kissed each other, and the king exclaimed, "Welcome, brother-in-law!" "I hope I find you well?" returned the prince courteously, and he told the Dragon King all his adventures from the beginning to the end.

Then the Dragon King cried out, "And where are you going, my poor fellow? The day before yesterday True Steel passed here carrying away your wife. I assailed him with seven thousand dragons, yet could do him no harm. Leave the devil in peace; I will give you as much money as you like, and then you may go home quietly." But the king's son would not hear of going back, and proposed next morning to continue his journey. When the Dragon King saw that he could not change his intention, he took one of his feathers, and gave it into his hand, saying, "Remember what I now say to you. Here you have one of my feathers, and if you find True Steel and are greatly pressed, burn this feather, and I will come in an instant to your help with all my forces." The king's son took the feather and continued his journey.

After long travelling about the world, he arrived at a great city, and, as he rode through the streets, a girl called to him from a kiosk, "Here, son of the king! Dismount and come into the courtyard!" The prince led his horse into the yard, and behold! the second sister came to meet him. They embraced and kissed each other, and the sister led the brother up into the kiosk, and had his horse taken to a stable. When they were in the kiosk, the sister asked her brother how he came there, and he told her all his adventures. He then asked her who her husband was. "I am married to the King of the Falcons," she said, "and he will come home tonight, so I must hide you somewhere, for he often threatens my brothers."

Shortly after she had concealed her brother, the Falcon King came home. As soon as he alighted, all the house shook. Immediately his supper was set before him, but he said to his wife, "There are human bones somewhere!" The wife answered, "No, my husband, there is nothing." After long talking, however, she asked him, "Would you harm my brothers if they came to see me?" The Falcon King answered, "The eldest brother and the second I would delight in torturing, but to the youngest I would do no harm." So she told him about her brother. Then he ordered that they should bring him immediately; and when he saw him he rose up, and they embraced and kissed each other. "Welcome, brother-in-law!" said the King of Falcons. "I hope you are happy, brother?" returned the prince, and then they sat down to sup together. After supper, the Falcon King asked his brother-in-law where he was travelling. He replied that he was going in search of True Steel, and told the king all that had happened.

On hearing this, the Falcon King began to advise him to go no further. "It is no use going on," said he. "I will tell you something of True Steel. The day he stole your wife, I assaulted him with four thousand falcons. We had a terrible battle with him, blood was shed till it reached the knees, but yet we could do him no harm! Do you think now that you alone could do anything with him? I advise you to return home. Here is my treasure; take with you as much as you like." But the king's son answered, "I thank you for all your kindness, but I cannot return. I shall go at all events in search of True Steel!" For he thought to himself, "Why should I not go, seeing I have three lives?" When the Falcon King saw that he could not persuade him to go back, he took a little feather and gave it him, saying, "Take this feather, and when you find yourself in great need, burn it and I will instantly come with all my powers to help you!" So the king's son took the feather and continued his journey, hoping to find True Steel.

After travelling for a long time about the world, he came to a third city. As he entered, a girl called to him from a kiosk: "Dismount, and come into the courtyard." The king's son went into the yard, and was surprised to find his youngest sister, who came to meet him. When they had embraced and kissed each other, the sister led her brother to the kiosk and sent his horse to the stables. The brother asked her, "Dear sister, whom have you married? What is your husband?" She answered, "My husband is the King of Eagles."

When the Eagle King returned home in the evening, his wife received him, but he exclaimed immediately, "What man has come into my palace? Tell me the truth instantly!" She answered, "No one is here." And they began their supper. By-and-by the wife said, "Tell me truly, would you do any harm to my brothers if they came here?" The Eagle King answered, "The eldest and second brother I would kill, but to the youngest I would do no harm! I would help him whenever I could!" Then the wife said, "My youngest brother, and your brother-in-law, is here; he came to see me." The Eagle King ordered that they should bring the prince instantly, received him standing, kissed him, and said, "Welcome, brother-in-law!" And the king's son answered, "I hope you are well?" They then sat down to their supper. During the repast they conversed about many things, and at last the prince told the king he was travelling in search of True Steel.

When the Eagle King heard that, he tried to dissuade him from going on, adding, "Leave the devil in peace, my brother-in-law; give up that journey and stay with me! I will do everything to satisfy you!" The king's son, however, would not hear of remaining, but next day, as soon as it was dawn, prepared to set out in search of True Steel. Then the Eagle King, seeing that he could not persuade him to give up his journey, plucked out one of his feathers and gave it him, saying, "If you find yourself in great danger, my brother, make a fire and burn this feather; I will then come to your help immediately with all my eagles." So the prince took the feather and went away.

After travelling for a very long time about the world, roaming from one city to another, and always going farther and farther from his home, he found his wife in a cavern.

When the wife saw him, she was greatly astonished, and cried, "In God's name, my husband, how did you come here?" He told her how it all happened, and then added, "Now let us fly!" "How can we fly," she asked, "when True Steel will reach us instantly? And when he does, he will kill you and carry me back." But the prince, knowing he had three other lives to live, persuaded his wife to flee, and so they did. As soon, however, as they started, True Steel heard it, and followed immediately. When he reached them, he shouted to the king's son, "So, prince, you have stolen your wife!" Then, after taking the wife back, he added, "Now, I forgive you this life, because I recollect that I promised to give you three lives; but go away directly, and never come here again after your wife, else you will be lost!" Thus saying, he carried the wife away, and the prince remained alone on the spot, not knowing what to do.

At length the prince resolved to go back to his wife. When he came near the cave, he found an opportunity when True Steel was absent, and took his wife again and tried to escape with her.

But True Steel learned their flight directly, and ran after them. When he reached them, he fixed an arrow to his bow, and cried to the king's son, "Do you prefer to die by the arrow or by the sword?" The king's son asked pardon, and True Steel said, "I pardon you also the second life. But I warn you! Never come here again after your wife, for I will not pardon you anymore! I shall kill you on the spot!" Saying that, he carried the wife back to the cave, and the prince remained, thinking all the time how he could save her.

At last he said to himself, "Why should I fear True Steel, when I have yet two lives? One of which he has made me a present, and one which is my own?" So he decided to return again to the cave next morning, when True Steel was absent. He saw his wife, and said to her, "Let us fly!" She objected, saying, "It is of no use to fly, when True Steel would certainly overtake us." However, her husband forced her to go with him, and they went away.

True Steel, however, overtook them quickly, and shouted, "Wait a bit! This time I will not pardon you!" The prince became afraid, and begged him to pardon him also this time, and True Steel said to him, "You know I promised to give you three lives, so now I give you this one, but it is the third and last. Now you have only one life, so go home, and do not risk losing the one life God gave you!"

Then the prince, seeing he could do nothing against this great power, turned back, reflecting, however, all the time, as to the best way of getting his wife back from True Steel.

At last, he remembered what his brothers-in-law had said to him when they gave him their feathers. Then he said to himself, "I will try this fourth time to get my wife back; if I come to trouble, I will burn the feathers, and see if my brothers-in-law will come to help me."

Hereupon he went back once more towards the cavern wherein his wife was kept, and, as he saw from a distance that True Steel was just leaving the cave, he went near and showed himself to his wife. She was surprised and terrified, and exclaimed, "Are you so tired of your life that you come back again to me?" Then he told her about his brothers-in-law, and how each of them had given him one of their feathers, and had promised to come to help him whenever he needed their assistance. "Therefore," added he, "I am come once more to take you away; let us start at once."

This they did. The same moment, however, True Steel heard of it, and shouted from afar, "Stop, prince! You cannot run away!" And then the king's son, seeing True Steel so near him, quickly took out a flint and tinderbox, struck some sparks, and burned all three feathers. Whilst he was doing this, however, True Steel reached him, and, with his sword, cut the prince in two parts.

That moment came the King of Dragons, rushing with his whole army of dragons, the King of Falcons, with all his falcons, and the King of Eagles, with his mighty host of eagles, and they all attacked True Steel. Torrents of blood were shed, but after all True Steel caught up the woman and fled away.

Then the three kings gave all their attention to their brother-in-law, and determined to bring him back to life. Thereupon they asked three of the most active dragons which of them could bring them, in the shortest time, some water from the river Jordan.

One said, "I could bring it in half an hour." The second said, "I can go and return in ten minutes." The third dragon said, "I can bring it in nine seconds." Then the three kings said to the last one, "Go, dragon, and make haste!" Then this dragon exhibited all his fiery might, and in nine seconds, as he had promised, he came back with water from the Jordan.

The kings took the water and poured it on the places where the prince was wounded, and, as they did so, the wound closed up, the body joined together, and the king's son sprang up alive.

Then the three kings counselled him, "Now that you are saved from death, go home!" But the prince answered, he would at all events yet once more try to get his wife back. The kings, his brothers-in-law, again spoke: "Do not try again! Indeed, you will be lost if you go, for now you have only one life which God gave you!"

The king's son, however, would not listen to their advice. So the kings told him, "Well, then, if you are still determined to go, at least do not take your wife away immediately, but tell her to ask True Steel where his strength lies, and then come and tell us, in order that we may help you to conquer him!"

So the prince went secretly and saw his wife, and told her how she could persuade True Steel to tell her where his strength was. He then left her and went away.

When True Steel came home, the wife of the king's son asked him, "Tell me, now, where is your great strength?" He answered, "My wife, my strength is in my sword!" Then she began to pray, and turned to his sword. When True Steel saw that, he burst out laughing, and said, "O foolish woman! My strength is not in my sword, but in my bow and arrows!" Then she turned towards the bow and arrows and prayed.

Then True Steel said, "I see, my wife, you have a clever teacher who has taught you to find out where my strength lies! I could almost say that your husband is living, and it is he who teaches you!"

But she assured him that no one taught her, for she had no longer anyone to do so.

After some days her husband came, and when she told him she could not learn anything from True Steel, he said, "Try again!" and went away.

When True Steel came home, she began again to ask him the secret of his strength. Then he answered her, "Since you think so much of my strength, I will tell you truly where it is." And he continued, "Far away from this place there is a very high mountain; in the mountain there is a fox; in the fox there is a heart; in the heart there is a bird, and in this bird is my strength. It is no easy task, however, to catch that fox, for she can transform herself into a multitude of creatures."

Next day, as soon as True Steel left the cave, the king's son came to his wife, and she told him all she had learned. Then the prince hurried away to his brothers-in-law, who waited, all three impatient to see him, and to hear where was the strength of True Steel. When they heard, all three went away at once with the prince to find the mountain.

Having got there, they set the eagles to chase the fox, but the fox ran to a lake, which was in the midst of the mountain, and changed herself into a six-winged golden bird. Then the falcons pursued her, and drove her out of the lake, and she flew into the clouds, but there the dragons hurried after her. So she changed herself again into a fox, and began to run along the earth, but the rest of the eagles stopped her, surrounded, and caught her.

The three kings then ordered the fox to be killed, and her heart to be taken out. A great fire was made, and the bird was taken out of the heart and burnt. That very moment True Steel fell down dead, and the prince took his wife and returned home with her.

The Dream of the King's Son

THERE WAS ONCE a king who had three sons. One evening, when the young princes were going to sleep, the king ordered them to take good note of their dreams and come and tell them to him next morning.

So the next day the princes went to their father as soon as they awoke, and the moment the king saw them he asked of the eldest, "Well, what have you dreamt?"

The prince answered, "I dreamt that I should be the heir to your throne."

And the second said, "And I dreamt that I should be the first subject in the kingdom."

Then the youngest said, "*I* dreamt that I was going to wash my hands, and that the princes, my brothers, held the basin, whilst the queen, my mother, held fine towels for me to dry my hands with, and Your Majesty's self poured water over them from a golden ewer."

The king, hearing this last dream, became very angry, and exclaimed, "What! I – the king – pour water over the hands of my own son! Go away this instant out of my palace, and out of my kingdom! You are no longer my son."

The poor young prince tried hard to make his peace with his father, saying that he was really not to be blamed for what he had only dreamed, but the king grew more and more furious, and at last actually thrust the prince out of the palace.

So the young prince was obliged to wander up and down in different countries, until one day, being in a large forest, he saw a cave, and entered it to rest. There, to his great surprise and joy, he found a large kettle full of Indian corn boiling over a fire and, being exceedingly hungry, began to help himself to the corn. In this way he went on until he was shocked to see he had eaten up nearly all the maize, and then, being afraid some mischief would come of it, he looked about for a place in which to hide himself. At this moment, however, a great noise was heard at the cave mouth, and he had only time to hide himself in a dark corner before a blind old man entered, riding on a great goat and driving a number of goats before him.

The old man rode straight up to the kettle, but as soon as he found that the corn was nearly all gone, he began to suspect someone was there, and groped about the cave until he caught hold of the prince.

"Who are you?" asked he sharply. And the prince answered, "I am a poor, homeless wanderer about the world, and have come now to beg you to be good enough to receive me."

"Well," said the old man, "why not? I shall at least have someone to mind my corn whilst I am out with my goats in the forest."

So they lived together for some time; the prince remained in the cave to boil the maize, whilst the old man drove out his goats every morning into the forest.

One day, however, the old man said to the prince, "I think you shall take out the goats today, and I will stay at home to mind the corn."

This the prince consented to very gladly, as he was tired of living so long quietly in the cave. But the old man added, "Mind only one thing! There are nine different mountains, and you can let the goats go freely over eight of them, but you must on no account go on the ninth. The Vilas (fairies) live there, and they will certainly put out your eyes as they have put out mine, if you venture on their mountain."

The prince thanked the old man for his warning, and then, mounting the great goat, drove the rest of the goats before him out of the cave.

Following the goats, he had passed over all the mountains to the eighth, and from this he could see the ninth mountain, and could not resist the temptation he felt to go upon it. So he said to himself, "I will venture up, whatever happens!"

Hardly had he stepped on the ninth mountain before the fairies surrounded him, and prepared to put out his eyes. But happily a thought came into his head, and he exclaimed quickly, "Dear Vilas, why take this sin on your heads? Better let us make a bargain, that if you spring over a tree that I will place ready to jump over, you shall put out my eyes, and I will not blame you!"

So the Vilas consented to this, and the prince went and brought a large tree, which he cleft down the middle almost to the root. This done, he placed a wedge to keep the two halves of the trunk open a little.

When it was fixed upright, he himself first jumped over it, and then he said to the Vilas, "Now it is your turn. Let us see if you can spring over the tree!"

One Vila attempted to spring over, but at the same moment the prince knocked the wedge out, and the trunk closing, at once held the Vila fast. Then all the other fairies were alarmed, and begged him to open the trunk and let their sister free, promising, in return, to give him anything he might ask. The prince said, "I want nothing except to keep my own eyes, and to restore eyesight to that poor old man." So the fairies gave him a certain herb, and told him to lay it over the old man's eyes, and then he would recover his sight. The prince took the herb, opened the tree a little so as to let the fairy free, and then rode back on the goat to the cave, driving the other goats before him. When he arrived there, he placed at once the herb on the old man's eyes, and in a moment his eyesight came back, to his exceeding surprise and joy.

Next morning the old man, before he drove out his goats, gave the prince the keys of eight closets in the cave, but warned him on no account to open the ninth closet, although the key hung directly over the door. Then he went out, telling the prince to take good care that the corn was ready for their suppers.

Left alone in the cave, the young man began to wonder what might be in the ninth closet, and at last he could not resist the temptation to take down the key and open the door to look in.

What was his surprise to see there a golden horse, with a golden greyhound beside him, and near them a golden hen and golden chickens were busy picking up golden millet seeds.

The young prince gazed at them for some time, admiring their beauty, and then he spoke to the golden horse: "Friend, I think we had better leave this place before the old man comes back again."

"Very well," answered the golden horse, "I am quite willing to go away, only you must take heed to what I am going to tell. Go and find linen cloth enough to spread over the stones at the mouth of the cave, for if the old man hears the ring of my hoofs he will be certain to kill you. Then you must take with you a little stone, a drop of water, and a pair of scissors, and the moment I tell you to throw them down you must obey me quickly, or you are lost."

The prince did everything that the golden horse had ordered him, and then, taking up the golden hen with her chickens in a bag, he placed it under his arm, and mounted the horse and rode quickly out of the cave, leading with him, in a leash, the golden greyhound. But the moment they were in the open air, the old man, although he was very far off tending his goats on a distant mountain, heard the clang of the golden hoofs, and cried to his great goat, "They have run away. Let us follow them at once."

In a wonderfully short time, the old man on his great goat came so near the prince on his golden horse that the latter shouted, "Throw now the little stone!"

The moment the prince had thrown it down, a high rocky mountain rose up between him and the old man, and before the goat had climbed over it, the golden horse had gained much ground. Very soon, however, the old man was so nearly catching them that the horse shouted, "Throw now the drop of water!" The prince obeyed instantly, and immediately saw a broad river flowing between him and his pursuer.

It took the old man on his goat so long to cross the river that the prince on his golden horse was far away before them. But for all that, it was not very long before the horse heard the goat so near behind him that he shouted, "Throw the scissors!" The prince threw them, and the goat, running over them, injured one of his forelegs very badly. When the old man saw this, he exclaimed, "Now I see I cannot catch you, so you may keep what you have taken. But you will do wisely to listen to my counsel. People will be sure to kill you for the sake of your golden horse, so you had better buy at once a donkey, and take the hide to cover your horse. And do the same with your golden greyhound."

Having said this, the old man turned and rode back to his cave. And the prince lost no time in attending to his advice, and covered with donkey hide his golden horse and his golden hound.

After travelling a long time, the prince came unawares to the kingdom of his father. There he heard that the king had had a ditch dug – three hundred yards wide and four hundred yards deep – and had proclaimed that whosoever should leap his horse over it should have the princess, his daughter, for wife.

Almost a whole year had elapsed since the proclamation was issued, but as yet no one had dared to risk the leap. When the prince heard this, he said, "I will leap over it with my donkey and my dog!" And he leapt over it.

But the king was very angry when he heard that a poorly dressed man on a donkey had dared to leap over the great ditch which had frightened back his bravest knights. So he had the disguised prince thrown into one of his deepest dungeons, together with his donkey and his dog.

Next morning the king sent some of his servants to see if the man was still living, and these soon ran back to him, full of wonder, and told him that they had found in the dungeon, instead of a poor man and his donkey, a young man, beautifully dressed, a golden horse, a golden greyhound, and a golden hen, surrounded by golden chickens, which were picking up golden millet seeds from the ground.

Then the king said, "That must be some powerful prince." So he ordered the queen, and the princes, his sons, to prepare all things for the stranger to wash his hands. Then he went down himself into the dungeon, and led the prince up with much courtesy, desiring thus to make amends for the past ill-treatment.

The king himself took a golden ewer full of water, and poured some over the prince's hands, whilst the two princes held the basin under them, and the queen held out fine towels to dry them on.

This done, the young prince exclaimed, "Now, my dream is fulfilled." And they all at once recognized him, and were very glad to see him once again amongst them.

The Three Brothers

I

THERE WAS ONCE upon a time an old man whose family consisted of his wife and three sons. They were exceedingly poor, and finding that they could not possibly all live at home, the three sons went out into the world in different directions to find some means of living. Thus the old man and his wife remained alone.

Having neither horses nor oxen, the old man was obliged to go every day to the forest for fuel, and carry home the firewood on his back.

On one occasion it was nearly evening when he started to go to the forest, and his wife, who was afraid to remain alone in the house, begged very hard to be permitted to go with him. He objected very much at first, but as she persisted in her entreaties, he at length consented to her following him, first bidding her, however, take good care to make the house door safe, lest someone should break into the house.

The old woman thought the door would be safest if she took it off its hinges, and carried it away on her back. So she took it off and followed her husband as fast as she was able. The old man, however, was not angry when he saw how she had mistaken his words, and the manner she had chosen to make sure of the door; for, he reflected, there was little or nothing at all in the house for anyone to steal.

When they had reached the forest, the husband began to cut wood, and his wife gathered the branches together in a heap. Meanwhile it had got very late, and they were anxious as to how they should pass the night, seeing their own house was so far off that they would be unable to reach it before morning, and there were no houses in the neighbourhood where they could sleep. At last they observed a very tall and widely spreading pine tree, and they resolved to climb up and pass the night on one of its branches.

The man got up first, and his wife followed him, drawing, with great difficulty, the door after her. Her husband advised her to leave the door on the ground under the tree, but she would not listen to him, and could not be persuaded to remain in the tree without her house door. Hardly had they settled themselves on a branch, the old woman holding fast her door, before they heard a great noise, which came nearer and nearer.

They were excessively frightened at the noise, and dared neither speak nor move.

In a short time they saw a captain of robbers, followed by twelve of his men, approach the tree. The robbers were dressed all alike, in gold and silver, and one of them carried a sheep killed and ready for roasting. When the old man and woman saw the band of robbers come and settle under the pine tree in which they had themselves taken refuge, they thought their time was come, and gave themselves up for lost.

As soon as the robbers had settled themselves, the youngest of them made a fire and put the sheep down to roast, whilst the captain conversed with the others. The sheep was already roasted and cut up, and the robbers had begun with great gaiety to eat it, when the old woman told her husband that she could not possibly hold the door any longer, but must let it fall. The old man begged her piteously not to let it go, but to hold it fast and keep quiet, lest the robbers should discover and kill them. The old woman said, however, that she was so exceedingly tired she could no longer by any possibility hold it. The old man, seeing it was no good talking about it, declared that, as he could not hold his corner of the door any longer when she had let go her corner, it was not worthwhile to complain. "Since," as he said, "what must be must be, and it is no use to be sorry for anything in this world." Thereupon they both loosened their holds of the door at once, and it fell down, making a great noise – especially with its iron lock – as it fell from branch to branch.

The door made so much noise in falling that the whole forest echoed with the sound.

The robbers, greatly astonished at the noise, and too frightened by the unexpected clashing above their heads to see what was the cause, took to their heels, without once thinking of the roast sheep they left behind, or of any of the treasures which they had brought with them. One of them alone did not run away far from the spot, but hid himself behind a tree, and waited to see what might come of so much noise.

The old couple, seeing the robbers did not return, came down from the tree, and, being exceedingly hungry, began to eat heartily, the old man all the time praising the wisdom of his wife in throwing down the door.

The robber who had hidden himself, seeing only the old people near the fire, came up to them, and begged to be allowed to share their meal, as he had not eaten anything for the last twenty-four hours. This they permitted, and spoke of all kinds of things, until the old man exclaimed suddenly to the robber, "Take care! you have a hair on your tongue! Do not choke yourself, for I have no means to bury you here!"

The brigand took this joke in earnest, and begged the old man to take the hair out of his mouth, and he would in return show him a cave wherein a great treasure was hidden. As he was describing the great heaps of gold ducats, thalers, shillings, and other coins which he said were in the cave, the old woman interrupted him, saying, "I will take the hair out of your mouth, without pay! Only put your tongue out and shut your eyes!" The robber very gladly did as she told him, and she caught up a knife, and in a moment cut off a piece of his tongue. Then she said, "Well, now! I have taken the hair out!" When the robber felt what had been done to him, he jumped up and down in pain, and at length ran away without hat or coat in the same direction as his companions had gone, shouting all the time, "Help! help! give me some plaster!" His companions, hearing imperfectly these words, misunderstood him, and thought he cried to them, "Help yourselves; here is the police-master!" especially as he ran as if the captain of police with a large force was at his heels. Accordingly, the robbers themselves ran faster and farther away.

Meanwhile the old couple thought it no longer safe to stay under the pine tree, so they gathered up quickly all the money, whether gold or silver, that they could carry, and hurried back to their home. When they got there, they found the hens of the neighbours had pulled off the thatch of their house. They were, however, the less sorry for this, since they had now money enough to build another and a better home. And this they did, and continued to live in their fine new house without once remembering their sons, who had been wandering about the world already some nine long years.

II

In the meantime, the sons had been working each in a different part of the world. When, however, they had been away from their home nine years, they all, as if by common consent, conceived an ardent desire to go back once more to their father's house. So they took the whole of the savings which they had laid up in their nine years' service, and commenced their journeys homeward.

On his travels the eldest brother met with three gypsies, who were teaching a young bear to dance by putting him on a red-hot plate of iron. He felt compassion for the creature in its sufferings, and asked the gypsies why they were thus tormenting the animal. "Better," he said, "let me have it, and I will give you three pieces of silver for it!" The gypsies accepted the offer eagerly, took the three pieces of silver, and gave him the bear. Travelling farther on, he met with some huntsmen who had caught a young wolf, which they were about to kill. He offered them also three pieces of silver for the animal, and they, pleased to get so much, readily sold it. A little further still, he met some shepherds, who were about to hang a little dog. He was sorry for the poor brute, and offered to give them two pieces of silver if they would give the dog to him, and this they very gladly agreed to.

So he travelled on homeward, attended by the young bear, the wolf-cub, and the little dog. As all his nine years' savings had amounted only to nine pieces of silver, he had now but a single piece left.

Before he reached his father's house, he met some boys who were about to drown a cat. He offered them his last piece of money if they would give him the cat, and they were content with the bargain and gave it up to him. So, at last he arrived at his home without any money, but with a bear, a wolf, a dog, and a cat.

Just so, it had happened with the other two brothers. By their nine years' work they had only saved nine pieces of silver, and on their way home they had spent them in ransoming animals, exactly as the eldest brother had done.

Soon after they had returned, the old father died. Then the three brothers consulted together, and decided to invest part of the money, which their father and mother had got from the robbers, in the purchase of four horses and one grass field.

A few days later, they all went into the fields to bring in the hay which the two elder ones had mown. They found, however, hardly the third part of the hay which they had left. At this they wondered greatly, and looked about to see who had stolen it, but, finding no one, after a little while they took up what was left and returned home.

At length the year, on which all this had happened, passed away. The next year, however, they dared not leave their mown grass unwatched. So they discussed which of them should first keep guard. Each of them offered to do it, but at last they agreed that the youngest brother should begin to watch. So he prepared himself, and at night went out into the field. Having come there, he climbed up into a tree and resolved to remain there until daybreak. About midnight, he heard a great noise and shouting, which frightened him so much that he dared not stir at all. Some creatures came into the field and ate up most of the hay, and what they did not eat they tossed about and spoiled, so that it was fit for nothing. When daylight came, the youngest brother came down from the tree and went home to tell what he had seen.

So that year they had no hay.

Next year, when hay harvest came, the three brothers took counsel together how to preserve their hay. The second brother now volunteered to watch in the field, and seemed quite sure he would be able to save the hay. Accordingly he went, and climbed into the tree, just as his brother had done the previous year. About midnight, three winged horses came into the field with a company of fairies. The winged horses began to eat the newly mown hay, and the fairies danced over it. After the greater part of the hay had been eaten by the horses and all the rest had been spoiled by the dancing of the fairies, the whole company left the field just as day began to dawn. The watcher in the tree had witnessed all this; he was, however, too frightened to do anything – indeed, he hardly dared to move. When he went home, he told his brothers all that he had seen, at which they were sad, since this year again they would have no hay.

However, the time passed, and the third summer came on. Again the three brothers cut the grass in their meadow, and consulted together anxiously how they should manage to keep their new hay.

At length it was settled that it was now the turn of the eldest brother to keep watch. If he also failed to save the hay, it was agreed that they should divide amongst them the little property which they had left, and go out again, separately, to seek their fortunes in the world, seeing they had no luck in their own country.

As had been agreed upon, the eldest brother now went out into the field at night; but, instead of going up into the tree as his brothers had done, he lay quietly down on a heap of hay, and waited to see what would happen. About midnight, he heard a great noise afar off and, by-and-by, a troop of fairies, with three winged horses, came straight towards the place where he lay. Having got there, the fairies began to dance, and the horses to eat the hay and canter about. The eldest brother looked on and, at first, felt much afraid, and wished heartily the whole company would go away without seeing him. As, however, they seemed in no hurry to do this, he considered what he should do and, at length, decided that it would be worthwhile to try to catch one of the three horses. So when they came near him, he jumped on the back of one of them, and clung fast to it. The other two horses instantly ran away, and the fairies with them.

The horse that the eldest brother had caught tried all sorts of tricks to throw off his unwelcome rider, but he could not succeed. Finding all his attempts to free himself quite useless, at last he said, "Let me go, my good man, and I will be of use to you some other time." The man answered, "I will set you free on one condition; that is, you must promise never more to come in this field, and you must give me some pledge that you will keep your promise."

The horse gladly agreed to this condition, and gave the man a hair from his tail, saying, "Whenever you happen to be in need, hold this hair to a fire, and I will instantly be at your service."

Thereupon the horse went off, and the eldest brother returned home. His brothers had waited impatiently for his return and, when they saw him, pressed him immediately to tell them all that had happened. So he told everything, except that he had got a hair from the horse's tail, because he did not believe that the horse would keep his promise and come to him in his need. The two younger brothers, however, had no confidence that the fairies and winged horses would fulfil their promise and never come again to ruin their hayfield, so they proposed that the property should be at once divided, and that they should separate. The eldest brother tried to persuade them to remain at least one other year longer, to see what would happen; he was not able, however, to succeed in this. Accordingly they divided the remnant of their property, took each their animals, that is, each his bear, his wolf, his dog, and his cat, and left their home for the second time to seek their fortunes in the world.

The first day they travelled together, but the second day they were obliged to separate because, having come to a crossway, and trying to keep on the same path, they found they could not take a step forward so long as they were together. They therefore left that path and tried another. It was, however, of no use, for they could not move a step forward as long as they were together. And when they tried the third path, the same happened there also. So they tried if two of them could go on in one road if one of them went before and the other behind. But this also they were unable to do; they could not get on one step, try as hard as they would, so nothing was left them but to separate and each of them to go alone by a different road. They were exceedingly sorry to part, but could not help themselves.

Before the brothers separated, the eldest brother said, "Now, brothers, before we part, let us stick our knives in this oak tree; as long as we live, our knives will remain where we stick them; when one of us dies, his knife will fall out. Let us, then, come here every third year to see if the knives are still in their places. Thus we shall know something, at least, about each other." The other two agreed to this, and, having stuck their knives in the oak tree and kissed each other, went, each one his own way, taking his animals with him.

III

Let us first follow the youngest brother in his wanderings. He travelled, with his attendant animals, all that day and the following night without stopping, and the next day saw before him a king's palace, and went straight towards it. Having been taken into the presence of the king, he begged His Majesty to employ him in watching his goats. The king consented to take him as goatherd, and from that day he had the charge of the king's goats and lived on thus quietly for a long time.

One day the new goatherd chanced to drive his flock to a high hill, not far from the king's palace. On the summit of the hill there was a very tall pine tree, and the instant he saw it he resolved to climb up and look about from its top on the surrounding country. Accordingly, he climbed up, and enjoyed exceedingly the extensive and beautiful prospect. As he looked in one direction he saw, a long way off, a great smoke arising from a mountain. The moment he saw the smoke he fancied that one of his brothers must be there, as he thought it unlikely that anyone else would be in such a wilderness. So he resolved at once to give up his place of goatherd, and travel to the mountain which he had seen in the distance. Coming down from the tree, therefore, he immediately collected his goats, which was a very easy task for him to do, since he had such good help from his bear, his wolf, his dog, and his cat.

No sooner had he reached the palace than he went straight to the king and said, "Sir, I can no longer be Your Majesty's goatherd. I must go away, for I saw today a smoking mountain, and I believe that one of my brothers is there, and I wish to go and see if this be so. I therefore beg Your Majesty to pay me what you owe me, and to let me go!" All this time he thought the king knew nothing about the smoking mountain.

When he had said this, however, the king immediately began to advise him on no account to go to the mountain – for, as he assured him, whoever went there never came back again. He told him that all who had gone thither seemed at once to have sunk into the earth, for no one ever heard anything more about them. All the king's warnings and counsels, however, availed nothing; the goatherd was bent on going to the smoking mountain, and looking after his two brothers.

After he had made all preparations for the journey, he set out, accompanied, as usual, by his four animals. He went straight to the mountain, but, having got there, he could not at first find the fire. Indeed, he had trouble enough before he discovered it. At length, however, he found a large fire burning under a beech tree, and went near it to warm himself. At the same time, he looked about on all sides to see who had made the fire. After looking about some time, he heard a woman's voice, and upon his looking up to see whence the sound came, he saw an old woman sitting on one of the branches above his head. She sat huddled together all of a heap and shaking with cold.

No sooner had he discovered her than the old woman begged him to allow her to come down to the fire and warm herself a little. So he told her she might come down and warm herself as soon as she pleased. She answered, however, "Oh, my son, I dare not come down because of your company. I am afraid of the animals you have with you – your bear, and wolf, and dog, and cat."

At this he tried to reassure her and said, "Don't be afraid! They will do you no harm." However, she would not trust them, so she plucked a hair from her head, and threw it down, saying, "Put that hair on their necks and then I shall not be afraid to come down."

Accordingly the man took the hair and threw it over his animals, and in a moment the hair was turned into an iron chain which kept his four-footed followers bound fast together.

When the old woman saw that he had done as she desired, she came down from the tree and took her place by the fire. She seemed at first a very little woman; as she sat by the fire, however, she began to grow larger. When he saw this, he was greatly astonished, and said to her, "But, my old woman, it seems to me that you grow bigger and bigger!" Thereupon she answered, shivering, "Ha! ha! no, no, my son! I am only warming myself!" But, nevertheless, she continued to grow taller and taller, and had already grown half as tall as the beech tree. The goatherd watched her growing with wide-open eyes, and, beginning to get frightened, said again, "But really you are getting a fearful size, and are growing taller and taller every moment."

"Ha, ha, my son," she coughed and shivered, "I am only warming myself!" Seeing, however, that she was now as tall as the tallest beech tree, and, fearing that his life was in danger, he called anxiously to his companions, "Hold her fast, my bear! Hold her fast, my wolf! Hold her fast, my dog! Hold her fast, my cat!" But it was all in vain that he called to them; none of them could move a step from his place. When he saw that, he endeavoured to run away, but found that he could no more move from his place than if he were fast chained to it. Then the old woman, seeing everything had gone on just as she wished, bent down a little, and, touching him with her little finger, said, "Go, you have lost your head!" And the self-same moment he turned to ashes. After that, she touched, with the little toe of her left foot, all his animals, one after the other, and they also turned at once to ashes as their master had done.

Having collected all the ashes, she buried them under an oak tree. Then as soon as she took the iron chain in her hand, it turned again into a hair, which she put back into its place on her head.

She had before done with many young and noble knights just as she had now done with this poor goatherd.

The second brother, after serving a long time in a strange place, was seized with a great desire to go to the oak tree at the crossroads, where he had parted with his brothers, in order to see if their knives were still sticking in the tree. When he got there, he found the knife of his eldest brother still firmly fixed in the trunk of the oak, but his youngest brother's knife had fallen to the ground. Then he knew that his younger brother was dead, or in great danger of death, and he resolved at once to follow the way he had gone and try to discover what had become of him. Going then along the same road which his younger brother had travelled, he came, on the third day, to the king's palace, and went in and begged the king to take him into his service. Whereupon the king took him as goatherd, exactly as he had taken before the youngest brother.

When the second brother had tended the king's goats a long time, he one day drove them up a high hill, and, finding there a very tall pine tree, resolved at once to climb up to its top and look about to see what kind of a country lay on the other side of the hill. When he had looked round a while from the tree, he noticed a great volume of smoke rising from a mountain afar off, and the thought came at once to his mind that his brothers might be there. Accordingly, he came down quickly, collected his goats, and went back to the king's palace, followed by his four companions – that is to say, by his bear, his wolf, his dog, and his cat. When he had reached the palace, he went straight to the king, and begged him to pay him his wages at once, and to let him go to look after his brothers, for he had seen a smoke upon a mountain, and he believed they were there. The king tried in vain to dissuade him by telling him that none who went there ever came back. But all His Majesty's words availed nothing. Thereupon, seeing he was decided on going, the king paid him what he owed him and let him go.

He at once set out and went straight to the mountain. But, when he got there, it was a long time before he could find any fire. At last, however, he found one burning under a beech tree, and he went up to it to warm himself, wondering all the time who had made it, since he saw no one near. As he warmed himself, he heard a woman's voice in the tree above his head and, looking up, saw there an old woman huddled up on a branch and shaking with cold.

As soon as he saw her, the old woman asked him to let her come down and warm herself by the fire, and he told her she might come and warm herself as long as she liked.

She said, however, "I am afraid of the company which you have with you. Take this hair and lay it over your bear, and wolf, and dog, and cat, and then I shall be able to come down."

So saying, she pulled a hair out of her head and threw it down. He laughed at her fears, and assured her that his companions would not hurt her. Finding, however, notwithstanding all he said, that she was still afraid to come down from the tree, he at last took the hair and laid it on the beasts as she had directed. In an instant the hair turned into an iron chain and bound the four animals fast together. Then the old woman came down and took a place by the fire to warm herself. As the second brother watched her warming herself, he saw her grow bigger and bigger, until she had grown half as tall as the beech tree.

Wondering greatly, he exclaimed, "Old woman, you are growing bigger and bigger." "Hy, hy! my son," said she, coughing and shivering, "I am only warming myself." But when he saw that she was already as tall as the beech tree, he became frightened, and called to his companions, "Hold her, my bear! Hold her, my wolf! Hold her, my dog! Hold her, my cat!" They were none of them, however, able to move, so fast were they held together by the iron chain.

Seeing that, the old woman stooped down and touched him with her little finger, and he fell immediately into ashes. Then she touched the four animals, one after the other, with the little toe of her left foot, and they also crumbled to ashes.

No sooner had the old woman done this than she collected all the ashes in a heap and buried them under an oak tree. As she had before done with the ashes of many a youthful knight and gentleman, so she did now with those of this poor simple man. Pity, if they were to die, that some more worthy means than one hair from the head of a miserable old woman had not brought about their deaths!

A very long time had passed, and yet the eldest brother never once thought of going back to the crossroads where he had parted with his brothers. He was engaged in the service of a good and honest master, and, finding himself so well off, fancied that his brothers were the same. His master was an innkeeper, and the whole work of the servant was to prepare, morning and evening, the beds of the guests. He did his duty so well that his master thought of adopting him for his son, as he himself was childless.

One day a gentleman of great distinction came to pass the night at the inn, and the servant thought that the stranger looked remarkably like his youngest brother. He wished to ask him his name, but could not for shame, partly because he feared his brother would reproach him for having forgotten to go to the crossroads; partly because the guest's manners were so polished and his clothes were of fine silk and velvet, whereas he had left his brother very poorly clad, and of rustic manners.

As he thought of the likeness which the guest bore to his youngest brother, he considered that, in his travels about the world, his brother might have found wisdom, and by his wisdom might have succeeded in some way of business, and by his business might have gained money; and then, having got money, that it would be easy for him to get as fine clothes as the stranger wore. Reasoning thus, he took courage at last to ask the gentleman about his family, and at length grew bold enough to ask him plainly if he was not his brother.

This, however, the stranger quickly and positively denied, and asked, in return, about the servant's family. To all the particulars which the servant gave him he listened with a smile.

Next morning, the guest left the inn very early. And when the servant went to arrange the bed in which he had slept, he found, under the pillow, a little stone.

He thought the stone must be valuable, having been in the possession of so rich a man, and yet he considered its loss could hardly be felt by one who went clothed in silks and velvets. He lifted it to his lips to kiss it, before putting it in his pocket. But the moment his lips touched it, two men started out and asked him, "What are your orders, sir?" He was frightened by the suddenness of their appearance, and answered, "I do not order anything." Then the men disappeared, and he put the stone in his pocket.

The more he thought of this, the more he marvelled at the wonderful stone, and considered what he should do with it. By-and-by, in order to find out what the two men could do, he took the stone out of his pocket and raised it again to his lips. The moment he did so, the men reappeared and asked him again, "What do you demand, sir?" He replied quickly, "I desire to have the finest clothes prepared for me, of which no two pieces must be made from the same kind of stuff." In a very few moments the men brought him the most beautiful clothes possible; so fine indeed were they all, that he could not decide which piece was the most beautiful. Then, dismissing the men, who disappeared in the stone, he dressed himself. He was admiring the fine fit of his clothes, when his master came to the door of his room, and, seeing a stranger in such an exceedingly rich dress, said humbly, "Excuse me, sir, where do you come from?"

"From not far off," the servant answered.

"Wait a moment, sir," said the innkeeper. "I will call my servant to take your orders." And, going outside, he called loudly for his servant.

Meanwhile, the servant quickly threw off his fine clothes and gave them back to the two men. Dressing himself hurriedly in his old clothes, he rushed out of his room. Then, finding the pantry open, he began to arrange the things.

His master found him employed in this way, and ordered him at once to leave that business, and to go into the house to make coffee for a distinguished guest who had that moment arrived.

The strange guest, however, was nowhere to be found. The innkeeper looked, with his servant, into all the rooms, but there was no sign of a guest anywhere. Then the master, greatly astonished, thought that some thieves had been playing him a trick, and bid the servant in future to look more sharply who came in and who went out of the inn. The servant listened quietly to his master. But, having once remembered his brothers, he had now an irresistible desire to look after them, and so he told the innkeeper that he had resolved to go away, and desired that he might be paid his wages.

The innkeeper was very sad at hearing this, and offered to raise his wages, and tried all means to keep him, but it was of no use. Seeing that the servant was resolved to go away, the master then paid him, and let him leave the inn. Then the eldest brother took with him his four animals – his bear, wolf, dog, and cat – and went away.

After travelling a very long time, his good fortune brought him to the crossroads where he had parted with his brothers. Instantly he rushed to the oak to see if the knives were still sticking in it, but his own knife alone stood in the tree. The two others had fallen out, and he was much grieved at this, believing that his brothers were dead or that they were in great danger. In his trouble he had quite forgotten the wonderful hair and stone which he possessed. He resolved to go and search after his brothers, and therefore went along the same road his youngest brother had taken when they parted.

As he travelled he remembered the hair which the winged horse had given him, and the stone which he had found at the inn. But these did not much console him, he was so exceedingly sorry for his brothers. After travelling some time, he found himself before a large palace, the doorkeeper of which asked him if he would take charge of the king's goats. He said he would, if the king could only tell him something about his two brothers, who had travelled that way with a similar company to that which he had. The king said that no men with such a company had passed that way during his reign. And this was quite true, inasmuch as he had only recently mounted the throne, the old king, under whom the two brothers had served, having lately died. However, though the eldest brother could learn nothing of his two younger brothers, he decided to stay some time there, and so engaged himself to the king as goat-keeper.

As he drove the goats out, day by day, he looked about on all sides for some trace of his brothers; for, although their knives had fallen out of the oak tree, he tried to believe that they were not dead.

One day, as he thus wandered about with his goats, he met an old man, who was going to the forest, with his axe on his shoulder, to cut wood.

So he asked him if he had seen anything of his two brothers. The old man answered, "Who knows? Perhaps they have been lost on that mountain where so many other men have lost their lives. Drive your goats up that high hill. From its top you will see a much higher mountain, which smokes, and never ceases to smoke. On that mountain many people have been lost. Perhaps your brothers also have perished there. I will, however, give you one piece of good advice: do not go, for anything in the world, to the place where it smokes. I am now an old man, but I never remember to have seen one man return who went there. Therefore, if your life is dear to you, do not go up that mountain." So saying, the old man went off.

The goat-keeper drove his goats up the hill, and from its top he saw, as he had been told, a very high mountain which smoked. He tried to discover if any living creature was thereon, but he could not see the traces of a single one there. He considered within himself whether he should go there or not, and, after revolving it over in his mind, he at length determined to go.

In the evening, when he drove the goats home, he told the king of his intention. The king tried hard to dissuade him, and promised to raise his wages if he would stay with him. However, nothing could turn him from his resolution. So the king paid him, and he went away.

Having come to the mountain, he found the fire, and wondered who lit it. As he thought over this, he heard a woman's voice, saying, "Hy, hy!" So he looked up, and was astonished at seeing, in the branches of the beech tree over his head, an old woman huddled there. Her hair was longer than her body, and as white as snow. When he looked up, she said to him, "My son, I am so cold. I should like to warm myself, but I am afraid of your beasts. I made that fire myself, but, seeing you coming with your animals, I was frightened, and got up here to save myself."

"Well, you can now come down again, and warm yourself as much as you please," said he. However, she protested, "I dare not – your beasts would bite me. But I will throw you a hair, and you shall bind them with it. *Then* I can come down." The eldest brother thought to himself that the hair must be a very singular hair indeed, if it could bind his bear, his wolf, his dog, and his cat. So, instead of throwing it over the animals, he threw it into the fire. Meanwhile the old woman came down from the tree, and they both sat by the fire. But he never moved his eyes from her.

Very soon she began to grow, and grow, and in a short time she was ten yards high. Then he remembered the words of the old woodcutter, and trembled. However, he only said to her, "How you are growing, auntie." "Oh, no, my son," she answered, "I am only warming myself." She still grew taller and taller, and had grown as tall as the beech tree, when he again exclaimed, "But how you *are* growing, old woman!"

"Oh, no, my son. I am only warming myself," she repeated as before.

But he saw that she meant him mischief, so he shouted to his companions, "Hold her, my dog! Hold her, my little bear! Hold her, my little wolf! Hold her, my pussy!" Thereupon they all jumped on the old woman and began to tear her. Seeing she was unable to help herself, she begged him to save her from her furious enemies, and promised she would give him whatever he asked. "Well," said he, "I demand that you bring back to life my two brothers, with their companions, and all those you have destroyed. Besides that, I demand ten loads of ducats. If you will not comply with these demands, I shall leave you to be torn to pieces by my animals." The old woman agreed to do all this, only she begged hard that one man should not be brought back to life, because she had said, when she had turned him to ashes, "When *you* arise, may *I* lie down in your place!" And, therefore, she was afraid she should be turned to ashes herself if *he* came back to life.

As the eldest brother, however, thought that she was trying to cheat him, he would not comply with her request.

Finding that she could not otherwise help herself, she at length said to him, "Take some ashes from that heap under the tree, and throw them over yourself and your company, and whilst you do so, say, 'Arise up, dust and ashes – what I am now may you also be!'"

Wonder of wonders! The moment he did as she told him, there arose up crowds of men – more than ten thousand of them. On seeing such a multitude of people coming from under the tree, he was almost struck senseless with astonishment. But he explained to them briefly what had happened. Most of them thanked him heartily. Some, however, would not believe him, and said with anger, "We would rather you had not awakened us." Then they went away in crowds; some took one way, some another, until they were all dispersed. Only his two brothers remained behind, though they, too, for some time could not believe that he was their brother. However, when they saw that their animals recognized his, they remembered that no one but themselves had had such a strange company of beasts. Having recognized each other, the brothers fell into each other's arms and embraced affectionately. Then they divided the ducats which the old woman had given to the eldest, loaded their animals with their treasures, and went straight away towards the place where they were born, and where their parents had died.

As for the old woman, when the last man arose from the ashes under the oak tree, she herself crumbled into ashes under it.

IV

The three brothers built three fine palaces for themselves, and lived therein some time unmarried. At length, however, they began to think what would become of all their property after their deaths, and said to each other that it would be a pity for them to die without heirs. So they resolved to marry, that their wealth might be left to their sons and daughters.

The eldest brother said, "Let me go and find the best wives I can for all three of us; meantime you two will remain here, and take care of our property." The others gladly agreed to this, as the eldest brother had given proofs enough that he was by far the wisest of the three, and they felt sure that he would be able also to bring this important business to a successful issue. So he made the needful preparations, and started on his journey to look out for three wives for himself and the two younger brothers who remained at home.

After long travelling, he arrived at a large city, and resolved to remain there all night, and to continue his journey in the morning.

It happened that the king of that place had just arranged a horserace, and promised his only daughter as the prize, and, with her, ten loads of treasure to the winner.

The very evening the eldest brother arrived, he heard the public bell-man proclaiming aloud through the streets that everyone who had a horse should come tomorrow to the royal field, and whoever should spring first over the ditch should be rewarded with the king's daughter, and should receive, with her, ten loads of gold.

He listened to the proclamation without saying anything. Next morning he went out into the king's field in order to see the racing, and found there already innumerable horses of all kinds.

A little later came also the princess, the king's daughter, and behind her were brought ten loads of treasures.

When he saw the king's daughter, he thought her so exceedingly beautiful that he went instantly a little aside from the crowd to get a better sight of her. He then remembered his wonderful stone. Taking it out, he now lifted it to his lips, and immediately the two men appeared and said, "Master, what do you command?" He replied, "Bring me clothes of silk and velvet, together with precious stones, and ten good horses! And bring them as soon as possible!" He had not winked twice before the men had placed before him everything which he had demanded. Then he took out the hair, and, striking fire with a flint, held the hair near it. The moment he did this, the same cream-coloured horse that had given him the hair stood beside him and asked, "Master, what do you command?" He answered, "I wish that today we leave all the other horses behind us in the race, so that I may gain the king's daughter. Therefore prepare yourself, and let us go at once, as the other horses are now ready for starting."

The instant he had spoken these words, the cream-coloured horse stood, pawing the earth, ready and eager to begin the race. The man then mounted it, and off they went. The other racers, having started a few moments before, were already pretty far from the starting point. In an instant, however, he had reached them, and in another had passed and left them far behind. When he reached the ditch – which was a hundred and five yards deep, and a hundred yards wide – the horse made so great a spring that it touched ground some fifty yards beyond the ditch, broad as it was.

Then he rode back and took the maiden, the king's daughter, and, placing her behind him on his horse, carried her off, together with the loads of gold. All the people, seeing this, wondered greatly who the strange knight could be who had left all the best horses so far behind in the race, and had won the beautiful princess, with all her rich treasures.

He rode along until he came to a wood pretty far from the city, and there he let his wonderful horse go until he should want him again. He then took off all his beautiful clothes, and put on his old dress, and in this manner went on with the maiden and the loads of gold.

About evening he arrived at a strange city, and decided to remain there. After he had rested a little while, the people in the inn told him that all day long the city bell-man had proclaimed that whoever had a good horse should go tomorrow to the horserace, for the king of the palace had offered his only daughter as a prize, together with a hundredweight of gold and jewels; but that there was a ditch to be sprung over, which was three hundred and fifty yards deep and a hundred and fifty yards wide. When he heard this, he was greatly pleased, for he was quite sure that he should win this race also.

Next morning, by the help of the little stone and the wonderful hair, he was again dressed in the finest clothes, and mounted on his cream-coloured horse, and so took his place amongst the racers.

Everyone wondered from what country this knight came, and were delighted at his rich dress; as for the horse, the people were never tired of admiring it. When the racehorses were arranged for the start, he remained purposely behind. He knew well enough that this was of no consequence to him, as in one moment he could reach and pass them all. At length he started, and in a moment distanced the fleetest horse, arriving at the ditch, and leaping over it as if it were nothing. Then, without waiting a minute, he took possession of the king's daughter and her treasures, and went straight to the city where he had left the first king's daughter and her loads of gold.

Taking the two princesses and all the wealth with him, he now thought that it was time for him to go back home. On his way, however, he had the great good luck to come again to a large city, where he resolved to remain during the night. There, also, the public crier had been proclaiming all day long that the king had determined to give his only daughter and fifteen hundredweight of gold to whoever should win the race which was to be run on the morrow. In this instance, however, the horses would have to leap over a ditch one thousand yards deep and four hundred and fifty yards wide. On hearing this proclamation, the eldest brother became very joyful, for he knew that no racer had any chance of beating his wonderful horse.

On the morrow, therefore, by means of his little stone and the hair, he ordered fifteen horses to be ready, to carry away the treasures he felt sure of winning, and, at the same time, directed the two men to bring him his fairy courser and dresses so splendid that not even a king could buy them.

Richly dressed in this way, and mounted, as he was, on his marvellous horse, all the world, who had gathered to see the great race, could look at nothing except at him.

When all the racers were arranged for the start, he lingered behind and let them all speed off like falcons. He wished everyone to see that he was the last to start, that they might not charge him afterwards with having in any way cheated. When they had already gone pretty far, he started himself, and in a moment he had reached them, passed them, and left them all a long, long distance behind. How could it be otherwise? When did the crow outfly the falcon?

Coming to the ditch, he touched the bridle a little, and, in an instant, his horse had leaped over the ditch, and they were safe on the other side. So, without any delay, he took away the maiden, together with all the gold, and went back to the city. Having collected his immense treasures, he now took with him the three princesses and went straight home.

As he travelled along with his company, everyone who met him asked him, "Where are you going?" For you see the princesses were exceedingly beautiful.

But beyond all others, his two brothers, when he reached home, wondered and were delighted at the sight of the three beautiful princesses. They did not rejoice half so much over the great riches he had gained for them as over the marvellous fairness of the king's daughters whom he had brought to be their wives.

Thus each of the three brothers married a beautiful princess. The eldest brother, however, who had shown himself so much the bravest and wisest of them, married the youngest and most beautiful of the three.

Animals as Friends and as Enemies

ONCE UPON A TIME, a long while ago, there lived in a very far-off country a young nobleman who was so exceedingly poor that all his property was an old castle, a handsome horse, a trusty hound, and a good rifle.

This nobleman spent all his time in hunting and shooting, and lived entirely on the produce of the chase.

One day he mounted his well-kept horse and rode off to the neighbouring forest, accompanied, as usual, by his faithful hound. When he came to the forest he dismounted, fastened his horse securely to a young tree, and then went deep into the thicket in search of game. The hound ran on at a distance before his master, and the horse remained all alone, grazing quietly. Now it happened that a hungry fox came by that way and, seeing how well-fed and well-trimmed the horse was, stopped a while to admire him. By and by she was so charmed with the handsome horse that she lay down in the grass near him to bear him company.

Some time afterward, the young nobleman came back out of the forest carrying a stag that he had killed, and was extremely surprised to see the fox lying so near his horse. So he raised his rifle with the intention of shooting her, but the fox ran up to him quickly and said, "Do not kill me! Take me with you, and I will serve you faithfully. I will take care of your fine horse whilst you are in the forest."

The fox spoke so pitifully that the nobleman was sorry for her, and agreed to her proposal. Thereupon he mounted his horse, placed the stag he had shot before him, and rode back to his old castle, followed closely by his hound and his new servant, the fox.

When the young nobleman prepared his supper, he did not forget to give the fox a due share, and she congratulated herself that she was never likely to be hungry again, at least so long as she served so skilful a hunter.

The next morning the nobleman went out again to the chase; the fox also accompanied him. When the young man dismounted and bound his horse, as usual, to a tree, the fox lay down near it to keep it company.

Now, whilst the hunter was far off in the depth of the forest looking for game, a hungry bear came by the place where the horse was tied, and, seeing how invitingly fat it looked, ran up to kill it. The fox hereupon sprang up and begged the bear not to hurt the horse, telling him if he was hungry, he had only to wait patiently until her master came back from the forest, and then she was quite sure that the good nobleman would take him also to his castle and feed him, and care for him, as he did for his horse, his hound, and herself.

The bear pondered over the matter very wisely and deeply for some time, and at length resolved to follow the fox's advice. Accordingly he lay down quietly near the horse, and waited for the return of the huntsman. When the young noble came out of the forest, he was greatly surprised to see so large a bear near his horse, and, dropping the stag he had shot from his shoulders, he raised his trusty rifle and was about to shoot the beast. The fox, however, ran up to the huntsman and entreated him to spare the bear's life, and to take him, also, into his service. This the nobleman agreed to do, and, mounting his horse, rode back to his castle, followed by the hound, the fox, and the bear.

The next morning, when the young man had gone again with his dog into the forest, and the fox and the bear lay quietly near the horse, a hungry wolf, seeing the horse, sprang out of a thicket to kill it. The fox and the bear, however, jumped up quickly and begged him not to hurt the animal, telling him to what a good master it belonged, and that they were sure, if he would only wait, he also would be taken into the same service, and would be well cared for. Thereupon the wolf, hungry though he was, thought it best to accept their counsel, and he also lay down with them in the grass until their master came out of the forest.

You can imagine how surprised the young nobleman was when he saw a great gaunt wolf lying so near his horse! However, when the fox had explained the matter to him, he consented to take the wolf also into his service. Thus it happened that this day he rode home followed by the dog, the fox, the bear, and the wolf. As they were all hungry, the stag he had killed was not too large to furnish their suppers that night, and their breakfasts next morning. Not many days afterward, a mouse was added to the company, and after that a mole begged so hard for admission that the good nobleman could not find it in his heart to refuse her. Last of all came the great bird, the kumrekusha – so strong a bird that she can carry in her claws a horse with his rider! Soon after, a hare was added to the company, and the nobleman took great care of all his animals and fed them regularly and well, so that they were all exceedingly fond of him.

The Animals' Council

One day the fox said to the bear, "My good Bruin, pray run into the forest and bring me a nice large log, on which I can sit whilst I preside at a very important council we are going to hold."

Bruin, who had a great respect for the quick wit and good management of the fox, went out at once to seek the log, and soon came back bringing a heavy one, with which the fox expressed herself quite satisfied. Then she called all the animals about her, and, having mounted the log, addressed them in these words:

"You know all of you, my friends, how very kind and good a master we have. But, though he is very kind, he is also very lonely. I propose, therefore, that we find a fitting wife for him."

The assembly was evidently well pleased with this idea, and responded unanimously, "Very good, indeed, if we only knew any girl worthy to be the wife of our master; which, however, we do not."

Then the fox said, "*I* know that the king has a most beautiful daughter, and I think it will be a good thing to take her for our lord; and therefore I propose, further, that our friend the kumrekusha should fly at once to the king's palace, and hover about there until the princess comes out to take her walk. Then she must catch her up at once, and bring her here."

As the kumrekusha was glad to do anything for her kind master, she flew away at once, without even waiting to hear the decision of the assembly on this proposal.

Just before evening set in, the princess came out to walk before her father's palace, whereupon the great bird seized her and placed her gently on her outspread wings, and thus carried her off swiftly to the young nobleman's castle.

The king was exceedingly grieved when he heard that his daughter had been carried off, and sent out everywhere proclamations promising rich rewards to anyone who should bring her back, or even tell him where he might look for her. For a long time, however, all his promises were of no avail, for no one in the kingdom knew anything at all about the princess.

At last, however, when the king was well-nigh in despair, an old gypsy woman came to the palace and asked the king, "What will you give me if I bring back to you your daughter, the princess?"

The king answered quickly, "I will gladly give you whatever you like to ask, if only you bring me back my daughter!"

Then the old gypsy went back to her hut in the forest, and tried all her magical spells to find out where the princess was. At last she found out that she was living in an old castle, in a very distant country, with a young nobleman who had married her.

The Magic Carpet

The gypsy was greatly pleased when she knew this and, taking a whip in her hand, seated herself at once in the middle of a small carpet, and lashed it with her whip. Then the carpet rose up from the ground and bore her swiftly through the air, toward the far country where the young nobleman lived, in his lonely old castle, with his beautiful wife, and all his faithful company of beasts.

When the gypsy came near the castle she made the carpet descend on the grass among some tress, and leaving it there went to look about until she could meet the princess walking about the grounds. By and by the beautiful young lady came out of the castle, and immediately the ugly old woman went up to her, and began to fawn on her and to tell her all kinds of strange stories. Indeed, she was such a good storyteller that the princess grew quite tired of walking before she was tired of listening; so, seeing the soft carpet lying nicely on the green grass, she sat down on it to rest awhile. The moment she was seated, the cunning old gypsy sat down by her and, seizing her whip, lashed the carpet furiously. In the next minute the princess found herself borne upon the carpet far away from her husband's castle, and before long the gypsy made it descend into the garden of the king's palace.

You can easily guess how glad he was to see his lost daughter, and how he generously gave the gypsy even more than she asked as a reward. Then the king made the princess live from that time in a very secluded tower with only two waiting-women, so afraid was he lest she would again be stolen from him.

Meanwhile the fox, seeing how miserable and melancholy her young master appeared after his wife had so strangely been taken from him, and having heard of the great precautions which the king was using in order to prevent the princess being carried off again, summoned once more all the animals to a general council.

When all of them were gathered about her, the fox thus began, "You know all of you, my dear friends, how happily our kind master was married. But you know, also, that his wife has been unhappily stolen from him, and that he is now far worse off than he was before we found the princess for him. *Then* he was lonely; *now* he is more than lonely – he is desolate! This being the case, it is clearly our duty, as his faithful servants, to try in some way to bring her back to him. This, however, is not a very easy matter, seeing that the king has placed his daughter for safety in a strong tower. Nevertheless, I do not despair, and my plan is this: I will turn myself into a beautiful cat, and play about in the palace gardens under the windows of the tower in which the princess lives. I dare say she will long for me greatly the moment she sees me, and will send her waiting-women down to catch me and take me up to her. But I will take good care that the maids do not catch me, so that, at last, the princess will forget her father's orders not to leave the tower, and will come down herself into the gardens to see if she may not be more successful. I will then make believe to let her catch me, and at this moment our friend, the kumrekusha, who must be hovering over about the palace, must fly down quickly, seize the princess, and carry her off as before. In this way, my dear friends, I hope we shall be able to bring back to our kind master his beautiful wife. Do you approve of my plan?"

Of course, the assembly were only too glad to have such a wise counsellor, and to be able to prove their gratitude to their considerate master. So the fox ran up to the kumrekusha, who flew away with her under her wing, both being equally eager to carry out the project, and thus to bring back the old cheerful look to the face of their lord.

When the kumrekusha came to the tower wherein the princess dwelt, she set the fox down quietly among the trees, where it at once changed into a most beautiful cat, and commenced to play all sorts of graceful antics under the window at which the princess sat. The cat was striped all over the body with many different colours, and before long the king's daughter noticed her, and sent down her two women to catch her and bring her up in the tower.

The two waiting-women came down into the garden, and called, "Pussy! pussy!" in their sweetest voices. They offered her bread and milk, but they offered it all in vain. The cat sprang merrily about the garden, and ran round and round them, but would on no account consent to be caught.

At length the princess, who stood watching them at one of the windows of her tower, became impatient, and descended herself into the garden, saying petulantly, "You only frighten the cat. Let me try to catch her!" As she approached the cat, who seemed now willing to be caught, the kumrekusha darted down quickly, seized the princess by the waist, and carried her high up into the air.

The frightened waiting-women ran to report to the king what had happened to the princess, whereupon the king immediately let loose all his greyhounds to seize the cat which had been the cause of his daughter's being carried off a second time. The dogs followed the cat closely, and were on the point of catching her, when she, just in the nick of time, saw a cave with a very narrow entrance and ran into it for shelter. There the dogs tried to follow her, or to widen the mouth of the cave with their claws, but all in vain. So, after barking a long time very furiously, they at length grew weary, and stole back ashamed and afraid to the king's stables.

When all the greyhounds were out of sight, the cat changed herself back into a fox, and ran off in a straight line toward the castle, where she found her young master very joyful, for the kumrekusha had already brought back to him his beautiful wife.

The King Makes War on the Animals

Now the king was exceedingly angry to think that he had again lost his daughter, and he was all the more angry to think that such poor creatures as a bird and a cat had succeeded in carrying her off after all his precautions. So, in his great wrath, he resolved to make a general war on the animals, and entirely exterminate them.

To this end he gathered together a very large army, and determined to be himself their leader. The news of the king's intention spread swiftly over the whole kingdom, whereupon for the third time the fox called together all her friends – the bear, the wolf, the kumrekusha, the mouse, the mole, and the hare – to a general council.

When all were assembled, the fox addressed them thus:

"My friends, the king has declared war against us, and intends to destroy us all. Now it is our duty to defend ourselves in the best way we can. Let us each see what number of animals we are able to muster. How many of your brother bears do you think *you* can bring to our help, my good Bruin?"

The bear got up as quickly as he could on his hind legs and called out, "I am sure I can bring a hundred."

"And how many of your friends can *you* bring, my good wolf?" asked the fox anxiously.

"I can bring at least five hundred wolves with me," said the wolf with an air of importance.

The fox nodded her satisfaction and continued, "And what can *you* do for us, dear master hare?"

"Well, I think, I can bring about eight hundred," said the hare cautiously.

"And what can *you* do, you dear little mouse?"

"Oh, *I* can certainly bring three thousand mice."

"Very well, indeed! And you, mister mole?"

"I am sure I can gather eight thousand."

"And now what number do you think you can bring us, my great friend, kumrekusha?"

"I fear not more than two or three hundred, at the very best," said the kumrekusha sadly.

"Very good. Now all of you go at once and collect your friends; when you have brought all you can, we will decide what is to be done," said the fox, whereupon the council broke up, and the animals dispersed in different directions throughout the forest.

Not very long after, very unusual noises were heard in the neighbourhood of the castle. There was a great shaking of trees, and the growling of bears and the short sharp barking of wolves broke the usual quiet of the forest. The army of animals was gathering from all sides at the appointed place. When all were gathered together, the fox explained to them her plans in these words: "When the king's army stops on its march to rest the first night, then you, bears and wolves, must be prepared to attack and kill all the horses. If, notwithstanding this, the army proceeds farther, you mice must be ready to bite and destroy all the saddle straps and belts while the soldiers are resting the second night, and you hares must gnaw through the ropes with which the men draw the cannon. If the king still persists in his march, you moles must go the third night and dig out the earth under the road they will take the next day, and must make a ditch, fifteen yards in breadth and twenty yards in depth, all round their camp. Next morning, when the army begins to march over this ground which has been hollowed out, you kumrekushas must throw down on them from above heavy stones while the earth will give way under them."

The plan was approved, and all the animals went off briskly to attend to their allotted duties.

When the king's army awoke, after their first night's rest on their march, they beheld, to their great consternation, that all the horses were killed. This sad news was reported at once to the king. But he only sent back for more horses, and, when they came late in the day, pursued his march.

The second night the mice crept quietly into the camp, and nibbled diligently at the horses' saddles and at the soldiers' belts, while the hares as busily gnawed at the ropes with which the men drew the cannon.

Next morning the soldiers were terrified, seeing the mischief the animals had done. The king, however, reassured them, and sent back to the city for new saddles and belts. When they were at length brought, he resolutely pursued his march, only the more determined to revenge himself on these presumptuous and despised enemies.

On the third night, while the soldiers were sleeping, the moles worked incessantly in digging round the camp a wide and deep trench underground. About midnight the fox sent the bears to help the moles, and to carry away the loads of earth.

Next morning the king's soldiers were delighted to find that no harm seemed to have been done on the previous night to their horses or straps, and started with new courage on their march. But their march was quickly arrested, for soon the heavy horsemen and artillery began to fall through the hollow ground, and the king, when he observed that, called out, "Let us turn back. I see God himself is against us, since we have declared war against the animals. I will give up my daughter."

Then the army turned back, amidst the rejoicings of the soldiers. The men found, however, to their great surprise and fear, that whichever way they turned, they fell through the earth. To make their consternation yet more complete, the kumrekushas now began to throw down heavy stones on them, which crushed them completely. In this way the king, as well as his whole army, perished.

Very soon afterward the young nobleman, who had married the king's daughter, went to the enemy's capital and took possession of the king's palace, taking with him all his animals. And there they all lived long and happily together.

The Lame Fox

THERE WAS A MAN who had three sons – two intelligent, and one a simpleton. This man's right eye was always laughing, while his left eye was weeping and shedding tears. This man's sons agreed to go to him one by one, and ask him why his right eye laughed and his left eye shed tears.

Accordingly the eldest went to his father by himself, and asked him, "Father, tell me truly what I am going to ask you. Why does your right eye always laugh and your left eye weep?" His father gave him no answer, but flew into a rage, seized a knife, and threw it at him, and he fled out of doors, and the knife stuck in the door. The other two were outside, anxiously expecting their brother, and when he came out, they asked him what his father had said to him. But he answered them, "If you're not wiser than another, go, and you will hear."

Then the middle brother went to his father by himself, and asked him, "Father, tell me truly what I am going to ask you. Why does your right eye always laugh and your left weep?" His father gave him no answer, but flew into a rage, seized a knife, and threw it at him, and he fled out of doors, and the knife stuck in the door. When he came out to his brothers, his brothers asked him, "Tell us, brother – so may health and prosperity attend you – what our father has said to you." He answered them, "If you're not wiser than another, go, and you will hear." But this he said to his elder brother on account of the simpleton, that he, too, might go to his father to hear and see.

Then the simpleton, too, went by himself to his father, and asked him, "Father, my two brothers won't tell me what you have said to them. Tell me why your right eye always laughs and your left eye weeps?" His father immediately flew into a rage, seized a knife, and brandished the knife to pierce him through. But as he was standing, so he remained standing where he was, and wasn't frightened in the least. When his father saw that, he came to him and said, "Well, you're my true son; I will tell you, but those two are cowards. The reason why my right eye laughs is that I rejoice and am glad because you children obey and serve me well. And why my left eye weeps, it weeps on this account: I had in my garden a vine, which poured forth a bucket of wine every hour, thus producing me twenty-four buckets of wine every day and night. This vine has been stolen from me, and I have not been able to find it, nor do I know who has taken it or where it is. And for this reason my left eye weeps, and will weep till I die, unless I find it." When the simpleton came out of doors, his brothers asked him what his father had said, and he told them all in order.

Then they prepared a drinking bout for their father and the domestics, and set out on their journey. On the journey they came to a crossroad, and three ways lay before them. The two elder brothers consulted together, and said to their youngest brother, the simpleton, "Come, brother, let us each choose a road, and let each go by himself and seek his fortune." "Yes, brothers," answered the simpleton. "You choose each a road; I will take that which remains to me." The two elder took two roads which ran into each other, started on their way, and afterwards met, came out into the road, and said, "Praise be to God that we're quit of that fool!" They then sat down to take their dinner. Scarcely had they sat down to eat, when up came a lame she-fox on three legs, which approached them, fawning and begging to obtain something to eat. But as soon as they saw the fox, they said, "Here's a fox. Come, let us kill it." Then, sticks in hand, they went after it. The fox limped away in the best fashion it could, and barely escaped from them. Meanwhile, shepherd-dogs came to their wallet and ate up everything that they had. When they returned to the wallet, they had a sight to see.

The simpleton took the third road right on, and went forward till he began to feel hungry. Then he sat down on the grass under a pear tree, and took bread and bacon out of his wallet to eat. Scarcely had he sat down to eat, when, lo! that very same lame fox which his two brothers had seen began to approach him, and to fawn and beg, limping on three feet. He had compassion for it because it was so lame, and said, "Come, fox, I know that you are hungry, and that it is hard lines for you that you have not a fourth foot." He gave it bread and bacon to eat, a portion for himself, and a portion for the fox. When they had refreshed themselves a little, the fox said to him, "But, brother, tell me the truth, whither are you going?" He said, "Thus and thus, I have a father and us three brothers. And one of my father's eyes always laughs because we serve him well, and the other eye weeps because there has been stolen from him a vine belonging to him, which poured forth a bucket of wine every hour. And now I am going to ask people all over the world whether someone cannot inform me about this vine, that I may obtain it for my father, that his eye may not weep any longer."

The fox said, "Well, I know where the vine is. Follow me." He followed the fox, and they came to a large garden. Then the fox said, "There is the vine of which you are in search, but it is difficult to get to it. Do you now mark well what I am going to say to you. In the garden, before the vine is reached, it is necessary to pass twelve watches, and in each watch twelve warders. When the warders are looking, you can pass them freely, because they sleep with their eyes open. If they have their eyes closed, go not, for they are awake, not sleeping, with their eyes closed. When you come into the garden, there under the vine stand two shovels – one of wood, and the other of gold. But mind you don't take the golden shovel to dig up the vine, for the shovel will ring, and will wake up the watch. The watch will seize you, and you may fare badly. But take the wooden shovel, and with it dig up the vine, and, when the watch is looking, come quietly to me outside, and you will have obtained the vine."

He went into the garden, arrived at the first watch, The warders directed their eyes towards him; one would have thought they would have looked him to powder. But he went past them as past a stone, came to the second, third, and all the watches in succession, and arrived in the garden at the vine itself. The vine poured forth a bucket of wine every hour. He was too lazy to dig with the wooden shovel, but took the golden one, and as soon as he struck it into the ground, the shovel rang and woke the watch. The watch assembled, seized him, and delivered him to their lord.

The lord asked the simpleton, "How did you dare to pass so many watches and come into the garden to take my vine away?" The simpleton said, "It is not your vine, but my father's; and my father's left eye weeps, and will weep till I obtain him the vine, and I must do it; and if you don't give me my father's vine, I shall come again, and the second time I shall take it away." The lord said, "I cannot give you the vine. But if you procure me the golden apple tree which blooms, ripens, and bears golden fruit every twenty-four hours, I will give it you."

He went out to the fox, and the fox asked him, "Well, how is it?" He answered, "No how. I went past the watch, and began to dig up the vine with the wooden shovel, but it was too long a job, and I took the golden shovel; the shovel rang and woke the watch; the watch seized me, and delivered me to their lord, and the lord promised to give me the vine if I procured him the golden apple tree which, every twenty-four hours, blooms, ripens, and bears golden fruit." The fox said, "But why did you not obey me? You see how nice it would have been to go to your father with the vine." He shook his head, "I see that I have done wrong, but I will do so no more." The fox said, "Come! now let us go to the golden apple tree." The fox led him to a far handsomer garden than the first one, and told him that he must pass similarly through twelve similar watches. "And when you come in the garden," said she, "to where the golden apple tree is, two very long poles stand there – one of gold, and the other of wood. Don't take the golden one to beat the golden apple tree, for the golden branch will emit a whistling sound, and will wake the watch, and you will fare ill. But take the wooden pole to beat the golden apple tree, and then mind you come out immediately to me. If you do not obey me, I will not help you further." He said, "I will, fox, only that it may be mine to acquire the golden apple tree to purchase the vine. I am impatient to go to my father." He went into the garden, and the fox stayed waiting for him outside. He passed the twelve watches, and also arrived at the apple tree. But when he saw the apple tree, and the golden apples on the apple tree, he forgot for joy where he was, and hastily took the golden pole to beat the golden apple tree. As soon as he had stripped a golden branch with the pole, the golden branch emitted a whistling sound, and woke the watch. The watch hastened up, seized him, and delivered him to the lord of the golden apple tree.

The lord asked the simpleton, "How did you dare, and how were you able, to go into my garden in face of so many watches of mine, to beat the golden apple trees?" The simpleton said, "Thus and thus, my father's left eye weeps because a vine has been stolen from him, which poured forth a bucket of wine every hour. That vine is kept in such and such a garden, and the lord of the garden and the vine said to me, 'If you procure me the golden apple tree which, every twenty-four hours, blooms, ripens, and produces golden fruit, I will give you the vine.' And, therefore, I have come to beat the golden apple tree, to give the apple tree for the vine, and to carry the vine to my father, that his left eye may not weep. And if you do not give me the golden apple tree now, I shall come again to steal it."

The lord said, "It is good, if it is so. Go you and procure me the golden horse which, in twenty-four hours, goes over the world, and I will give you the golden apple tree. Give the apple tree for the vine, and take the vine to your father, that he may weep no more."

Then he went outside, and the fox, awaiting him, said, "Now, then, how is it?" "Not very well. The golden apple trees are so beautiful that you can't look at them for beauty. I forgot myself, and couldn't take the wooden pole, as you told me, but took the golden pole to beat the golden apple tree; the branch emitted a whistling sound, and woke the watch; the watch seized me, and delivered me to their lord, and the lord told me if I procured him the golden horse which goes over the world in twenty-four hours, he would give me the golden apple tree, that I may give the apple tree for the vine to take to my father, that he may weep no more."

Again the fox began to scold and reproach him. "Why did you not obey me? You see that you would have been by now at your father's. And thus you torment both yourself and me." He said to the fox, "Only procure me the horse, fox, and I will always henceforth obey you."

The fox led him to a large and horrible forest, and in the forest they found a farmyard. In this farmyard twelve watches, as in the case of the vine and the apple tree, guarded the golden horse. The fox said, "Now you will pass the watches as before. Go if they are looking; do not go if they have their eyes shut. When you enter the stable, there stands the golden horse, equipped with golden trappings. By the horse are two bridles – one of gold, and the other plaited of tow. Mind you don't take the golden bridle, but the one of tow; if you bridle him with the golden bridle, the horse will neigh and will wake the watch; the watch will seize you, and who will be worse off than you? Don't come into my sight without the horse!" "I won't, fox," said he, and went. He passed all the watches, and entered the stable where the horse was. When he was there, golden horse! golden wings! so beautiful, good heavens! that you couldn't look at them for beauty! He saw the golden bridle; it was beautiful and ornamented; he saw also that of tow; it was dirty, and couldn't be worse. Now he thought long what to do and how to do. "I can't put that nasty thing" – the tow bridle – "it's so nasty! – on that beauty; I had rather not have him at all than put such a horse to shame." He took the golden bridle, bridled the golden horse, and mounted him. But the horse neighed, and woke the watch; the watch seized him and delivered him to their lord.

Then the lord said, "How did you have resolution to pass my numerous warders into my stable to take away my golden horse?" The simpleton replied, "Need drove me; I have a father at home, and his left eye continually weeps, and will weep till I obtain for him a vine which in a day and night poured forth twenty-four buckets of wine; this vine has been stolen from him. Well, I have found it, and it has been told me that I shall obtain the vine if I procure the golden apple tree for the lord of the vine; and the lord of the golden apple tree said if I procured him the golden horse, he would give me the golden apple tree; and I came from him to take away the golden horse, that I might give the golden horse for the golden apple tree, and the golden apple tree for the vine, to take it home and give it my father, that he may weep no more." The lord said, "Good. If it is so, I will give you my golden horse, if you procure me the golden damsel in her cradle, who has never yet seen either the sun or the moon, so that her face is not tanned." And the simpleton said, "I will procure you the golden damsel, but you must give me your golden horse, on which to seek the golden damsel and bring her to you. And a golden horse properly appertains to a golden damsel." The lord said, "And how will you guarantee that you will return to me again?" The simpleton said, "Behold, I swear to you by my father's eyesight that I will return to you again, and either bring the horse, if I do not find the damsel, or give you the damsel, if I find her, for the horse." To this the lord agreed, and gave him the golden horse. He bridled it with the golden bridle, and came outside to the fox. The fox was impatiently expecting him, to know what had happened.

The fox said, "Well, have you obtained the horse?" The simpleton said, "I have, but on condition that I procure for him the golden damsel in her cradle, who has never yet seen the sun or the moon, so that her face is not tanned. But if you know what need is, good friend, in the world, say whether she is anywhere, and whether you know of such a damsel." The fox said, "I know where the damsel is. Only follow me." He followed, and they came to a large cavern. Now the fox said, "There the damsel is. You will go into that cavern, deep into the earth. You will pass the watches as before. In the last chamber lies the golden damsel in a golden cradle. By the damsel stands a huge spectre, which says, "No! No! No!" Now, don't be at all afraid; it cannot do anything to you in anywise. But her wicked mother has placed it beside her daughter, that no one may venture to approach her to take her away. And the damsel is impatiently waiting to be released and freed from her mother's cruelty. When you come back with the damsel in the cradle, push all the doors to behind you, that they may be shut, that the watch may not be able to come out after you in pursuit." He did so. He passed all the watches, entered the last chamber, and in the chamber was the damsel, rocking herself in a golden cradle, and on the way to the cradle stood a huge spectre, which said, "No! No! No!" But he paid no attention to it. He took the cradle in his hands, seated himself with the cradle on the horse, and proceeded, pushed the doors to, and the doors closed from the first to the last, and out he flew with the damsel in the cradle before the fox. The fox was anxiously expecting him.

Now the fox said to him, "Are you not sorry to give so beautiful a damsel for the golden horse? But you will not otherwise be able to acquire the golden horse, because you have sworn by your father's eyesight. But come! let me try whether I can't be the golden damsel." She bounded hither and thither, and transformed herself into a golden damsel; everything about her was damsel-like, only her eyes were shaped like a fox's eyes.

He put her into the golden cradle, and left the real damsel under a tree to take charge of the golden horse. He went, he took away the golden cradle, in which was the fox-damsel, and delivered her to the lord of the golden horse, and absolved himself from the oath by his father's eyesight. He returned to the horse and the damsel. Now that same lord of the golden horse, full of joy at acquiring the golden damsel, assembled all his lordship, prepared a grand banquet for their entertainment, and showed them what he had acquired in exchange for his golden horse. While the guests were gazing at the damsel, one of them scrutinized her attentively, and said, "All is damsel-like, and she is very beautiful, but her eyes are shaped like a fox's eyes." No sooner had he said this, when up sprang the fox and ran away. The lord and the guests were enraged that he had said "fox's eyes", and put him to death.

The fox ran to the simpleton, and on they went to give the golden horse for the golden apple tree. They arrived at the place. Here again the fox said, "Now, you see, you have got possession of the golden damsel, but the golden horse properly appertains to the golden damsel. Are you sorry to give the golden horse?" "Yes, fox, but though I am sorry, yet I wish my father not to weep." The fox said, "But stay; let me try whether I can be the golden horse." She bounded hither and thither, and transformed herself into a golden horse, only she had a fox's tail. Then she said, "Now lead me; let them give you the golden apple tree, and I know when I shall come to you."

He led off the fox-horse, delivered it to the lord of the golden apple tree, and obtained the golden apple tree. Now, the lord of the golden apple tree was delighted at having acquired so beautiful a horse, and invited his whole lordship to a feast, to boast to them what a horse he had acquired. The guests began to gaze at the horse, and to wonder at how beautiful he was. All at once, one scrutinized his tail attentively, and said, "All is beautiful and all pleases me, only I should say that it is a fox's tail!" The moment he said that, the fox jumped up and ran away. But the guests were enraged at him for using the expression "fox's tail", and put him to death. The fox came to the simpleton, and proceeded with the golden damsel, the horse, and the golden apple tree to the vine.

Now again the fox said, "You see, now you have acquired the golden apple tree. But the golden damsel is not appropriate without the golden horse, or the golden horse without the golden apple tree. Are you sorry to give the golden apple tree?" The simpleton said, "Yes, fox; but I must, to obtain the vine, that my father may not weep. I had rather that my father did not weep than all that I have." The fox said, "Stay! I will try whether I can be the golden apple tree." She bounded hither and thither, and transformed herself into a golden apple tree, and told him to take it away and give it for the vine. He took off the golden fox-apple tree, and gave it to the lord of the vine, obtained the vine, and went away.

The lord for joy assembled his whole lordship, and prepared a grand feast, to display what a golden apple tree he had acquired. The guests assembled and began to gaze at the apple tree. But one scrutinized it attentively, and said, "All is beautiful, and cannot be more beautiful, only the fruit is in the shape a fox's head, and not like other apples." No sooner had he said this when up jumped the fox and ran away. But they were enraged at him and slew him, because he had said "fox's head".

Now the simpleton took leave of the fox and went home, having with him the golden damsel, the golden horse, the golden apple tree, and the vine. When he arrived at the crossroad, where he had parted from his brothers when he went from home to seek the vine, he saw a multitude of people assembled, and he, too, went thither to see what was the matter. When he got there, his two brothers were standing condemned, and the people were going to hang them. He told the damsel that they were his brothers, and that he would like to ransom them. The damsel took a large quantity of treasure out of her bosom, and he ransomed his brothers, the malefactors, who had thought to acquire the vine by slaying, burning, and plundering. They envied him, but could not help themselves. They proceeded home. The simpleton planted the vine in the garden where it had been. The vine began to pour forth wine, and his father's left eye ceased to weep and began to laugh. The apple tree began to blossom, the golden horse to neigh, the damsel to sing, and there was love and beauty at the farmhouse. Everything was merry; everything was rejoicing and making progress.

All at once the father sent his sons to bring him from the country three ears of rye, that he might see what manner of season it would be. When they came to a well in the country, they told their simpleton brother to get them some water to drink. He stooped over the well to reach the water for them. They pushed him into the water and he was drowned. Immediately the vine ceased to pour forth wine, the father's eye began to weep, the apple tree drooped, the horse ceased to neigh, the damsel began to weep, and everything lost its cheerful appearance. Thereupon that self-same lame fox came up, got down into the well, gently drew her adopted brother out, poured the water out of him, placed him on the fresh grass, and he revived. As soon as he revived, the fox was transformed into a very beautiful damsel. Then she related to him how her mother had cursed her because she had rescued her greatest enemy from death. She was cursed, and was transformed into a cunning fox, and limped on three feet until she should rescue her benefactor from a watery death. "And, lo! I have rescued you, my adopted brother. Now, adieu!" She went her way, and the simpleton his way to his father, and when he arrived at the farmhouse, the vine began again to pour forth wine, his father's eye to laugh, the golden apple tree to bloom, the golden horse to neigh, and the golden damsel to sing. He told his father what his brothers had done to him on the way, and how a damsel had rescued him and freed herself from a curse. When his father heard this, he drove the two villains out into the world. But he married the simpleton to the golden damsel, with whom he lived long in happiness and content.

The Dragon and the Prince

THERE WAS AN EMPEROR who had three sons. One day the eldest son went out hunting, and when he got outside the town, up sprang a hare out of a bush, and he after it, and hither and thither, till the hare fled into a watermill, and the

prince after it. But it was not a hare, but a dragon, and it waited for the prince and devoured him. When several days had elapsed and the prince did not return home, people began to wonder why it was that he was not to be found. Then the middle son went hunting, and as he issued from the town, a hare sprang out of a bush, and the prince after it, and hither and thither, till the hare fled into the watermill and the prince after it. But it was not a hare, but a dragon, which waited for and devoured him. When some days had elapsed and the princes did not return, either of them, the whole court was in sorrow. Then the third son went hunting, to see whether he could not find his brothers. When he issued from the town, again up sprang a hare out of a bush, and the prince after it, and hither and thither, till the hare fled into the watermill. But the prince did not choose to follow it, but went to find other game, saying to himself, "When I return I shall find you."

After this he went for a long time up and down the hill, but found nothing, and then returned to the watermill. But when he got there, there was only an old woman in the mill. The prince invoked God in addressing her: "God help you, old woman!" The old woman replied, "God help you, my son!" Then the prince asked her, "Where, old woman, is my hare?" She replied, "My son, that was not a hare, but a dragon. It kills and throttles many people." Hearing this, the prince was somewhat disturbed, and said to the old woman, "What shall we do now? Doubtless my two brothers also have perished here." The old woman answered, "They have indeed, but there's no help for it. Go home, my son, lest you follow them." Then he said to her, "Dear old woman, do you know what? I know that you will be glad to liberate yourself from that pest." The old woman interrupted him: "How should I not? It captured me, too, in this way, but now I have no means of escape." Then he proceeded: "Listen well to what I am going to say to you. Ask it whither it goes and where its strength is, then kiss all the places where it tells you its strength is, as if from love, till you ascertain it, and afterwards tell me when I come." Then the prince went off to the palace, and the old woman remained in the watermill.

When the dragon came in, the old woman began to question it: "Where in God's name have you been? Whither do you go so far? You will never tell me whither you go." The dragon replied, "Well, my dear old woman, I do go far." Then the old woman began to coax it: "And why do you go so far? Tell me where your strength is. If I knew where your strength is, I don't know what I should do for love; I would kiss all those places." Thereupon the dragon smiled and said to her, "Yonder is my strength, in that fireplace." Then the old woman began to fondle and kiss the fireplace, and the dragon on seeing it burst into a laugh, and said to her, "Silly old woman, my strength isn't there; my strength is in that tree-fungus in front of the house." Then the old woman began again to fondle and kiss the tree, and the dragon again laughed, and said to her, "Away, old woman! My strength isn't there." Then the old woman inquired, "Where is it?" The dragon began to give an account in detail: "My strength is a long way off, and you cannot go thither. Far in another empire under the emperor's city is a lake, in that lake is a dragon, and in the dragon a boar, and in the boar a pigeon, and in that is my strength."

The next morning when the dragon went away from the mill, the prince came to the old woman, and the old woman told him all that she had heard from the dragon. Then he left his home, and disguised himself; he put shepherd's boots on his feet, took a shepherd's staff in his hand, and went into the world. As he went on thus from village to village and from town to town, at last he came into another empire and into the imperial city, in a lake under which the dragon was. On going into the town, he began to inquire who wanted a shepherd. The citizens told him that the emperor did. Then he went straight to the emperor. After he announced himself, the emperor admitted him into his presence, and asked him, "Do you wish to keep sheep?" He replied, "I do, illustrious crown!" Then the emperor engaged him, and began to inform and instruct him: "There is here a lake, and alongside the lake very beautiful pasture, and when you call the sheep out, they go thither at once, and spread themselves round the lake. But whatever shepherd goes off there, that shepherd returns back no more. Therefore, my son, I tell you, don't let the sheep have their own way and go where they will, but keep them where you will."

The prince thanked the emperor, got himself ready, and called out the sheep, taking with him, moreover, two hounds that could catch a boar in the open country, and a falcon that could capture any bird, and carrying also a pair of bagpipes. When he called out the sheep, he let them go at once to the lake, and when the sheep arrived at the lake, they immediately spread round it, and the prince placed the falcon on a stump, and the hounds and bagpipes under the stump, then tucked up his hose and sleeves, waded into the lake, and began to shout, "Dragon! dragon! come out to single combat with me today, that we may measure ourselves together, unless you're a woman." The dragon called out in reply, "I will do so now, prince – now!"

Erelong, behold the dragon! It was large, it was terrible, it was disgusting! When the dragon came out, it seized him by the waist, and they wrestled a summer day till afternoon. But when the heat of afternoon came on, the dragon said, "Let me go, prince, that I may moisten my parched head in the lake, and toss you to the sky." But the prince replied, "Come, dragon, don't talk nonsense; if I had the emperor's daughter to kiss me on the forehead, I would toss you still higher." Thereupon the dragon suddenly let go of him, and went off into the lake. On the approach of evening, he washed and got himself up nicely, placed the falcon on his arm, the hounds behind him, and the bagpipes under his arm, then drove the sheep and went into the town playing on the bagpipes.

When he arrived at the town, the whole town assembled as to see a wondrous sight because he had come, whereas previously no shepherd had been able to come from the lake. The next day the prince got ready again, and went with his sheep straight to the lake. But the emperor sent two grooms after him to go stealthily and see what he did, and they placed themselves on a high hill whence they could have a good view. When the shepherd arrived, he put the hounds and bagpipes under the stump and the falcon upon it, then tucked up his hose and sleeves, waded into the lake and shouted, "Dragon, dragon! come out to single combat with me, that we may measure ourselves once more together, unless you are a woman!" The dragon replied, "I will do so, prince, now, now!" Erelong, behold the dragon! It was large, it was terrible, it was disgusting! And it seized him by the waist and wrestled with him a summer's day till afternoon. But when the afternoon heat came on, the dragon said, "Let me go, prince, that I may moisten my parched head in the lake, and may toss you to the sky." The prince replied, "Come, dragon, don't talk nonsense; if I had the emperor's daughter to kiss me on the forehead, I would toss you still higher." Thereupon the dragon suddenly left hold of him, and went off into the lake. When night approached, the prince drove the sheep as before, and went home playing the bagpipes.

When he arrived at the town, the whole town was astir and began to wonder because the shepherd came home every evening, which no one had been able to do before. Those two grooms had already arrived at the palace before the prince, and related to the emperor in order everything that they had heard and seen. Now when the emperor saw that the shepherd returned home, he immediately summoned his daughter into his presence and told her all, what it was and how it was. "But," said he, "tomorrow you must go with the shepherd to the lake and kiss him on the forehead." When she heard this, she burst into tears and began to entreat her father. "You have no one but me, and I am your only daughter, and you don't care about me if I perish." Then the emperor began to persuade and encourage her: "Don't fear, my daughter. You see, we have had so many changes of shepherds, and of all that went out to the lake, not one has returned. But he has been contending with the dragon for two whole days and it has done him no hurt. I assure you, in God's name, that he is able to overcome the dragon, only go tomorrow with him to see whether he will free us from this mischief which has destroyed so many people."

When on the morrow the day dawned and the sun came forth, up rose the shepherd, and up rose the maiden too, to begin to prepare for going to the lake. The shepherd was cheerful, more cheerful than ever, but the emperor's daughter was sad, and shed tears. The shepherd comforted her: "Lady sister, I pray you, do not weep, but do what I tell you. When it is time, run up and kiss me, and fear not." As he went and drove the sheep, the shepherd was thoroughly cheery, and played a merry tune on his bagpipes. But the damsel did nothing but weep as she went beside him, and he several times left off playing and turned towards her. "Weep not, golden one; fear nought."

When they arrived at the lake, the sheep immediately spread round it, and the prince placed the falcon on the stump, and the hounds and bagpipes under it, then tucked up his hose and sleeves, waded into the water, and shouted, "Dragon! dragon! come out to single combat with me, that we may measure ourselves once more, unless you're a woman!" The dragon replied, "I will, prince, now, now!" Erelong, there was the dragon! It was huge, it was terrible, it was disgusting! When it came out, they seized each other by the middle, and wrestled a summer's day till afternoon. But when the afternoon heat came on, the dragon said, "Let me go, prince, that I may moisten my parched head in the lake, and toss you to the skies." The prince replied, "Come, dragon, don't talk nonsense; if I had the emperor's daughter to kiss me on the forehead, I would toss you much higher." When he said this, the emperor's daughter ran up and kissed him on the face, on the eye, and on the forehead. Then he swung the dragon, and tossed it high into the air, and when it fell to the ground, it burst into pieces.

But as it burst into pieces, out of it sprang a wild boar, which started to run away. But the prince shouted to his shepherd dogs, "Hold it! Don't let it go!" And the dogs sprang up and after it, caught it, and soon tore it to pieces. But out of the boar flew a pigeon, and the prince loosed the falcon, and the falcon caught the pigeon and brought it into the prince's hands. The prince said to it, "Tell me now, where are my brothers?" The pigeon replied, "I will, only do me no harm. Immediately behind your father's town is a watermill, and in the watermill are three wands that have sprouted up. Cut these three wands up from below, and strike with them upon their root. An iron door will immediately open into a large vault. In that vault are many people, old and young, rich and poor, small and great, wives and maidens, so that you could settle a populous empire. There, too, are your brothers." When the pigeon had told him all this, the prince immediately wrung its neck.

The emperor had gone out in person, and posted himself on the hill from which the grooms had viewed the shepherd, and he, too, was a spectator of all that had taken place. After the shepherd had thus obtained the dragon's head, twilight began to approach. He washed himself nicely, took the falcon on his shoulder, the hounds behind him, and the bagpipes under his arm, played as he went, drove the sheep, and proceeded to the emperor's palace, with the damsel at his side still in terror.

When they came to the town, all the town assembled as to see a wonder. The emperor, who had seen all his heroism from the hill, called him into his presence, and gave him his daughter, went immediately to church, had them married, and held a wedding festival for a week. After this, the prince told him who and whence he was, and the emperor and the whole town rejoiced still more. Then, as the prince was urgent to go to his own home, the emperor gave him a large escort, and equipped him for the journey. When they were in the neighbourhood of the watermill, the prince halted his attendants, went inside, cut up the three wands, and struck the root with them, and the iron door opened at once. In the vault was a vast multitude of people. The prince ordered them to come out one by one, and go whither each would, and stood himself at the door. They came out thus one after another, and lo! there were his brothers also, whom he embraced and kissed. When the whole multitude had come out, they thanked him for releasing and delivering them, and went each to his own home. But he went to his father's house with his brothers and bride, and there lived and reigned to the end of his days.

The Birdcatcher

NEAR CONSTANTINOPLE there lived a man who knew no other occupation but that of catching birds; his neighbours called him the birdcatcher. Some he used to sell, others served him for food, and thus he maintained himself. One day he caught a crow, and wanted to let it go, but then he had nothing to take home. "If I can't catch anything today, I'll take my children the crow, that they may amuse themselves, and they have no other birds at hand." So he intended, and so he did. His wife, on seeing the crow, said, "What mischief have you brought me? Wring the worthless thing's neck!" The crow, on hearing that sentence, besought the birdcatcher to let her go, and promised to be always at his service. "I will bring birds to you; through me

you will become prosperous." "Even if you're lying, it's no great loss," said the birdcatcher to himself, and set the crow at liberty.

On the morrow the birdcatcher went out birdcatching as usual, and the crow kept her word; she brought him two nightingales, and he caught them both, and took them home. The nightingales were not long with the birdcatcher, for the grand vizier heard of them, sent for the birdcatcher, took the two nightingales from him, and placed them in the new mosque. The nightingales were able to sing sweetly and agreeably. The people collected in front of the mosque and listened to their beautiful singing, and the wonder came to the ears of the emperor.

The emperor summoned the grand vizier, took the birds from him, and inquired whence he had got them. When the emperor had thought the matter over, he sent his kavasses, and they summoned the birdcatcher. "It's no joke to go before the emperor! I know why he summons me; no half torture will be mine. I am guilty of nothing, I owe nothing, but the emperor's will, that's my crime!" said the birdcatcher, and went into the emperor's presence all pale with fear. "Birdcatcher, sirrah! are you the catcher of those nightingales that were at the new mosque?" "Padishah! both father and mother! where your slipper is, there is my face! – I am." "Sirrah!" again said the emperor. "I wish you to find their mother. Doubtless your reward will be forthcoming. But do you hear? You may be quite sure of it; if you don't, there will be no head on your shoulders. I'm not joking."

Now the poor fellow went out of the emperor's presence, and how he got home he didn't know. A good two hours afterwards, he came to himself and began to lament. "I'm a fool! I thought my trade led nowhither, and not to misfortune for me, but now see! To find the mother of the birds – none but a fool could imagine it – and to catch her!" To this lamentation there was neither limit nor end. It was getting dark, and his wife summoned him to supper. Just then the crow was at the window. "What's this?" the crow asked. "What are these lamentations? What's the distress?" "Let me alone, don't add to my torture. I'm done for owing to you!" said the birdcatcher, and told her all, what it was and how it was. "That's easy," answered she.

"Go to the emperor tomorrow, and ask for a thousand loads of wheat; then pile up the corn in one heap, and I will inform the birds that the emperor gives them a feast; they will all assemble; their mother, too, will doubtless come; the one with regard to which I give you a sign is she; bring a cage, put the two nightingales in it; the mother, seeing her two young birds, will fly up; let your snare be ready, and then we shall find and catch her."

As the crow instructed him, so he did. The emperor gave him the corn; he feasted the birds, caught the mother of the nightingales, and took her to the emperor. He received a handsome reward, but he would gladly have gone without such reward when he remembered how many tears he had shed. The crow, too, received a reward, for she persuaded the birdcatcher to give his wife a good beating, which he did, to the satisfaction of the crow, in her presence.

Time after time, behold some of the emperor's kavasses! "Come, the emperor summons you!" sounded from the door. "A new misfortune! A new sorrow!" thought the birdcatcher in his heart, and went before the emperor. Do you hear, sirrah? Just now I paid you a good recompense; now a greater one awaits you. I wish you to seek the mistress of those birds, otherwise, valah! bilah! your head will be in danger! Do you understand me?" At these words of the emperor, the birdcatcher either could not or dared not utter a word. He shrugged his shoulders and went out of his presence. As he went home he talked to himself, weeping, "I see that he is determined to destroy me, and some devil has put it into his head to torture me first."

On arriving at home, he found his crow at the window. "Has some misfortune again occurred to you?" "Don't ask," replied the birdcatcher. "One still blacker and more miserable!" And he told her all in detail, what it was and how it was. "Don't trouble your head much about that," said the crow. "Be quick; ask the emperor for a boat full of all manner of wares; then we will push off on the deep sea; when people hear that the emperor's agent is bringing wares, the people will assemble, and that lady is sure to come; the one on which I perch is she; up anchor and off with the boat!" This the birdcatcher remembered well. What he asked of the emperor, that he gave him, and he pushed the boat over the sea; his bringing wares for sale went from mouth to mouth; people came and purchased the wares; at last came the mistress of the birds also, and began to examine the wares; the crow perched on her shoulder; the anchor was raised, and in a short time the birdcatcher brought the boat to under the emperor's quay. When the birdcatcher brought her before the emperor, the emperor was astounded. He didn't know which to admire most, the birdcatcher's cleverness or her beauty. Her beauty overpowered the emperor's mind. He rewarded the birdcatcher handsomely, and placed the sultana in his house. "You are the dearest to me of all," said the emperor several times to her. "If I were to banish all the sultanas, you should never go out of my seraglio."

The birdcatcher was again in evil case. The new sultana was in a perpetual state of irritation, for it was poor luck to be obliged to be affectionate to an elderly longbeard. The emperor comforted her, and asked her what failed her, when she had everything in abundance with him. A woman's revenge is worse than a cat's. Not daring to tell the emperor the truth, she wanted to revenge herself on the poor birdcatcher. "Dear Padishah, I had a valuable ring on my hand when that birdcatcher deluded me into the boat, and pushed it from the shore. I began to wring my hands in distress, the ring broke, and one half fell into the sea, just where it was my hap to be. But, dear sultan, if I am a little dear to you, send that birdcatcher, let him seek that half for me, that I may unite it to this one." "All shall be done," said the emperor; and the kavasses soon brought the birdcatcher. "My son," said the emperor, "if you do not intend to lose my love and favour, hearken to me once more. At the place where you captured that lady, she broke a ring; it fell into the sea. I know that you can do so – find her that half; your reward will not fail. Otherwise, you know…"

When the poor fellow got home, a fit of laughter seized him from distress. "I knew that the devil was teaching him how to torment and torture me before he put me to death. If hell were to open, all the devils wouldn't find it!" "What's the matter, friend?" said the crow. "Till now you were weeping and complaining, and now in a rage you are laughing." He told her all, what it was, and how it was. "Don't fret yourself," continued the crow. "Have you given your wife a good thrashing? I wish you to give her a good hiding again, when we go down to the sea. And now come, ask the emperor for a thousand barrels of oil." The emperor had stores of oil and felt; he gave him as much as he required. Everybody thought that he was going to trade with the oil.

When he arrived at the place where he captured the young lady, the crow gave the word of command, and they poured out all the oil into the sea. The sea became violently agitated, the crow darted in, and found the missing fragment of the ring. The birdcatcher took the boat back thence under the emperor's palace, and delivered the ring to the emperor. He passed it on to the lady, and she fitted it to the other half. Both she and the emperor were astonished at the birdcatcher's cleverness, commended him, and sent him home with a present.

The emperor wished by every means to induce the young lady to marry him, and to have a formal wedding. She for a long time declined, but at last said, "If it is your will, I consent, but only on condition that before our wedding you destroy that birdcatcher." The emperor now found himself between two fires. It was agony to destroy his benefactor; it was worse agony not to be able to withstand his heart, and to give up the love of the young lady. Love is eternal, and is often stronger even than truth. He summoned the birdcatcher, commended him for having so often fulfilled his will, and told him that he deserved to sit in the grand vizier's seat. "But there is nothing else for it; you must go home, and take leave of your wife, children, and friends, of whom I will undertake the care. In the afternoon come; you must of necessity jump into the fire."

He went home, and the crow came to meet him. He told her all that was to be done with him in the afternoon, and said to her, "If you do not help me as usual now, I am done for, not through my fault, nor through the emperor's, but owing to you." The crow informed him what to do, but before he went, he was to give his wife a thoroughly good beating. His wife departed this life from so many blows. A fire was flaming before the great mosque. The Turks came out of the mosque, the emperor came, and the people swarmed round the fire. The birdcatcher came cheerfully before the emperor.

Everyone deemed him a malefactor. "Fortunate Padishah, it is your pleasure to burn me to death. I am happy to be able to be a sacrifice for you. It has occurred to my mind, I am anxious to have a ride on a good horse. Permit me so to do before I jump into the fire." The emperor smiled, and ordered his best horse to be brought for him. He mounted, and made the horse gallop well.

When the horse sweated, he dismounted, anointed himself with the horse's foam, remounted, darted up to the fire, then dismounted, and darted into the fire. The people looked on. Five times, six times he crossed the flames, sprang out of the fire, and stood before the emperor as a youth of twenty years of age, sound, young, goodly, and handsome. The people cried, "Mercy, emperor! He has fulfilled his penalty." And the emperor graciously pardoned him.

The emperor now longed to become young and handsome also. He made the birdcatcher grand vizier, merely that he might tell him the secret. He said to him, "My lord, it is easy. Take a good horse, gallop about an hour as I did, dismount when the horse sweats, anoint yourself with his perspiration, jump into the fire, and you will come out such as I am."

Friday dawned. The emperor's best horse was saddled for him. Everybody thought that he was going to the mosque. A fire was burning furiously in front of the mosque. The people said, "There's somebody going to jump in again," and they were under no delusion. The emperor darted up to the fire all alone, and the people looked on to see what was going to happen.

The emperor dismounted with great speed, and sprang into the fire. The people crowded to rescue the emperor – 'twas all in vain. The emperor was burned to death. "He was crazy!" shouted the chief men and soldiers. They conducted the birdcatcher into the mosque, and girt him with the emperor's sword. Then the birdcatcher became emperor, the damsel he selected sultana, and the crow the chief lady at court.

Tales of Magic

Magic tales are the focus of this chapter, by and large featuring male protagonists. The world of magic is key in these tales is key, which range from the 'floating kiosk' in the sky, representing the Other World (where princesses are captured), to a magic flying carpet, a marvellous telescope and a miraculous ointment (in 'The Three Suitors').

The hero of another tale, 'Animal's Language', is gifted the ability to understand the language of animals by the King of the Snakes, father of a snake the hero rescued from a fire. He thus becomes privy to what animals know and say, a power that has intrigued humans for centuries. Finally, Pepelyouga's mother becomes a magical cow after her death, with astonishing powers.

The Wonderful Kiosk

ONCE UPON A TIME there lived a king, who had three sons and one daughter. The daughter was kept by her father for safety in a cage, since he cared for her as for his own eyes. When the girl grew up, she one evening asked her father to let her walk a little with her brothers in the front of the palace, and her father granted her request. She had hardly, however, taken a step outside the door of the palace before a dragon came down, caught her away from her brothers, and flew up with her into the clouds.

The three brothers ran as quickly as they could, and told their father what had happened to their sister, and asked him to let them go in search of her. To this their father consented, and gave each of them a horse, and other needful things for their travelling, and they went away to find their sister. After they had travelled a long time, they came in sight of a kiosk, which was neither in the sky nor yet on the earth, but hung midway between both. On coming near it, they began to think that their sister might be in it, and they consulted together how they might contrive to reach it.

After much deliberation they settled that one of them should kill his horse, make a thong out of the hide, and, fastening one end of the thong to an arrow, shoot it from the bow so that it should strike deep in the side of the kiosk, and that thus they might be able to climb up to it. The youngest brother proposed to the eldest that he should kill his horse, but this he refused to do. In like manner the second brother refused, so that nothing remained but that the youngest should kill his horse, which he did and made a long thong out of the hide; to this he tied an arrow, which he shot towards the kiosk.

The question was then asked, who would climb up the thong? The eldest brother declared that he would not; the second also refused, and thus it was the youngest was forced to climb up. When he had reached the kiosk, he went from room to room, until at length he found his sister sitting with the dragon sleeping with his head upon her knee, while she passed her fingers through the hair of his head.

When she saw her brother, she was very much frightened, and made signs for him to go away before the dragon woke up. But this her brother would not do, and instead of going away took his mace and struck with all his might on the head of the dragon. The dragon moved his paw a little towards the place where he had been struck, and said to the maiden, "I felt something bite me just here."

As he spoke, the king's son gave him another blow, and the dragon said again, "I felt something bite me just here." When the brother lifted his mace to strike the third time, the sister pointed and showed him where to strike at the life of the dragon. So he struck at the life, and the dragon immediately fell down dead, and the king's daughter pushed him from her knee and ran quickly to her brother and kissed him. Then she took him by the hand and began to show him the various rooms of the kiosk.

First, she took him into a room where a black horse stood ready to be mounted, with all his riding gear on him, and the whole of the harness was of pure silver.

She then led him to a second room, and in it stood a white horse, also saddled and bridled, and his harness was entirely of pure gold.

At last the sister took her brother into a third room, and there stood a cream-coloured horse, and the reins and stirrups and saddle, which were on him, were all thickly studded with precious stones.

After passing through these three rooms, she led him to a room where a young maiden sat behind a golden tambourette, busily engaged in embroidering with golden thread.

From this room they went into another, where a girl was spinning gold thread, and again into another room where a girl sat threading pearls, and before her, on a golden plate, was a golden hen with her chickens, sorting the pearls.

Having seen all these things, the brother went back to the room where the dragon lay dead, and threw him down to the earth, and the two brothers, who were below, were almost frightened to death at the sight of the dragon's carcass. The young prince then let his sister slowly down, and, after her, the three young maidens, each of them with the work on which she was employed. As he let them down, one after the other, he shouted to his brothers and told them to whom each of the maidens should belong – reserving for himself the third one, whom he also let down to the ground. This was the maiden who was engaged in threading pearls with the help of the golden hen and chickens. His brothers, however, were envious at the success of his courage, and at his having found his sister and saved her from the dragon, so they cut the thong in order that he might not be able to get down from the kiosk.

Then they found, in the fields nearby, a young shepherd, whom they disguised and took to their father, but forbad their sister and the three maidens, with many threats, to tell what they had done. After some time, the youngest brother, who had been left in the kiosk, received the news that his two brothers and the shepherd were to marry the three maidens. On the day when his eldest brother was married, the youngest brother mounted his black horse, and just as the wedding party came back from the church, the young prince came down from the kiosk, rushed into the midst, and struck his eldest brother slightly in the back, so that he fell down from his horse; he then immediately flew back again to the kiosk.

On the day that his second brother was married, the youngest again came down among the wedding party, as they left the church. He was mounted on the white horse, and he struck his second brother as he had done the eldest, so that he also fell down, and then he returned again to the kiosk. At last, on hearing that the young shepherd was going to be married to the maiden whom the prince had selected for himself, he mounted on the cream-coloured horse, descended again, and rode among the wedding guests as they came out of the church, and struck the bridegroom with his mace on his head so that he at once fell down dead.

When the guests gathered round him to catch him, which he permitted them to do, making no attempt to escape from them, he soon proved to them that he himself was the third son of the king, and that the shepherd was an imposter, and that his brothers, out of envy, had left him in the kiosk, when he had found his sister and killed the dragon. His sister and the three young maidens confirmed all that he said, so that the king, in his anger at the two elder brothers, drove them away from his court. However, he married the youngest brother to the third maiden, and, at his death, left him his kingdom.

The Three Suitors

IN A VERY REMOTE COUNTRY there formerly lived a king who had only one child – an exceedingly beautiful daughter. The princess had a great number of suitors, and amongst them were three young noblemen, whom the king loved much. As, however, the king liked the three nobles equally well, he could not decide to which of the three he should give his daughter as a wife. One day, therefore, he called the three young noblemen to him, and said, "Go, all of you, and travel about the world. The one of you who brings home the most remarkable thing shall become my son-in-law!"

The three suitors started at once on their travels, each of them taking opposite ways, and going in search of remarkable things into distant and different countries.

A long time had not passed before one of the young nobles found a wonderful carpet which would carry rapidly through the air whoever sat upon it.

Another of them found a marvellous telescope, through which he could see everybody and everything in the world, and even the many-coloured sands at the bottom of the great deep sea.

The third found a wonder-working ointment, which could cure every disease in the world, and even bring dead people back to life again.

Now the three noble travellers were far distant from each other when they found these wonderful things. But when the young man who had found the telescope looked through it, he saw one of his former friends and present rivals walking with a carpet on his shoulder, and so he set out to join him. As he could always see, by means of his marvellous telescope, where the other nobleman was, he had no great difficulty in finding him, and when the two had met, they sat side by side on the wonderful carpet, and it carried them through the air until they had joined the third traveller.

One day, when each of them had been telling of the remarkable things he had seen in his travels, one of them exclaimed suddenly, "Now let us see what the beautiful princess is doing, and where she is." Then the noble who had found the telescope looked through it and saw, to his great surprise and dismay, that the king's daughter was lying very sick, and at the point of death. He told this to his two friends and rivals, and they, too, were as thunderstruck at the bad news – until the one who had found the wonder-working ointment, remembering it suddenly, exclaimed, "I am sure I could cure her, if I could only reach the palace soon enough!" On hearing this, the noble who had found the wonderful carpet, cried out, "Let us sit down on my carpet, and it will quickly carry us to the king's palace!"

Thereupon the three nobles gently placed themselves on the carpet, which rose instantly in the air, and carried them direct to the king's palace.

The king received them immediately, but said very sadly, "I am sorry for you, for all your travels have been in vain. My daughter is just dying, so she can marry none of you!"

But the nobleman who possessed the wonder-working ointment said respectfully, "Do not fear, sire, the princess will not die!" And on being permitted to enter the apartment where she lay sick, he placed the ointment so that she could smell it. In a few moments the princess revived, and when her waiting-women had rubbed a little of the ointment on her skin, she recovered so quickly that in a few days she was better than she had been before she was taken ill.

The king was so glad to have his daughter given back to him, as he thought, from the grave, that he declared that she should marry no one but the young nobleman whose wonderful ointment had cured her.

But now a great dispute arose between the three young nobles; the one who possessed the ointment affirmed that, had he not found it, the princess would have died and could not, therefore, have married anyone; the noble who owned the telescope declared that, had he not found the wonderful telescope, they would never have known that the princess was dying, and so his friend would not have brought the ointment to cure her; whilst the third noble proved to them that, had he not found the wonderful carpet, neither the finding of the ointment nor the telescope would have helped the princess, since they could not have travelled such a great distance in time to save her.

The king, overhearing this dispute, called the young noblemen to him, and said to them, "My lords, from what you have said, I see that I cannot, with justice, give my daughter to any of you; therefore, I pray you to give up altogether the idea of marrying her, and that you continue friends as you always were before you became rivals."

The three young nobles saw that the king had decided justly; so they all left their native country, and went into a far-off desert to live like hermits. And the king gave the princess to another of his great nobles.

Many, many years had passed away since the marriage of the princess, when her husband was sent by her father to a distant country with which the king was waging war. The nobleman took his wife, the princess, with him, as he was uncertain how long he might be forced to remain abroad. Now it happened that a violent storm arose just as the vessel, in which the princess and her husband were, was approaching a strange coast, and in the height of the great tempest the ship dashed on some rocks, and went to pieces instantly. All the people on board perished in the waves, excepting only the princess, who clung very fast to a boat, and was carried by the wind and the tide to the seashore. There she found what seemed to be an uninhabited country, and, finding a small cave in a rock, she lived in it alone three years, feeding on wild herbs and fruits. She searched every day to find some way out of the forest which surrounded her cave, but could find none. One day, however, when she had wandered farther than usual from the cave where she lived, she came suddenly on another cave, which had, to her great astonishment, a small door. She tried over and over again to open the door, thinking she would pass the night in the cave, but all her efforts were unavailing, it was shut so fast. At length, however, a deep voice from within the cave called out, "Who is at the door?"

At this the princess was so surprised that she could not answer for some moments. When, however, she had recovered a little, she said, "Open me the door!" Immediately the door was opened from within, and she saw, with sudden terror, an old man with a thick grey beard reaching below his waist, and long white hair flowing over his shoulders.

What frightened the princess the more was her finding a man living here in the same desert where she had lived herself three years without seeing a single soul.

The hermit and the princess looked at each other long and earnestly without saying a word. At length, however, the old man said, "Tell me, are you an angel or a daughter of this world?"

Then the princess answered, "Old man, let me rest a moment, and then I will tell you all about myself, and what brought me here!" So the hermit brought out some wild pears, and when the princess had taken some of them, she began to tell him who she was, and how she came to be in that desert. She said, "I am a king's daughter, and once, many years ago, three young nobles of my father's court asked the king for my hand in marriage. Now the king had such an equal affection for all these three young men that he was unwilling to give pain to any of them, so he sent them to travel into distant countries, and promised to decide between them when they returned.

"The three noblemen remained a long time away, and whilst they were still abroad somewhere, I fell dangerously ill. I was just at the point of death, when they all three returned suddenly, one of them bringing a wonderful ointment which cured me at once, the two others bringing each equally remarkable things – a carpet that would carry whoever sat on it through the air, and a telescope with which one could see everybody and everything in the world, even to the sands at the bottom of the sea."

The princess had gone on thus far with her story, when the hermit suddenly interrupted her, saying, "All that happened afterwards I know as well as you can tell me. Look at me, my daughter! I am one of those noblemen who sought to win your hand, and here is the wonderful telescope." And the hermit brought out the instrument from a recess in the side of his cave before he continued, "My two friends and rivals came with me to this desert. We parted, however, immediately, and have never met since. I know not whether they are living or dead, but I will look for them."

Then the hermit looked through his telescope, and saw that the other two noblemen were living in caves like his, in different parts of the same desert. Having found this out, he took the princess by the hand, and led her on until they found the other hermits. When all were reunited, the princess related her adventures since the ship, in which her husband was, had gone down, and she alone had been saved.

The three noble hermits were pleased to see her alive once again, but at once decided that they ought to send her back to the king, her father.

Then they made the princess a present of the wonderful telescope, and the wonder-working ointment, and placed her on the wonderful carpet, which carried her and her treasures quickly and safely to her father's palace. As for the three noblemen, they remained, still living like hermits in the desert, only they visited each other now and then, so that the years seemed no longer so tedious to them, for they had many adventures to relate to each other.

The king was exceedingly glad to receive his only child back safely, and the princess lived with her father many years, but neither the king nor his daughter could entirely forget the three noble friends who, for her sake, lived like hermits in a wild desert in a far-off land.

Fate

ONCE UPON A TIME there were two brothers who lived together in a house. The one did all the work, whereas the other went about idling and never did anything but eat and drink. And they had abundance of everything, and were blessed with cattle, horses, sheep, pigs, and bees.

Then the brother who did all the work one day said to himself, "Why should I work for that lazy bones as well? It is much better we separate; I shall work for myself and he may do what he likes." And so he told his brother, "It is not fair that I have to manage everything whilst you never lend me a hand. You think of nothing but eating and drinking. I have, therefore, made up my mind. We are going to part." The brother, however, tried to dissuade him and said, "You have the management of everything, both of your property and of mine. And you know I am quite content and agree with everything you do." But the industrious brother insisted, so that the other one had to give in, and he said, "Very well, I shall not be cross with you about it. Go and give me my share according to what you think is mine." Then everything was divided up. The lazy brother took his share, and at once he appointed a cow-keeper for his cattle, a stableboy for his horses, a goatherd, a swineherd, and a beekeeper, and he said to them, "All my property I leave in your hands and God's." And after that he stayed at home, unconcerned, and without troubling himself about anything. The other brother went on working hard as before, looked after his herds, and was most careful. Yet in spite of that, he did not thrive, but suffered many losses, and his affairs became daily worse and worse. At last he was so poor that he had not even a pair of latchet shoes, and had to walk about barefooted. Then he said to himself, "I will go to my brother to see how he is getting on."

His way led him past the meadow, in which there was a flock of sheep, and when he came nearer he saw there was no shepherd, but an exceedingly beautiful maiden who was spinning a golden thread. After he had greeted the girl with a friendly "God be with you", he asked her whose were those sheep. She replied, "To whom I belong, his are also the sheep." Then he asked her, "Who are you?" whereupon she answered, "I am your brother's Good Luck." Then, overcome with violent anger, he asked, "Where is my Good Luck?" The maiden said, "Oh, that is very far from you." "And could I find it?" he asked. "You may," she said. "Go and search for it." And when he had heard this and seen that his brother's sheep were so fine that one cannot possibly imagine any sheep more valuable, then he was no longer inclined to view the other herds, but he went straightaway to his brother. When the latter beheld him, he pitied him, and with tears in his eyes he said, "Where have you been all this time?" And noticing the poor garments and bare feet, he gave him a pair of latchet shoes and some money. After he had been entertained for a few days, the poor brother started again for home. Arrived there, he took a knapsack over his shoulders, put some bread in it, took a staff in his hands, and went into the wide world to find his Good Luck.

When he had been walking for some time, he came into a big forest, and there he found an ugly trollop sleeping underneath a shrub. Then he lifted his stick and struck her on the back to awaken her. She got up with difficulty, could hardly open her bleared eyes, and said, "You may thank God that I had fallen asleep here, for had I been awake, you would not have received those lovely shoes." Then he asked her, "Who are you that on your account I should not have been given these shoes?" The slut said, "I am your Good Luck." When he heard this, he grew very angry, saying, "So you are my Good Luck? I wish God would kill you. Who is it that has given you unto me?" The slut, however, interrupted him. "Fate has given me unto you." Then he asked, "Where is this Fate?" And she said, "Go and search for it!" With which words she disappeared.

Thereupon the man started again on his way in order to find Fate. And whilst he was thus going along, he came to a village, and there stood a fine house in which a large fire was burning. Then he thought to himself, "Here must be a wedding, or they are celebrating some other feast day!" He entered, and saw hanging over the fire a big kettle in which the supper was cooking, and the master of the house sat by the fire. He wished him a good evening, to which the master of the house replied, "May God bestow on you all good things!" He invited him to take a seat near him, and asked him who he was and whither he was going. Then he told everything, how he, too, had been a householder, how he had become poor, and that he was now on his way to ask Fate herself why just he himself should remain so poor. Hereupon he asked the master of the house why and for whom he was cooking such a big meal. Then the latter said, "Alas, my brother! I am the master of a house and have abundance of everything, but nevertheless I am unable to appease the hunger of my people; it is as though dragons were hidden in their stomachs. Just observe my people when we are going to supper, then you will see it." And when they sat down for supper, the men snatched and grabbed one another's food, and in a few minutes the large cauldron was empty. After supper, the host's young wife collected all the bones and threw them on a heap behind the stove. And when the stranger was wondering at this, suddenly two very old persons thin as skeletons crawled forth in order to suck the bones. Then the stranger asked the master of the house, "Who are those behind the stove?" And he answered, "They are my father and my mother, and they will not die, just as though they were chained to this world."

The next morning when they parted, the stranger was requested kindly to ask Fate why the people in his house could not be sufficiently fed, and why his father and mother were so long in dying. The visitor promised to do so, and took his leave in order to find Fate.

After he had been on the road for ever such a long time, one evening he came into another village, entered one of the houses, and asked for a night's shelter. Readily he was received, and when asked what was his destination, he told them everything. Then the people in the house said, "For God's sake, brother, when you have reached your goal, do ask why our cattle do not thrive but are getting thinner and thinner." He promised to ask Fate about it, and the next morning he set out again.

And he came to a river and called out, "Oh, water, water, carry me over to the other bank." The water asked him, "Where are you going?" And he told the water. Then the water carried him across and said, "Please, brother, ask Fate why nothing can live within me." And he promised to do the water this favour and went on.

After ever such a long time, at last he came into a forest, and here he met a hermit, whom he asked whether he could give him any information about Fate. And the hermit said to him, "Go from here straight across the mountains, then you will arrive exactly in front of Fate's castle. But there you must not say a word, only do all the time precisely the same thing Fate is doing until she puts questions to you." The man thanked the hermit, and set out on his journey across the mountains. When he arrived at the castle of Fate, what things he did behold! Everywhere imperial splendour, and a great number of servants, men and women, were running about. But Fate sat quite alone at a table eating her supper. When the man saw her for whom he had been searching such a long time, he sat down by her side and shared the supper. After supper, Fate lay down to rest. So did he. Toward midnight, there was the most awful noise and turmoil in the castle, but above all the turmoil a voice was audible that said, "O Fate! O Fate! One hundred thousand souls have been born today. Give them something according to your pleasure!" Then Fate rose, opened a treasure box full of gold, took out of it glittering sovereigns, and scattered them all over the floor of the room. At the same time she said, "As I am faring today, they shall fare all their lives."

At daybreak the magnificent castle was gone, and in its place stood quite a small house of modest appearance. Yet there was in it enough and to spare of everything. When evening fell, Fate again sat down to supper; so did our friend, and neither spoke a word. And after supper both lay down to rest. Towards midnight there was again the most awful noise and turmoil, and above all the turmoil a voice was again audible that said, "O Fate! O Fate! One hundred thousand souls have been born today. Give them something according to your pleasure!" Then Fate rose, and opened a money box, but there were no sovereigns, only silver coins with an occasional sovereign hidden away amongst them, and Fate scattered silver coins all over the floor of the room. At the same time she said, "As I am faring today they shall fare all their lives."

And at daybreak that small but comfortable house was gone too, and in its place stood one ever so much smaller. So it happened every night and every morning the house was smaller, until at last there remained but a wretched hut, and Fate took a spade and began digging. Then the man, our friend, likewise took a spade and began digging, and both kept on digging throughout the day. When evening fell, Fate took a piece of bread, halved it, and gave one half to the man. That was their supper, and when they had eaten it they lay down to rest. Toward midnight, there was again the most awful noise and turmoil, and above all the turmoil a voice was yet again audible that said, "O Fate! O Fate! One hundred thousand souls have been born today. Give them something according to your pleasure!" Then Fate rose, opened a box, and began scattering about small potsherds like those with which children play, and amongst them a very few coins. At the same time she said, "As I am faring today they shall fare all their lives."

But when day broke again, the hut had once more been changed into a large palace, just as grand as the one which the man found when he arrived. And now at last Fate spoke to him and asked him, "Why did you come here?" And then he related all the particulars of his distress and his troubles, and that he had come to ask Fate personally why she had given unto him such a Bad Luck. Then Fate said to him, "You have seen how during the first night I was scattering sovereigns, and you have noticed, I hope, everything that happened during that night. Exactly as

I am faring during the night in the course of which a man is born, thus he will fare throughout his life. You have been born in a night of poverty, and therefore you will remain poor as long as you live. Your brother, on the other hand, has seen the light of the world during a fortunate night, and he will be a fortunate man until the end of his days. But since you have taken so much trouble and come in quest of me, I will tell you how you can help yourself. Your brother has a daughter; her name is Milica, and she is just as fortunate as her father. When you get home again, take her to you into your house, and of everything that you may gain say, "It is Milica's!"

Then he thanked Fate and said, "I know of a rich farmer who has more than enough of everything, yet he never succeeds in feeding his household well; at every meal they empty a brewer's copper full of food, and even that is not enough for them. And the father and the mother of this farmer, as though they were chained to this earth, have grown quite black with age and they are shrivelled up like ghosts, yet they cannot die. Therefore he begged me when I was his guest for a night to ask you what is the reason of all that." Then Fate replied, "All that happens because he does not honour his father and mother, and just throws some food at them behind the stove. If he would put them in the place of honour at his table and hand to them the first glass of wine and the first glass of whisky, they would soon breathe their last, and the people of the farmer's household would no longer eat so much."

Then he asked Fate, "In another village where I was staying a night, a man complained to me that his cattle would not thrive, and he urged me to find out from you whose fault it is." And Fate said, "It is because on the day of the patron saint of his house, he slaughters the most wretched cow he has. If, on the other hand, he would kill the very best, all his cattle would thrive." Finally, he also inquired on behalf of the water. "And how is it that nothing can live in that water?" And Fate answered, "Because no human being has yet been drowned in it. But take heed not to tell the water about this secret before you have been carried across, lest the water should at once drown you!"

Once again he thanked Fate, and started on his journey home. When he came to the water, it asked, "Well, what did Fate say?" And he answered, "First carry me across, and then I will tell you." Hardly had the water carried him across than he began running, and when he was a good distance away, he turned round and called out, "O, Water, it is because you have never drowned a human being that nothing will live in you." On hearing this, the water rushed after him over the fields and meadows, and only with great difficulty he escaped.

When he came into the village to the man whose cattle were not thriving, he was already impatiently awaited. "What news do you bring me, brother? Have you questioned Fate?" Whereupon he replied, "Yes, I have done so, and Fate said it is because you always offer up the worst cow on the feast day of your household saint. But if you would sacrifice your best, all your cattle would thrive." Having heard this, the farmer said, "Brother, stay with us! There are but three days to the feast of our patron saint, and if that is true which you tell me, I'll show you my gratitude." When now the feast day came, the father of the family killed the finest bullock which he had, and from that moment onwards his cattle began to thrive. Then he gave the man five oxen as a present. And the man set out again.

And when he arrived in the village where the ever-hungry household was, he was greeted with the words, "For God's sake, tell me, brother, how are you and what did Fate say?" And he replied, "Fate says you are not honouring your father and your mother, and you always throw the food at them behind the stove. If you would put them at the table, and, moreover, in the place of honour at the top of the table, and hand them the first glass of wine and the first glass of whisky, the inmates of your house would not eat half as much, and your father and mother would depart this life." When the master of the house had heard this, he told his wife at once to wash and to comb her father- and mother-in-law and to dress them nicely. When the evening came, the two were placed at the top of the table, and the first glass of wine and the first glass of whisky were handed to them. From that moment onwards the inmates of that household could no longer eat so much, and the father and mother in a few days died peaceably. Then the grateful master of the house gave our friend two bullocks, and the latter, after thanking his host, went home.

When he came into his native place, his acquaintances met him and asked him, "Whose are these beautiful cattle?" And he said each time, "My friend, they belong to Milica, my brother's daughter." When he arrived home, he went at once to his brother and begged him, "Do give me Milica, brother, as you know I have no one to care for me." And his brother replied, "I do not mind at all. Go and take Milica with you." Then he led his brother's daughter to his house. From that moment onwards, he prospered much, but of everything gained, he said, "It is Milica's."

One day he went out over his fields to see how the corn was going on. It was most lovely to look at. Then a wanderer came along, who asked him, "Whose is this corn field?" And, forgetting himself for a moment, he said, "It's mine." In the moment he said that, flames burst out of the corn and the fire spread rapidly. Quickly he ran after the wanderer and exclaimed, "Stop, my friend, the corn does not belong to me at all; it is Milica's." At once the fire ceased. Henceforth he lived happily with Milica, and to the end of his days all he did prospered.

Solomon Cursed by His Mother

ONCE UPON A TIME the very wise Solomon, in a conversation with his mother, said that every woman on earth at the bottom of her heart was thoroughly bad. His mother scolded him very much, and said it was not true; and when he proved in some fashion that she, too, was like other women, she grew infuriated and cursed him, and said he was not to die until he had seen the depths of the sea and the heights of heaven.

When Solomon had reached a very great age, and became tired of life and this world, he bethought himself how he could break the spell of his mother's curse so that he might die. First of all he wrought a big iron box, big enough to allow him to sit inside. To the lid of the box he fastened an iron chain, long enough in his opinion to reach the bottom of the sea.

Then he climbed into the box, and asked his wife to lock it, and to throw it into the sea, but to keep in her hands the end of the chain so that she might be able to pull it up again after the box and the chain had reached the bottom of the sea. Solomon's wife put the lid on, locked the box, and threw it into the sea. Whilst she was now holding in her hands the end of the chain, someone came and deceived her by telling her that the wise Solomon, together with his box, had been swallowed by a great fish already ever such a long time ago, and that she could do no better than let the chain drop and go home. She did so, and the heavy chain pressed the box with the wise Solomon inside firmly onto the bottom of the sea.

Some time after this event, the devils found the staff, cap, and stole of St. Johannes, and started a quarrel amongst themselves when dividing these things. At last they agreed to go to the wise Solomon, and he was to settle their differences. When they came to him at the bottom of the sea and told him what they wanted him to do, he said, "How can I decide your case here from within the box, where I cannot see either you or the object of your disputes? Carry me up to the surface and put me on the shore, and I will be your umpire." At once the devils carried him up in his box. As soon as the wise Solomon had got out, he took into his hands the things about which the devils were quarrelling just as if he was going to examine them and see what they were worth. All of a sudden he made the sign of the cross with the staff of the saint, and then the devils fled, so that all the things became his.

In this way the wise Solomon had beheld the bottom of the sea. Now he bethought himself how he might get a sight of the heights of heaven. For this purpose he caught two ostriches, starved them for a few days, and then he tied to their feet a big basket. Then he sat down in that basket, and in his hands he held on a long spit a roasted lamb just above the heads of the ostriches. Eager to seize the roasted lamb, up flew the ostriches, up and up, and they never stopped till the wise Solomon touched with his spit the vault of heaven. Then he turned his spit downwards, and thus the ostriches carried him again down to earth. And now that he had seen the depths of the sea and the heights of heaven, he could die at last.

Animals' Language

A **WEALTHY PEASANT had a shepherd, who served him for a great number of years most honestly and faithfully. One day, as he drove his sheep through a forest to the pasture, he heard a hissing sound, and wondered what it could be. Listening carefully, he went nearer and nearer to the spot whence the sound came, and he saw that the forest was on fire and that the hissing proceeded from a snake that was surrounded by flames. The shepherd watched to see what the poor creature would do in its trouble: and when the snake saw the shepherd, it exclaimed from the midst of the flames, "O shepherd, I pray of you, save me from this fire!" Then the shepherd reached out his crook, and the snake entwined itself swiftly round the stick, round his arm, on to his shoulders, and round his neck.**

When the shepherd realized what was happening, he was seized with horror, and cried out, "What are you about to do, ungrateful creature! Did I save your life only to lose my own?" And the snake answered him, "Have no fear, my saviour! But take me to my father's house! My father is the king of the snake-world."

The shepherd endeavoured to move the snake to pity and prayed it to excuse him, for he could not leave his sheep. Thereupon the snake said to him, "Be comforted, my friend! Do not trouble about your sheep; nothing amiss will happen to them, but now do hasten to my father's house!" So the shepherd went with the snake round his neck through the forest, till he came at length to a doorway constructed entirely of serpents. When they came near the gate, the shepherd's guide hissed to its servants, whereupon all the snakes instantly untwined themselves, leaving a way open for the shepherd, who passed through unmolested. Then the snake said to its preserver, "When we come before my father, he will surely give you, as reward for your kindness to me, whatever you may wish – gold, silver and precious stones – but you should not accept anything of that kind. I would advise you to ask for the language of animals. He will undoubtedly be opposed to your wish, but finally he will yield."

They now entered the apartments of the king, who, with evident relief, inquired, "My son, where have you been all this time?" The reptile then told all about the fire in the forest and of the kindness of the shepherd, who had saved his life. At this the snake-king turned with emotion to the shepherd. "What reward can I give you for having saved the life of my son?" he said. The shepherd answered, "I desire nothing but the power of understanding and speaking the language of animals." But the monarch said, "That is not for you, for if I give you that power, and you should impart the secret to another, you will instantly die. Therefore choose some other gift." But the shepherd insisted: "If you wish to reward me, give me the language of animals; if you do not care to gratify my wish, no more need be said. I bid you farewell!" And indeed he turned to go, but the king, seeing his determination, stopped him, exclaiming, "Come here, my friend! Since you so strongly desire the language of animals, the gift shall not be withheld. Open your mouth!" The shepherd obeyed, and the snake-king blew into his mouth, and said, "Now, blow into my mouth!" The shepherd did as he was told, and the snake-king blew a second time in the shepherd's mouth, and then said, "Now you have the language of animals. Go in peace, but be sure not to impart your secret to another, else you will die that very moment!"

The shepherd took leave of his friends, and as he returned through the woods, he heard and understood everything the birds, plants and other living creatures were saying to each other. When he reached his flock and found all his sheep safe as had been promised, he lay on the grass to rest.

The Buried Treasure

Hardly had he settled himself when two ravens alighted on a tree nearby and began to converse: "If this shepherd knew what is under the spot where that black lamb is lying, he would surely dig in the earth; he would discover a cave full of silver and gold."

The shepherd at once went to his master and told him of the buried treasure. The latter drove a cart to the place indicated, dug deeply in the earth and lo! he found a cave full of silver and gold, the contents of which he placed in his cart and carried home. This master was an honest and generous man, and he gave the entire treasure to his shepherd, saying, "Take this, my son; it was to you that God gave it! I would advise you to build a house, to marry and start some good business with this gold."

The shepherd did as his kindly master advised him, and, little by little he multiplied his wealth and became the richest man, not only in his village, but in the whole district. He now hired his own shepherds, cattle-drivers and swineherds to keep his great property in good order. One day, just before Christmas, he said to his wife, "Prepare wine and food, for tomorrow we will go to our farms and feast our servants." His wife did as he bade, and the next morning they went to their farms, and the master said to his men, "Now come one and all, eat and drink together. As for the sheep, I will myself watch them tonight."

So the kind man went to guard his sheep. About midnight, wolves began to howl, and his dogs barked a defiance. Said the wolves in their own language to the dogs, "Can we come and kill the sheep? There will be enough for you also." Thereupon the dogs answered in their own tongue, "O come by all means, we also would like to have a feast!" But amongst the dogs there was a very old one who had only two teeth left. That faithful animal barked furiously at the wolves, "To the devil with you all! So long as I have these two teeth, you shall not touch my master's sheep!" And the master heard and understood every word they uttered. Next morning he ordered his servants to kill all his dogs, except the old one. The servants began to implore their master, saying, "Dear master, it is a pity to kill them!" But the master would not suffer any remonstrance, and sternly ordered, "Do as I bid you!" Then he and his wife mounted their horses and started for home, he on a horse and she on a mare. As they journeyed, the horse left the mare a little behind, and he neighed, saying, "Hurry up, why do you dawdle behind?" And the mare answered, "Eh, it is not hard for you – you are carrying only your master, and I am carrying a despotic woman whose rules are a burden to the whole household."

The Importunate Wife

Hearing this, the master turned his head and burst into laughter. His wife, noticing his sudden mirth, spurred on her mare, and when she reached her husband she asked him why he had laughed. He answered, "There is no reason, I just laughed." But the woman was not satisfied with this reply and would not give her husband any peace. He endeavoured in vain to excuse himself, saying, "Don't keep on asking me. If I tell you the true reason why I laughed, I shall instantly die!" But she did not believe her husband, and the more he refused to tell her, the more she insisted that he should do so, until at last the poor man was worn out by her persistence.

Directly when they arrived home, therefore, the man ordered a coffin to be made, and, when it was ready and he had it placed in front of the house door, he said to his wife, "I shall lie down in this coffin, for the moment I tell you why I laughed, I shall die." So he laid himself in the coffin, and as he took a last look around, he saw his faithful old dog, coming from the fields. The poor animal approached his master's coffin and sat near his head, howling with grief. When the master saw this, he requested his wife to give it food. The woman brought bread and gave it to the dog, who would not even look at it, much less eat it. The piece of bread attracted a cock, which came forward and began to peck at it. The dog reproached him saying, "You insatiable creature! You think of nothing but food, and you fail to see that our dear master is about to die!"

To this reprimand the cock retorted, "Let him die, since he is such a foolish man! I have a hundred wives, and I gather them all round a grain of corn, which I happen to find; and then, when they have all assembled, I swallow it myself! If any of them should protest, I just peck at them. But he, the fool, is not able to rule a single wife."

At this the man jumped out of the coffin, took a stick and called to his wife, "Come in the house, wife, and I shall tell you why I laughed!"

Seeing the obvious intention of her husband, the woman begged him to desist, and promised that nevermore would she be curious, or try to pry into his affairs.

Pepelyouga

ON A HIGH PASTURE LAND, near an immense precipice, some maidens were occupied in spinning and attending to their grazing cattle, when an old strange-looking man with a white beard, reaching down to his girdle, approached and said, "O fair maidens, beware of the abyss, for if one of you should drop her spindle down the cliff, her mother would be turned into a cow that very moment!"

So saying, the aged man disappeared, and the girls, bewildered by his words, and discussing the strange incident, approached near to the ravine which had suddenly become interesting to them. They peered curiously over the edge, as though expecting to see some unaccustomed sight, when suddenly the most beautiful of the maidens let her spindle drop from her hand, and ere she could recover it, it was bounding from rock to rock into the depths beneath. When she returned home that evening, she found her worst fears realized, for her mother stood before the door transformed into a cow.

A short time later, her father married again. His new wife was a widow, and brought a daughter of her own into her new home. This girl was not particularly well-favoured, and her mother immediately began to hate her stepdaughter because of the latter's good looks. She forebade her henceforth to wash her face, to comb her hair or to change her clothes, and in every way she could think of she sought to make her miserable.

One morning she gave her a bag filled with hemp, saying, "If you do not spin this and make a fine top of it by tonight, you need not return home, for I intend to kill you."

The poor girl, deeply dejected, walked behind the cattle, industriously spinning as she went, but by noon when the cattle lay down in the shade to rest, she observed that she had made but little progress, and she began to weep bitterly.

Now, her mother was driven daily to pasture with the other cows, and, seeing her daughter's tears, she drew near and asked why she wept, whereupon the maiden told her all. Then the cow comforted her daughter, saying, "My darling child, be consoled! Let me take the hemp into my mouth and chew it. Through my ear a thread will come out. You must take the end of this and wind it into a top." So this was done. The hemp was soon spun, and when the girl gave it to her stepmother that evening, she was greatly surprised.

Next morning the woman roughly ordered the maiden to spin a still larger bag of hemp, and as the girl, thanks to her mother, spun and wound it all, her stepmother, on the following day, gave her twice the quantity to spin. Nevertheless, the girl brought home at night even that unusually large quantity well spun, and her stepmother concluded that the poor girl was not spinning alone, but that other maidens, her friends, were giving her help. Therefore she, next morning, sent her own daughter to spy upon the poor girl and to report what she saw. The girl soon noticed that the cow helped the poor orphan by chewing the hemp, while she drew the thread and wound it on a top, and she ran back home and informed her mother of what she had seen. Upon this, the stepmother insisted that her husband should order that particular cow to be slaughtered. Her husband at first hesitated, but as his wife urged him more and more, he finally decided to do as she wished.

The Promise

On learning what had been decided, the stepdaughter wept more than ever, and when her mother asked what was the matter, she told her tearfully all that had been arranged. Thereupon the cow said to her daughter, "Wipe away your tears, and do not cry any more. When they slaughter me, you must take great care not to eat any of the meat, but after the repast, carefully collect my bones and inter them behind the house under a certain stone; then, should you ever be in need of help, come to my grave and there you will find it."

The cow was killed, and when the meat was served, the poor girl declined to eat of it, pretending that she had no appetite. After the meal, she gathered with great care all the bones and buried them on the spot indicated by her mother.

Now, the name of the maiden was Marra, but, as she had to do the roughest work of the house, such as carrying water, washing, and sweeping, she was called by her stepmother and stepsister Pepelyouga (Cinderella). One Sunday, when the stepmother and her daughter had dressed themselves for church, the woman spread about the house the contents of a basketful of millet, and said, "Listen, Pepelyouga; if you do not gather up all this millet and have dinner ready by the time we return from church, I will kill you!"

When they had gone, the poor girl began to weep, reflecting, "As to the dinner I can easily prepare it, but how can I possibly gather up all this millet?" But that very moment she recalled the words of the cow, that, if she ever should be struck by misfortune, she need but walk to the grave behind the house, when she would find instant help there. Immediately she ran out, and, when she approached the grave, lo! a chest was lying on the grave wide open, and inside were beautiful dresses and everything necessary for a lady's toilet. Two doves were sitting on the lid of the chest, and as the girl drew near, they said to her, "Marra, take from the chest the dress you like the best, clothe yourself and go to church. As to the millet and other work, we ourselves will attend to that and see that everything is in good order!"

Marra Goes to Church

Marra needed no second invitation; she took the first silk dress she touched, made her toilet and went to church, where her entrance created quite a sensation. Everybody, men and women, greatly admired her beauty and her costly attire, but they were puzzled as to who she was, and whence she came. A prince happened to be in the church on that day, and he, too, admired the beautiful maiden.

Just before the service ended, the girl stole from the church, went hurriedly home, took off her beautiful clothes and placed them back in the chest, which instantly shut and became invisible. She then rushed to the kitchen, where she discovered that the dinner was quite ready, and that the millet was gathered into the basket. Soon the stepmother came back with her daughter, and they were astounded to find the millet gathered up, dinner prepared, and everything else in order. A desire to learn the secret now began to torment the stepmother mightily.

Next Sunday everything happened as before, except that the girl found in the chest a silver dress, and that the prince felt a greater admiration for her, so much so that he was unable, even for a moment, to take his eyes from her.

On the third Sunday, the mother and daughter again prepared to go to church, and, having scattered the millet as before, she repeated her previous threats. As soon as they disappeared, the girl ran straight to her mother's grave, where she found, as on the previous occasions, the open chest and the same two doves. This time she found a dress made of gold lace, and she hastily clad herself in it and went to church, where she was admired by all, even more than before.

As for the tsar's son, he had come with the intention not to let her this time out of his sight, but to follow and see whither she went. Accordingly, as the service drew near to its close, and the maiden withdrew quietly as before, the enamoured prince followed after her. Marra hurried along, for she had none too much time, and, as she went, one of her golden slippers came off, and she was too agitated to stop and pick it up. The prince, however, who had lost sight of the maiden, saw the slipper and put it in his pocket. Reaching home, Marra took off her golden dress, laid it in the chest, and rushed back to the house.

The Prince's Quest

The prince now resolved to go from house to house throughout his father's realm in search of the owner of the slipper, inviting all fair maidens to try on the golden slipper. But, alas! his efforts seemed to be doomed to failure; for some girls the slipper was too long, for others too short, for others, again, too narrow. There was no one whom it would fit.

Wandering from door to door, the sad prince at length came to the house of Marra's father. The stepmother was expecting him, and she had hidden her stepdaughter under a large trough in the courtyard. When the prince asked whether she had any daughters, the stepmother answered that she had but one, and she presented the girl to him. The prince requested the girl to try on the slipper, but, squeeze as she would, there was not room in it even for her toes! Thereupon the prince asked whether it was true that there were no other girls in the house, and the stepmother replied that indeed it was quite true.

That very moment a cock flew on to the trough and crowed out lustily, "*Kook-oo-ryeh-koooo!* Here she is under this very trough!"

The stepmother, enraged, exclaimed, "Shhh! Go away! May an eagle seize you and fly off with you!" The curiosity of the prince was aroused. He approached the trough, lifted it up, and, to his great surprise, there was the maiden whom he had seen thrice in church, clad in the very same golden dress she had last worn, and having only one golden slipper.

When the prince recognized the maiden, he was overcome with joy. Quickly he tried the slipper on her dainty foot; it not only fitted her admirably, but it exactly matched the one she already wore on her left foot. He lifted her up tenderly and escorted her to his palace. Later he won her love, and they were happily married.

The Golden-Haired Twins

ONCE UPON A TIME, a long, long while ago, there lived a young king who wished very much to marry, but could not decide where he had better look for a wife.

One evening as he was walking disguised through the streets of his capital, as it was his frequent custom to do, he stopped to listen near an open window, where he heard three young girls chatting gaily together.

The girls were talking about a report which had been lately spread through the city, that the king intended soon to marry.

One of the girls exclaimed, "If the king would marry me, I would give him a son who should be the greatest hero in the world."

The second girl said, "And if I were to be his wife, I would present him with two sons at once – the twins with golden hair."

And the third girl declared that were the king to marry *her*, she would give him a daughter so beautiful that there should not be her equal in the whole wide world!

The young king listened to all this, and for some time thought over their words, and tried to make up his mind which of the three girls he should choose for a wife. At last he decided that he would marry the one who had said she would bring him twins with golden hair.

Having once settled this in his own mind, he ordered that all preparations for his marriage should be made forthwith, and shortly after, when all was ready, he married the second girl of the three.

Several months after his marriage, the young king, who was at war with one of the neighbouring princes, received tidings of the defeat of his army, and heard that his presence was immediately required in the camp. He accordingly left his capital and went to his army, leaving the young queen in his palace to the care of his stepmother.

Now the king's stepmother hated her daughter-in-law very much indeed, so when the young queen was near her confinement, the old queen told her that it was always customary in the royal family for the heirs to the throne to be born in a garret.

The young queen (who knew nothing about the customs in royal families except what she had learnt from hearing or seeing since her marriage to the king) believed implicitly what her mother-in-law told her, although she thought it a great pity to leave her splendid apartments and go up into a miserable attic.

Now when the golden-haired twins were born, the old queen contrived to steal them out of their cradle, and put in their place two ugly little dogs. She then caused the two beautiful golden-haired boys to be buried alive in an out-of-the-way spot in the palace gardens, and then sent word to the king that the young queen had given him two little dogs instead of the heirs he was hoping for. The wicked stepmother said in her letter to the king that she herself was not surprised at this, though she was very sorry for his disappointment. As to herself, she had a long time suspected the young queen of having too great a friendship for goblins and elves, and all kinds of evil spirits. When the king received this letter, he fell into a frightful rage, because he had only married the young girl in order to have the golden-haired twins she had promised him as heirs to his throne.

So he sent word back to the old queen that his wife should be put at once into the dampest dungeon in the castle, an order which the wicked woman took good care to see carried out without delay. Accordingly the poor young queen was thrown into a miserably dark dungeon under the palace, and kept on bread and water.

The Plight of the Young Queen

Now there was only a very small hole in this prison – hardly enough to let in light and air – yet the old queen managed to cause a great many people to pass by this hole, and whoever passed was ordered to spit at and abuse the unhappy young queen, calling out to her, "Are you really the queen? Are you the girl who cheated the king in order to be a queen? Where are your golden-haired twins? You cheated the king and your friends, and now the witches have cheated you!"

But the young king, though terribly angry and mortified at his great disappointment, was, at the same time, too sad and troubled to be willing to return to his palace. So he remained away for fully nine years. When he at last consented to return, the first thing he noticed in the palace gardens were two fine young trees, exactly the same size and the same shape.

These trees had both golden leaves and golden blossoms, and had grown up of themselves from the very spot where the stepmother of the king had buried the two golden-haired boys she had stolen from their cradle.

The king admired these two trees exceedingly, and was never weary of looking at them. This, however, did not at all please the old queen, for she knew that the two young princes were buried just where the trees grew, and she always feared that by some means what she had done would come to the king's ears. She therefore pretended that she was very sick, and declared that she was sure she should die unless her stepson, the king, ordered the two golden-leaved trees to be cut down, and a bed made for her out of their wood.

As the king was not willing to be the cause of her death, he ordered that her wishes should be attended to, notwithstanding he was exceedingly sorry to lose his favourite trees.

A bed was soon made from the two trees, and the seemingly sick old queen was laid on it as she desired. She was quite delighted that the golden-leaved trees had disappeared from the garden. But when midnight came, she could not sleep a bit, for it seemed to her that she heard the boards of which her bed was made in conversation with each other!

At last it seemed to her that one board said, quite plainly, "How are you, my brother?" And the other board answered, "Thank you, I am very well. How are you?"

"Oh, I am all right," returned the first board, "but I wonder how our poor mother is in her dark dungeon! Perhaps she is hungry and thirsty!"

The wicked old queen could not sleep a minute all night, after hearing this conversation between the boards of her new bed. So next morning she got up very early and went to see the king. She thanked him for attending to her wish, and said she already was much better, but she felt quite sure she would never recover thoroughly unless the boards of her new bed were cut up and thrown into a fire. The king was sorry to lose entirely even the boards made out of his two favourite trees. Nevertheless he could not refuse to use the means pointed out for his stepmother's perfect recovery.

So the new bed was cut to pieces and thrown into the fire. But whilst the boards were blazing and crackling, two sparks from the fire flew into the courtyard, and in the next moment two beautiful lambs with golden fleeces and golden horns were seen gambolling about the yard.

The king admired them greatly, and made many inquiries as to who had sent them there, and to whom they belonged. He even sent the public crier many times through the city, calling on the owners of the golden-fleeced lambs to appear and claim them. But no one came, so at length he thought he might fairly take them as his own property.

The king took very great care of these two beautiful lambs, and every day directed that they should be well fed and attended to. This, however, did not at all please his stepmother. She could not endure even to look on the lambs with their golden fleeces and golden horns, for they always reminded her of the golden-haired twins. So, in a little while she pretended again to be dangerously sick, and declared she felt sure that she should soon die unless the two lambs were killed and cooked for her.

The king was even fonder of his golden-fleeced lambs than he had been of the golden-leaved trees, but he could not long resist the tears and prayers of the old queen, especially as she seemed to be very ill. Accordingly, the lambs were killed, and a servant was ordered to carry their golden fleeces down to the river and to wash the blood well out of them. But whilst the servant held them under the water, they slipped, in some way or other, out of his fingers, and floated down the stream, which just at that place flowed very rapidly.

Now it happened that a hunter was passing near the river a little lower down, and, as he chanced to look in the water, he saw something strange in it. So he stepped into the stream, and soon fished out a small box which he carried to his house, and there opened it. To his unspeakably great surprise, he found in the box two golden-haired boys. Now the hunter had no children of his own; he therefore adopted the twins he had fished out of the river, and brought them up just as if they had been his own sons. When the twins were grown up into handsome young men, one of them said to his foster-father, "Make us two suits of beggars' clothes, and let us go and wander a little about the world!" The hunter, however, replied and said, "No, I will have a fine suit made for each of you, such as is fitting for two such noble-looking young men." But as the twins begged hard that he should not spend his money uselessly in buying fine clothes, telling him that they wished to travel about as beggars, the hunter – who always liked to do as his two handsome foster-sons wished – did as they desired, and ordered two suits of clothes, like those worn by beggars, to be prepared for them. The two sons then dressed themselves up as beggars, and as well as they could hid their beautiful golden locks, and then set out to see the world. They took with them a goussle and cymbal, and maintained themselves with their singing and playing.

The King's Sons

They had wandered about in this way some time when one day they came to the king's palace. As the afternoon was already pretty far advanced, the young musicians begged to be allowed to pass the night in one of the out-buildings belonging to the court, as they were poor men, and quite strangers in the city. The old queen, however, who happened to be just then in the courtyard, saw them, and, hearing their request, said sharply that beggars could not be permitted to enter any part of the king's palace. The two travellers said they had hoped to pay for their night's lodging by their songs and music, as one of them played and sung to the goussle, and the other to the cymbal.

The old queen, however, was not moved by this, but insisted on their going away at once. Happily for the two brothers, the king himself came out into the courtyard just as his stepmother angrily ordered them to go away, and at once directed his servants to find a place for the musicians to sleep in, and ordered them to provide the brothers with a good supper. After they had supped, the king commanded them to be brought before him that he might judge of their skill as musicians, and that their singing might help him to pass the time more pleasantly.

Accordingly, after the two young men had taken the refreshment provided for them, the servants took them into the king's presence, and they began to sing this ballad:

"The pretty bird, the swallow, built her nest with care in the palace of the king. In the nest she reared up happily two of her little ones. A black, ugly-looking bird, however, came to the swallow's nest to mar her happiness and to kill her two little ones. And the ugly black bird succeeded in destroying the happiness of the poor little swallow. The little ones, however, although yet weak and unfledged, were saved, and, when they were grown up and able to fly, they came to look at the palace where their mother, the pretty swallow, had built her nest."

This strange song the two minstrels sung so very sweetly that the king was quite charmed, and asked them the meaning of the words.

Whereupon the two meanly dressed young men took off their hats, so that the rich tresses of their golden hair fell down over their shoulders, and the light glanced so brightly upon it that the whole hall was illuminated by the shining. They then stepped forward together, and told the king all that had happened to them and to their mother, and convinced him that they were really his own sons.

The king was exceedingly angry when he heard all the cruel things his stepmother had done, and he gave orders that she should be burnt to death. He then went with the two golden-haired princes to the miserable dungeon, wherein his unfortunate wife had been confined so many years, and brought her once more into her beautiful palace. There, looking on her golden-haired sons, and seeing how much the king, their father, loved them, she soon forgot all her long years of misery. As to the king, he felt that he could never do enough to make amends for all the misfortunes his queen had lived through, and all the dangers to which his twin sons had been exposed. He felt that he had too easily believed the stories of the old queen, because he would not trouble himself to inquire more particularly into the truth or falsehood of the strange things she had told him.

After all this mortification, and trouble, and misery, everything came right at last. So the king and his wife, with their golden-haired twins, lived together long and happily.

Morality Tales & Fables

EXAMPLES OF EACH TYPE of folktale genre represented in the present book are found in this chapter, and each serves a purpose. Religious tales repeatedly proclaim the virtues of being a morally upright person, as in 'Good Deeds Are Never Lost', 'One Good Turn Deserves Another' and 'He Who Asks Little Receives Much'. Satirical anecdotes such as 'The Emperor Trojan's Goat's Ears' and the fable 'Why the Priest was Drowned' are darkly entertaining.

Finally, a number of legends in this chapter explain everyday things and conditions familiar to their audience: why Serbs are poor, why a certain village is sandy and why the sole of a man's foot is flat.

Good Deeds Are Never Lost

IN DAYS GONE BY there lived a married couple who had only one son. When he grew up, they made him learn something which would be of use to him in the afterlife. He was a kind, quiet boy, and feared God greatly. After his schooling was finished, his father gave him a ship, freighted with various sorts of merchandise, so that he might go and trade about the world, and grow rich, and become a help to his parents in their old age. The son put to sea, and one day the ship he was in met with a Turkish vessel, in which he heard great weeping and wailing. So he demanded of the Turkish sailors, "Pray tell me why there is so much wailing on board your ship?" And they answered, "We are carrying slaves which we have captured in different countries, and those who are chained are weeping."

Then he said, "Please, brothers, ask your captain if he would give me the slaves for ready cash."

The captain gladly agreed to the proposal, and after much bargaining the young man gave to the captain his vessel full of merchandise, and received in exchange the ship full of slaves.

Then he called the slaves before him, and demanded of each whence he came, and told them all they were free to return to their own countries. At last he came to an old woman who held close to her side a very beautiful girl, and he asked them from what country they came. The old woman told him, weeping, that they came from a very distant land, saying, "This young girl is the only daughter of the king, and I am her nurse, and have taken care of her from her childhood. One day, unhappily, she went to walk in a garden far away from the palace, and these wicked Turks saw her and caught her. Luckily I happened to be near, and, hearing her scream, ran to her help, and so the Turks caught me too, and brought us both on board this ship." Then the old woman and the beautiful girl, being so far from their own country, and having no means of getting there, begged him that he would take them with him. So he married the girl, took her with him, and returned home.

When he arrived, his father asked him about his ship and merchandise, and he told him what had happened, how he had given his vessel with its cargo, and had bought the slaves and set them free. "This girl," continued he, "is a king's daughter, and the old woman her nurse. As they could not get back to their country, they prayed to remain with me, so I married the girl."

Thereupon the father was very angry, and said, "My foolish son! What have you done? Why have you made away with my property without cause and of your own will?" And he drove him out of the house.

Then the son lived with his wife and her old nurse a long time in the same village, trying always, through the good offices of his mother and other friends, to obtain his father's forgiveness, and begging him to let him have a second ship full of merchandise, promised to be wiser in future. After some time, the father took pity on him, and received him again into his house with his wife and her old nurse. Shortly after, he fitted him out another ship, larger than the first one and filled with more valuable merchandise. In this he sailed, leaving his wife and her nurse in the house of his parents. He came one day to a city, where he found the soldiers very busy carrying some unlucky villagers away to prison. So he asked them, "Why are you doing this, my brethren? Why are you driving these poor people to prison?" And the soldiers answered, "They have not paid the king's taxes, that is why we take them to prison." Then he went to the magistrate and asked, "Please tell me how much these poor prisoners owe?"

When the magistrate told him, he sold his goods and ship, and paid the debts of all the prisoners, and returned home without anything. Falling at the feet of his father, he told him what he had done, and begged him to forgive him. But the father was exceedingly angry, more so than before, and drove him away from his presence. What could the unhappy son do in this great strait? How could he go begging, he whose parents were so rich? After some time his friends again prevailed upon the father to receive him back, because, they urged, so much suffering had made him wiser. At last the father yielded, took him again into his house, and prepared a ship for him finer and richer than the two former ones. Then the son had the portrait of his wife painted on the helm, and that of the old nurse on the stern, and, after taking leave of his father and mother and wife, he sailed away the third time.

After sailing for some days, he came near a large city, in which there lived a king, and, dropping anchor, he fired a salute to the city. All the citizens wondered, as did also their king, and no one could say who the captain of the strange ship might be. In the afternoon the king sent one of his ministers to ask who he was, and why he came. And the minister brought a message that the king himself would come at nine o'clock the next morning to see the ship. When the minister came, he saw on the helm the portrait of the king's daughter, and on the stern that of her old nurse, and in his surprise and joy dared not believe his own eyes. For the princess had been promised to him in marriage while she was yet a child, and long before she was captured by the Turks. But the minister did not tell anyone what he had seen.

Next morning, at nine o'clock, the king came with his ministers on board the ship, and asked the captain who he was, and whence he came. Whilst walking about the vessel, he saw there the portrait of the girl on the helm and that of the old woman on the stern, and recognized the features of his own daughter and her old nurse who had been captured by the Turks. But his joy was so great he dared not believe his eyes, so he invited the captain to come that afternoon to his palace to relate his adventures, hoping thus to find out if his hopes were well founded.

In the afternoon, in obedience to the king's wish, he went to the palace, and the king at once began to inquire why the figure of the girl was painted on the helm and that of the old woman on the stern. The captain guessed at once that this king must be his wife's father, so he told him everything that had happened – how he had met the Turkish ship filled with slaves, and had ransomed them and set them free. "This girl, alone," he continued, "with her old nurse, had nowhere to go, as her country was so far off, so they asked to remain with me, and I married the girl."

When the king heard this he exclaimed, "That girl is my only child, and the accursed Turks took her and her old nurse. You, since you are her husband, will be the heir to my crown. But go – go at once to your home and bring me your wife that I may see her, my only daughter, before I die. Bring your father, your mother, bring all your family. Let your property all be sold in that country, and come all of you here. Your father shall be my brother, and your mother my sister, as you are my son and the heir to my crown. We will all live together here in one palace." Then he called the queen, and all his ministers, and told them all about his daughter. And there was great rejoicing and festivity in the whole court.

After this the king gave his son-in-law his own large ship to bring back the princess and the whole family. So the captain left his own ship there, but he asked the king to send one of his ministers with him – "lest they should not believe me," he said. And the king gave him as a companion for his voyage the same minister to whom he had formerly promised the princess in marriage. They arrived safely in port, and the captain's father was surprised to see his son return so soon, and with such a splendid vessel.

Then he told all that had happened, and his mother and wife, and especially the old nurse, rejoiced greatly when they heard the good news. As the king's minister was there to witness the truth of this strange news, no one could doubt it. So the father and mother consented to sell all their property and go to live in the king's palace.

But the minister resolved to kill this new heir to the king and husband of the princess who had been promised to him for wife. So, when they had sailed a long distance, he called him on deck to confer with him. The captain had a quiet conscience, and did not suspect any evil, so he came up at once, and the minister caught him quickly and threw him overboard.

The ship was sailing fast, and it was rather dark, so the captain could not overtake her, but was left behind in the deep waters. The minister, however, went quietly to sleep.

Fortunately the waves carried the king's young heir to a rock near the shore. It was, however, a desert country, and no one was near to help him. Those he had left on board the ship, seeing next morning that he had disappeared, began to weep and wail, thinking he had fallen overboard in the night and been drowned. His wife especially lamented him, because they had loved each other very much. When the ship arrived at the king's city, bringing news of the disaster, the king was troubled, and the whole court mourned greatly. The king kept the parents and family of the young man by him as he had engaged to do, but they could not console themselves for their great loss.

Meanwhile, the king's unhappy son-in-law sat on the rock, and lived on the moss which grew there, and was scorched by the hot sun, from which he had no shelter. His garments were soiled and torn, and no one would have recognized him. Still not a living soul was to be seen anywhere to help him. At last, after fifteen days and fifteen nights, he noticed an old man on the shore, leaning on a staff, and engaged in fishing. Then the king's heir shouted to the old man, and begged him to help him off the rock. The old fisherman consented –

"If you will pay me for it," said he.

"How can I pay you when, as you see, I have nothing, and even my clothes are only rags?" answered the young man sadly.

"Oh, that matters nothing," exclaimed the old man. "I have here pen and paper, so, if you know how to use them, write a promise to give me half of everything you may ever possess, and then sign the paper."

To that the young man gladly consented. So the old man walked through the water to him, and he signed the paper, and then the old man took him over to the shore. After that he journeyed from village to village, barefoot, hungry, and sorrowful, and begged some garments to cover him.

After thirty days' wandering his good luck led him to the city of the king, and he went and sat at the door of the palace, wearing on his finger his wedding ring, on which were his own name and the name of his wife. At eventide the king's servants took him into the courtyard, and gave him to eat what remained of their supper. Next morning he took his stand by the garden door, but the gardener came and drove him away, saying that the king and his family were soon coming that way. So he moved away a little, and sat down near a corner of the garden, and shortly afterwards he saw the king walking with his mother, his father leading the queen, and his wife walking with the minister, his great enemy. He did not yet desire to show himself to them, but as they passed near him and gave him alms, his wife saw the wedding ring on a finger of the hand which he held out to take the money. Still she could not think the beggar could be her husband, so she said, "Let me see the ring you have on your finger."

The minister, who was walking by her, was a little frightened, and said, "Go on, how can you speak to that ragged beggar?"

But she would not hear him. She took the ring and read thereon her own and her husband's names. Her heart was greatly troubled by the sight of the ring, but she controlled her feelings and said nothing. As soon as they returned to the palace, she told the king, her father, that she had recognized her husband's ring on the hand of the beggar who sat by the side of the garden. "So please send for him," said she, "that we may find out how the ring came into his hands."

Then the king sent his servants to find the beggar, and they brought him to the palace. And the king asked him whence he came, and how he got that ring. Then he could no longer restrain himself, but told them how he had been thrown overboard by the treacherous minister, and spent fifteen days and nights on the naked rock, and how he had been saved.

"You see now how God and my right-dealing have brought me back to my parents and my wife."

When they heard that, they could hardly speak, so rejoiced were they. Then the king summoned the father and mother, and related what had happened to their son.

The servants quickly brought him fine new garments, and bathed and clothed him. Then for many days there were great rejoicings, not only in the palace, but also in all the city, and he was crowned as king. The minister was seized by the king's order, and given up to the king's son-in-law, that he might punish him after his own will. But the young king would not permit him to be put to death, but forgave him, on condition that he leave the kingdom instantly.

A few days after, the old man who had saved the young king came, bringing with him his written promise. The young king took the paper and, reading it, said, "My old man, sit down. Today I am king, but if I were a beggar I would fulfil my word, and acknowledge my signature. Therefore we will divide all that I have."

So he took out the book and began to divide the cities.

"This is for me; that is for you." So saying, he wrote all on a chart, till all was divided between them, from the greatest city to the poorest barrack.

The old man accepted his half, but immediately made a present of it again to the young king, saying, "Take it. I am not an old man, but an angel from God. I was sent by God to save thee, for the sake of thy good deeds. Now reign and be happy, and may thy prosperity last long."

The angel disappeared, and the king reigned there in great happiness.

One Good Turn Deserves Another

IT HAPPENED once upon a time, many years ago, that a certain king went into his forest to hunt, when instead of the usual game he caught a wild man. This wild man the king had taken to his castle, and locked up for safety in a dungeon. This done, he put out a proclamation that whosoever should dare to set the wild man free should be put to death.

As luck would have it, the dungeon where the creature was confined was just below the sleeping-room of the king's youngest son. Now, the wild man cried and groaned incessantly to be set free, and these unceasing lamentations at length so moved the young prince that one night he went down and opened the dungeon door, and let out the prisoner.

Next morning the king and all the courtiers and servants were exceedingly astonished to hear no longer the usual sounds of wailing from the dungeon, and the king, suspecting something amiss, went down himself to see what had become of his captive. When he found the den empty, he flew into a great passion, and demanded fiercely who had presumed to disobey his commands and let out the wild man. All the courtiers were so terrified at the sight of the king's angry countenance that not one of them dared speak, not even to assert their innocence. However, the young prince, the king's son, went forward at last and confessed that the pitiful crying of the poor creature had so disturbed him day and night, that at length he himself had opened the door. When the king heard this, it was his turn to be sorry, for he found himself compelled to put his own son to death or give his own proclamation the lie.

However, some of his old counsellors, seeing how greatly the king was perplexed and troubled, came and assured His Majesty that the proclamation would in reality be carried out if the prince, instead of being put to death, was simply banished from the kingdom for ever.

The king was very glad to find this way of getting out of the dilemma, and so ordered his son to leave the country, and never come back to it; at the same time he gave him many letters of recommendation to the king of a very distant kingdom, and directed one of the court servants to go with the young prince to wait upon him. Then the unhappy young prince and his servant started on their long journey.

After travelling some time, the young prince became very thirsty, and, seeing a well not far off, went up to it to drink. However, there happened to be no bucket at the well, nor anything in which to draw water, though the well was pretty full. Seeing this, the young prince said to his servant, "Hold me fast by the heels, and let me down into the pit that I may drink." So saying, he bent over the well, and the servant let him down as he was directed.

When the prince had quenched his thirst, and wished to be pulled back, the servant refused, saying, "Now I can let you fall into the pit in a moment, and I shall do so unless you consent at once to change clothes and places with me. I will be the prince henceforth, and you shall be my servant."

The king's son, seeing that he had foolishly placed himself in the power of the servant, promised readily everything his servant asked, and begged only to be drawn up.

But the faithless servant, without noticing his master's prayers, said roughly, "You must make a solemn oath that you will not speak a word to anyone about the change we are going to make."

Of course, since the prince could not help himself, he took the oath at once, and then the servant drew him up, and they changed clothes. Then the wicked servant dressed himself in his master's fine clothes, mounted his master's horse, and rode forward on the journey, whilst the unfortunate prince, disguised in his servant's dress, walked beside him.

In this way they went on until they came to the court of the king to which the exiled son had been recommended by his father.

Faithful to his promise, the unfortunate prince saw his false servant received at the court with great honours as the son of a great king, whilst he himself, all unnoticed, stood in the waiting room with the servants, and was treated by them with all familiarity as their equal.

After having some time enjoyed to his heart's content the hospitalities the king lavished upon him, the false servant began to be afraid that his master's patience might be wearied out soon, under all the indignities to which he was exposed, and that one day he might be tempted to forget his oath and proclaim himself in his true character. Filled with these misgivings, the wicked man thought over all possible ways by which he could do away with his betrayed master without any danger to himself.

One day he thought he had found out a way to do this, and took the first opportunity to carry out his cruel plan.

Now you must know that the king, at whose court this unhappy prince and the false servant were staying, kept in his gardens a great number of wild beasts fastened up in large cages. One morning, as the pretended prince was walking in these gardens with the king, he said suddenly, "Your Majesty has a large number of very fine wild beasts, and I admire them very much. I think, however, it is a pity that you keep them always fastened up, and spend so much money over their food. Why not send them under a keeper to find their own food in the forest? I dare say Your Majesty would be very glad if I recommended a man to you who could take them out in the morning and bring them back safely at night?"

The king asked, "Do you really think, prince, that you can find me such a man?"

"Of course, I can," replied unhesitatingly the cruel man. "Such a man is now in Your Majesty's court. I mean my own servant. Only call him and threaten that you will have his head cut off if he does not do it, and compel him to accept the task. I dare say he will try to excuse himself, and say the thing is impossible, but only threaten him with the loss of his head whether he refuses or fails. For my part, I am quite willing Your Majesty should have him put to death if he disobeys."

When the king heard this, he summoned the disguised prince before him, and said, "I hear that you can do wonders: that you are able to drive wild beasts out like cattle to find their own food in the forest, and bring them back safely at night into their cages. Therefore, I order you this morning to drive all my bears into the forest, and to bring them back again in the evening. If you don't do this, your head will pay for it, so beware!"

The unlucky prince answered, "I am not able to do this thing, so Your Majesty had better cut off my head at once."

But the king would not listen to him, only saying, "We will wait until evening; *then* I shall surely have your head cut off unless you bring back all my bears safely to their cages."

Now nothing was left for the poor prince to do but open the cage doors and try his luck in driving the bears to the forest. The moment he opened the doors, all the bears rushed out wildly and disappeared quickly among the trees.

The prince followed them sadly into the forest, and sat down on a fallen tree to think over his hard fortunes. As he sat thus, he began to weep bitterly, for he saw no better prospect before him than to lose his head that night.

As he sat thus crying, a creature in form like a man, but covered all over with thick hair, came out of a neighbouring thicket, and asked him what he was crying for. Then the prince told him all that had happened to him, and that, as all the bears had run away, he expected to be beheaded at night when he returned without them. Hearing this, the wild man gave him a little bell, and said kindly, "Don't be afraid! Only take care of this bell, and when you wish the bears to return, just ring it gently, and they will all come back and follow you quietly into their cages." And having said this he went away.

When the sun began to go down, the prince rang the little bell gently, and, to his great joy, all the bears came dancing awkwardly round him, and let him lead them back to the gardens, following him like a flock of sheep, whilst he, pleased with his success, took out a flute and played little airs as he walked before them. In this way he was able to fasten them up again in their dens without the least trouble.

Everyone at the court was astonished at this, and the false servant more than all the others, though he concealed his surprise, and said to the king, "Your Majesty sees now that I told you the truth. I am quite sure the man can manage the wolves just as well as the bears, if you only threaten him as before."

Thereupon, the next morning the king called the poor prince, and ordered him to lead out the wolves to find their food in the forest, and to bring them back to their cages at night. "Unless you do this," said His Majesty as before, "you will lose your head."

The prince pleaded vainly the impossibility of his doing such a thing, but the king would not hear him, only saying, "You may as well try, for whether you refuse or fail, you will certainly lose your head."

So the prince was obliged to open the cages of the wolves, and the moment he did this, the wild animals sprang past him into the thickets just as the bears had done, and he, following them slowly, went and sat down to bewail his ill-luck.

Whilst he sat thus weeping, the wild man came out of the wood and asked him, just as he had done the day before, what he was crying for. The prince told him, whereupon the creature gave him another little bell, and said, "When you want the wolves to come back, just ring this bell, and they will all come and follow you." Having said this, he went back into the wood, and left the prince alone.

Just before it grew dark, the prince rang his bell, and to his great joy all the wolves came rushing up to him from all quarters of the forest, and followed him quietly back to their cages.

Seeing this, the false servant advised the king to send out the birds also, and to threaten the disguised prince with the loss of his head if he failed to bring them also back in the evening.

Accordingly, the next morning the king ordered the prince to let out all the wild doves, and to bring them all safely to their different cages before night set in.

The instant the poor young man opened the cage doors, the wild doves rose like a cloud into the air and vanished over the tops of the trees. So the prince went into the forest and sat down again on the fallen tree. As he sat there, thinking how hopeless a task he had now before him, he could not help crying aloud and bewailing all his past misfortunes and present miserable fate.

Hardly had he begun to lament, however, before the same wild man came from the bushes near him and asked what fresh trouble had befallen him. Then the prince told him. Thereupon the wild man gave him a third bell, saying, "When you wish the wild doves to return to their cages, you have only to ring this little bell." And so it indeed happened, for the moment the prince began ringing softly, all the doves came flying about him, and he walked back to the palace gardens and shut them up in their different cages without the least trouble.

Now, happily for the prince, the king had just at this time much more important business on his hands than finding his wild beasts and birds in food without paying for it. No less a matter, in fact, began to occupy him than finding a suitable husband for his daughter. For this purpose he sent out a proclamation that he would hold races during three days, and would reward the victor of each day with a golden apple. Whosoever should succeed in winning all three apples should have the young princess for his wife. Now this princess was far more beautiful than any other princess in the world, and an exceeding great number of knights prepared to try and win her. This, the poor prince in his servant's dress watched with great dismay, for he had fallen deeply in love with the fair daughter of the king. So he puzzled himself day and night with plans for how he, too, could try his luck in the great race.

At last he determined to go into the forest and ask the wild man to help him. When the wild man heard the prince calling, he came out of the thicket, and listened to all he had to say about the matter. Seeing how much the prince was interested in the young princess, who was to be the prize of the victor, the wild man brought out some handsome clothes and a fine horse, and gave them to the prince, saying, "When you start in a race, do not urge your horse too much, but at the end, when you are getting near the goal, spur him, and then you will be sure to win. Don't forget, however, to bring me the golden apple as soon as you receive it."

All came to pass just as the wild man had said. The prince won the apples the two first days. But as he disappeared as soon as he received them from the king, no one in the court recognized him in his fine attire, and all wondered greatly who the strange knight might be. As for the king, he was more perplexed and curious than all the rest, and determined not to let the stranger escape so easily the third day. So he ordered a deep, wide ditch to be dug at the end of the racecourse, and a high wall built beyond it, thinking thus to stop the victor and find out who he was.

The prince, hearing of the king's orders, and guessing the reason of them, went once again into the forest to ask help from his wild friend. The wild man, thereupon, brought out to him a still more beautiful racer, and a suit of splendid clothes. And, thus prepared, the prince took his place as before among the knights who were going to try for the prize. He won the golden apple this third time also. But, to the surprise of the king and the whole court, who hoped now to find out who he was, he made his horse spring lightly over the ditch and the great wall, and vanished again in the forest.

The king tried every way to find out who had won the three golden apples, but all in vain. At last, one day the princess, walking in the gardens of the palace, met the prince disguised in his servant's dress, and saw the shining of the three apples which he carried concealed in his bosom. Thereupon she ran at once to her father, and told him what she had seen, and the king, wondering very much, called the servant before him.

Now the prince thought it time to put an end to all his troubles, and therefore told the king frankly all his misfortunes. He related how he had offended the king, his father, and been exiled for life; how his false servant had betrayed him; and how the wild man he had set free had come to help him out of the fearful snares the wicked servant had spread for him.

After hearing all this, the king very gladly gave him the princess for wife, and ordered the false servant to be put to death immediately.

As for the prince, he lived with his beautiful princess very happily for many years after this, and when the king, his father-in-law, died, he left to them both the kingdom.

The Legend of St. George

ONCE UPON A TIME, all the saints assembled in order to divide amongst themselves the treasures of the world. And, in this division, each saint obtained something which satisfied him.

The beautiful summer, with all its wealth of flowers, fell to the lot of St. George, to St. Elias fell the clouds and the thunder; and to St. Pantelija the tempest; St. Peter obtained the keys of heaven; to St. Nicholas fell the seas, and the ships upon them; and to the Archangel Michael fell the right of gathering and guarding the souls of the dying; St. John was chosen to preside over friendship and "*koom-ship*"; and to the holy Lady Mary the saints committed the charge of the lawless country of the cursed Troyan, in order that she might bring it to a state of peace, and establish therein the true religion.

About a year had passed away since the saints had thus divided amongst themselves the treasures of the world, when one day the holy Lady Mary entered the assembly, evidently greatly afflicted, and with large tears falling over her white cheeks. She greeted "*in the name of God!*" her brethren the saints, and these gave her back her greeting. Then St. Elias addressed her, saying, "*Our* sister, holy Mary, wherefore are you grieving? Why are you shedding these tears? You are, perhaps, dissatisfied with the lot which fell to you when we divided the treasures?"

But the holy Mary answered, "My brethren, ye who are the righteousness of God, when you divided the treasures you gave me also a share therein, and therewith I am satisfied. Yet I have good cause, nevertheless, to be sorely grieved. I come but now from the city of the Troyan, and I have been unable to bring it to peace and the true faith. There the young people do not reverence their elders; there the brother challenges his own brother to mortal combat; there the *koom* is pursuing his *koom* in the law courts; there the brother intermarries with his own sister, and the *koom* with his *kooma*; there the holy Sabbath is violated; and, worst of all, there they do not pray to the true God. The people have made to themselves a god of silver, and to this idol do they pray. Now, what can I do, my dear brethren, except to pray that the true God should send his lightnings from heaven to destroy the fortress and fortifications, and to burn down the cities and villages? Then, perhaps, the people of the Troyan country may come to see their great wickedness and repent."

St. Elias said to her these words: "Our sister, holy Mary, do not do this thing! Rather let us all pray God to allow us to give some warning to the people; that He orders snow to fall on Mitrovdan, and remain until St. George's day; and another snow to fall on St. George's day, and lie on the earth until Mitrovdan; so that no seeds can be sown, and no ewes can rear their lambs. In this way, perhaps, the pride of the earth may be subdued, and the people brought at last to repentance."

All the saints approved the proposal of St. Elias, and acted as he had said. Then a great snow fell on Mitrovdan, and remained until St. George's day, and a second snowfall came on St. George's day, and lay on the earth until Mitrovdan. No seed could be sown, therefore, and no lambs could be reared. The people suffered greatly throughout the year. They would not, however, repent and mend their ways. Some of them had part of last year's corn in their garners, and shiploads of grain were brought from countries beyond the seas, and so they got somehow through the year, and went on living just as wickedly as before.

The holy Mary, seeing this, went a second time to the assembled saints weeping. After the exchange of the customary greeting, St. Elias asked her what was the reason of her tears, and she told him that she was sorely grieved because the people of the Troyan country, notwithstanding the chastisement they had suffered, still continued living in wickedness. Then the saints resolved to send down a second warning. So they prayed God to send down the curse of the smallpox. Thereupon the smallpox appeared amongst the Troyans, and raged in their country for three full years, carrying off all the strength and beauty of the people, so that only the old remained to cough, and the little babes to cry.

But, when the children grew up, they behaved just as their parents had done, and neither improved nor repented. Weeping bitter tears over her white cheeks, the holy Mary went the third time to the assembly of the saints, and reported how disorderly and madly the people of the Troyan land were still living. She said it was quite evident that they could not be brought to repentance, and that, therefore, she intended now to pray God to send down his lightnings and destroy the cities and villages.

But St. Elias said again, "Not so, my dear sister! Not so! Let us give them yet a third warning." So the saints prayed to God for the third warning, and God granted their request.

Next morning, close by the king's palace in the chief city of the Troyans, a green lake appeared, and therein was an insatiable dragon feeding on young men and maidens. Every morning, for breakfast, the monster required a young man who had never been wedded; and every evening, for supper, he demanded a youthful and blooming maiden.

This went on for seven years, until, at length, the turn came to the only daughter of the king. Then the queen cried loudly and bitterly, and clasped her arms closely round the neck of her child. Mother and daughter wept together three days, and when the fourth day dawned, the queen fell into a light slumber by her daughter's side. As she slept, she dreamed that a man appeared to her, and said, "O queen of the Troyan city! do not send your daughter this evening to the lake; but send her tomorrow, when the day dawns, and the sun shines. Tell her, when she goes to the lake, she must bathe her face, and then, turning towards the east, let her call on the name of the true God. She must, however, be careful not to mention the idol of silver. This done, she must wait patiently, ready to accept whatsoever the true God ordereth for her."

The queen, awakening from her sleep, related at once her dream to her daughter, and impressed on her the necessity of carrying out faithfully her instructions. Weeping bitterly, the king's daughter took leave of her mother at daybreak, begging the queen to forgive her the milk with which she had been nourished in her babyhood. Then she went down to the lake shore, bathed her face, and, turning eastwards, prayed to the true God. This done, according to her mother's instructions, she sat down and awaited whatever might happen to her.

Suddenly there appeared a strange knight mounted on a magnificent charger. He greeted the maiden "in the name of God!", and she, springing up quickly, returned the greeting courteously. Then the strange knight, seeing she had been weeping, asked what it was that troubled her, and wherefore she sat waiting there alone. In answer to these questions the maiden related the whole sad story of the dragon, and the fearful fate which seemed to await her.

When she had finished her narration, the knight dismounted, and, removing his kalpak from his head, said, "Now I desire to sleep a little, and I wish you to pass your hand through my hair that I may sleep more pleasantly." The girl tried to dissuade him from this, lest the dragon should come whilst he slept and devour him also. She said it would be a pity for him to perish thus needlessly. However, she could not prevail on him to abandon his purpose, and he fell at once into a gentle slumber, and slept as quietly as a young lamb.

Very soon, however, the waters of the lake were agitated, and the terrible dragon appeared, coming towards them. Then the unknown knight sprang up quickly into his saddle, and, stretching out his arms, lifted the maiden up and placed her behind him on his charger. This done, with one stroke of his lance, he pinned the dragon down to the bottom of the lake, where it remained bleeding, but not dead. Then the knight took the girl back to the palace of the king, her father, and the queen, who had been watching anxiously everything that passed, met him at the gate and delivered up to him the keys of the city.

The knight, who was no other than St. George, now walked through the streets of the Troyan city, and, having gathered the people around him, spoke to them thus: "Listen to me, my children! Pray no more to the idol of silver, pray only to the one true God! And you, young people, revere your elders. All of you remember that near relatives cannot be permitted to intermarry. Keep holy the Sabbath, as well as all the other holy days and saint days."

Having thus admonished them, the holy knight ordered that the temple should be opened, and when his commands had been obeyed, he took out of it the silver idol, and melted it into a variety of ornaments. In the place of the silver idol he placed a holy picture, and then consecrated the temple, and it became a church. When this was done, he turned again to the people and said, "If you will promise to do as I have told you, I will kill the dragon in the lake; but if you refuse to do what I have asked of you, I will let him loose again, and I think he will soon make an end of you."

Then all the people bowed themselves to the earth before the holy knight and shouted aloud, "O good and unknown knight! Our brother in God! Deliver us from the dragon in the lake, and we will do and live just as you have counselled us!" Whereupon they received the true faith. When they had so done, St. George returned to the lake, and made the sign of the cross over it with a stick, and at that very moment both the lake and dragon disappeared as if they had never been.

Having done all this, St. George went back to the heavenly kingdom to recount to the saints there assembled the conversion of the Troyan people.

The Stepmother and Her Stepdaughter

O NCE UPON A TIME there was a girl who lived with her stepmother. The woman hated her stepdaughter exceedingly, because she was more beautiful than her own daughter, whom she had brought with her to the house. She did her utmost to turn the poor girl's own father against her, and with such success that he soon began to scold and even to hate his own child.

One day the woman said to her husband, "We must send your daughter away. She must go into the world to seek her fortune!" And he answered, "How can we send the poor girl away? Where could she go alone?" But the wicked stepmother replied, "Tomorrow you must take her far into the woods, leave her there and hurry home, or I will no longer live with you."

The unfortunate father at length gave way, and said, "At least prepare the girl something for her journey, that she may not die of hunger." The stepmother therefore made a cake, and gave it to the girl next morning as she was leaving the house. The man and his daughter trudged on until they were right in the depth of the woods, and then the father stole away and returned home.

The girl, alone in the woods, wandered all the rest of that day in search of a path, but could not find one. Meanwhile it grew darker and darker, and at length she climbed a tree, fearing lest some wild beast should devour her if she remained through the night on the ground. And indeed, all night long the wolves howled under the tree so ravenously that the poor girl, in her nervous terror, could hardly keep from falling.

Next morning she descended the tree and wandered on again in search of some way out, but the more she walked the denser grew the forest, and there seemed to be no end to it. When it grew dark again, she looked about for another suitable tree in the branches of which she might safely pass the night, but suddenly she noticed something shining through the darkness. She thought it might, perhaps, be a dwelling, and she went toward it. And indeed, she came soon to a large fine house, the doors of which were open. She entered and saw many elegant rooms, in one of which was a large table with lights burning on it. She thought this must be the dwelling of brigands, but she had no fear at all, for she reasoned with herself, "Only rich people need fear robbers. I, a poor simple girl, have nothing to be afraid of. I shall tell them that I am ready to work for them gladly if they will give me something to eat."

A Strange Dwelling

Then she took the cake from her bag, made the sign of the cross, and began her meal. No sooner had she begun to eat than a cock appeared and flew near her as if begging for a share. The good girl crumbled a piece of her cake and fed him. Shortly afterward a little dog came and began in his own way to express friendly feeling toward her. The girl broke another piece of her cake, gently took the little dog in her lap, and began feeding and caressing it. After that a cat came in too, and she did the same with her.

Suddenly she heard a loud growling, and she was terrified to see a lion coming toward her. The great beast waved his tail in such a friendly manner, and looked so very kind, however, that her courage revived, and she gave him a piece of her cake, which the lion ate, and then he began to lick her hand. This proof of gratitude reassured the girl completely, and she stroked the lion gently, and gave him more of the cake.

All at once the girl heard a great clashing of weapons, and nearly swooned as a creature in a bearskin entered the room. The cock, the dog, the cat and the lion all ran to meet it, and frisked about it affectionately, showing many signs of pleasure and rejoicing. She, poor creature, did not think this strange being could be anything but cruel, and expected it would spring upon her and devour her. But the seeming monster threw the bearskin from its head and shoulders, and at once the whole room gleamed with the magnificence of its golden garments. The girl almost lost her senses when she saw before her a handsome man of noble appearance. He approached her and said, "Do not fear! I am not a lawless man, I am the tsar's son. And when I wish to hunt, I usually come here, disguised in this bearskin, lest the people should recognize me. Save you, no one knows that I am a man; people think I am an apparition, and flee from me. No one dares to pass near this house, still less to enter it, for it is known that I dwell in it. You are the first who has ventured to come in. Probably you knew that I was not a ghost?"

Thereupon the girl told the prince all about her wicked stepmother, and declared that she knew nothing of this dwelling or who lived in it. When the young prince heard her story, moved with indignation and pity, he said, "Your stepmother hated you, but God loved you. I love you very much, too, and if you feel you could return my love, I would like to marry you. Will you be my wife?" "Yes," replied the maiden.

Next morning the prince took the girl to his father's palace and they were married. After some time the prince's bride begged to be allowed to go and pay a visit to her father. The prince gladly allowed her to do as she wished, and, donning a fine robe embroidered with gold, she went to her old home. Her father happened to be absent, and her stepmother, seeing her coming, feared that she had come to revenge herself. Therefore she hurried out to meet her, saying, "You see now that I sent you on the road of happiness?" The stepdaughter embraced the woman and kissed her; she also embraced her stepsister. Then she sat down to await her father's return, but at length, as he did not come, she was compelled reluctantly to leave without seeing him. On going away, she gave much money to her stepmother, but nevertheless when she had got some distance from the house, the ungrateful woman stealthily shook her fist at her, muttering, "Wait a little, you accursed creature, you shall certainly not be the only one so elegantly dressed. Tomorrow I shall send my own daughter the same way!"

The Envy of the Stepmother

The husband did not return until late in the evening, when his wife met him, saying, "Listen, husband! I propose that my own daughter should be sent out into the world that she may also seek her fortune, for your girl came back to visit us today and lo! she was glittering in gold." The man sighed and agreed.

Next morning the woman prepared for her daughter several cakes and some roast meat, and sent her with the father into the forest. The unfortunate man guided her as he had led his own daughter into the heart of the forest, and then stole off, leaving her alone. When the girl saw that her father had disappeared, she walked on slowly through the woods, till she came to the gates of the same house in which her stepsister had found happiness. She entered, closed the door, and resolved not to open it for anybody. Then she took a cake out of her bag and began her meal. Meanwhile the cock, the dog, and the cat came in, and began to frisk about her playfully, expecting that she would give them something to eat, but she exclaimed angrily, "Get away, you ugly creatures! I have hardly enough for myself. I will not give you any!" Then she began to beat them, whereat the dog howled, and the lion, hearing his friend's lamentation, rushed in furiously and killed the unkind girl.

Next morning the prince rode out with his wife to hunt. They came to the house and saw what had happened, and when the princess recognized her stepsister's dress, she gathered up the torn garment and carried it to her father's house. This time she found her father at home, and he was indeed very happy to learn that his dear daughter was married to a handsome prince. When, however, he heard what had befallen his wife's daughter, he was sad indeed, and exclaimed, "Her mother has deserved this punishment from the hand of God, because she hated you without reason. She is at the well. I will go and tell her the sad news."

When his wife heard what had happened, she said, "O husband! I cannot bear the sight of your daughter. Let us kill both her and the tsar's son! Do this thing or I will jump at once into the well." The man indignantly answered, "Well then, jump! I shall not murder my own child!"

And the wicked woman said, "If you cannot kill her, I cannot bear to look at her!" Thereupon she jumped into the well and was killed.

Justice and Injustice

THERE WAS A KING who had two sons, one of whom was cunning and unjust, and the other good and just. In due time the king died, and the unjust son said to his brother, "As you are younger than I, you cannot expect me to share the throne with you, so you had better go away from the palace. Take these three hundred *tzechins* and a horse to ride. This is to be your share of the inheritance." The younger brother took the gold and his horse, and, reflecting, he said, "God be praised! How much of the entire kingdom has fallen to me!"

Some time later the two brothers met by chance on a road, and the younger saluted the elder thus: "God help you, brother!" And the elder answered, "May God send you a misfortune! Why do you for ever mention the name of God to me? Injustice is better than justice." Thereupon the good brother said, "I wager that injustice is not better than justice!"

So they laid as a wager one hundred *tzechins* and agreed to accept the decision of the first passer-by whom they should happen to meet. Riding on a little farther, they met Satan, who had disguised himself as a monk, and they requested him to decide their contest. Satan immediately answered that injustice is better than justice; so the just brother lost one hundred *tzechins*. Then they made another wager in the same sum, and again a third; and each time the Devil – differently disguised on each occasion – pronounced for injustice. Finally the good brother lost even his horse, but he was quite unconvinced, and he reflected, "Ah, well! I have lost all my *tzechins*, it is true, but I have still my eyes, and I shall wager my eyes this time." So they made the bet once more, but the unjust brother did not even wait for anybody's arbitration. He took out his poniard and pierced his brother's eyes, saying, "Now, let justice help you, when you have no eyes!"

The poor youth said to his cruel brother, "I have lost my eyes for the sake of God's justice, but I pray you, my brother, give me a little water in a vessel that I may wash my wounds and take me under the pine tree, near the spring!" The unjust brother did as he was asked and then he departed.

The Healing Water

The unfortunate youth sat without moving until late in the night, when some veele came to the spring to bathe, and he heard one of them say to her sisters, "Do you know, O sisters, that the royal princess suffers from leprosy, and the king, her father, has consulted all the famous physicians, but no one can cure her? But if the king knew the healing qualities of this water, he would surely take a little and bathe his daughter with it, and she would recover perfect health." When the cocks began to crow, the veele disappeared and the prince crept to the spring to test its wonderful properties. He bathed his eyes, and lo! his sight was instantly restored. Then he filled his vessel with the water and hurried to the king, whose daughter was suffering from leprosy. Arriving at the palace, he told the officers on guard that he could cure the princess in a day and a night. The officers informed the king, who at once allowed him to try his method, and the suffering princess was restored. This pleased the king so much that he gave the young prince half of his kingdom, as well as his daughter for his wife. So the just brother became the king's son-in-law, and a Councillor of State.

The tidings of this great event spread all over the kingdom, and finally came to the ears of the unjust prince. He thought that his brother must have found his good fortune under the pine tree, so he went there himself to try his luck. Arrived there, he pierced his own eyes. Late in the night, the veele came to bathe, and the prince heard them discuss with astonishment the recovery of the royal princess. "Someone must have spied upon us," said one of them, "when we discussed about the qualities which this water possesses. Perhaps somebody is watching us even now. Let us look around us!" When they came under the pine tree, they found there the young man who had come seeking good fortune, and they immediately tore him into four.

And thus was the wicked prince recompensed for his injustice.

He Who Asks Little Receives Much

ONCE UPON A TIME there lived three brothers, who instead of much property had only a pear tree. Each would watch that tree in turn, whilst the other two went away from home to work for hire. One night God sent His angel to see how the brothers lived, and, should they be in misery, to improve their position. The angel came disguised as a beggar, and when he found one of the brothers watching the tree, he went forward and asked him for a pear. The youth plucked some of the fruit from his own part of the tree, handed them to the beggar, and said, "Accept these pears from my share of the tree, but I cannot give you those belonging to my brothers." The angel took the fruit, thanked the youth, and disappeared.

The next day it was the turn of the second brother to watch the fruit, and the angel, again in the semblance of a beggar, came and asked for a pear. This brother likewise gave from his own part of the tree, saying, "Take these; they are my own. But of those belonging to my brothers I dare not offer you." The angel took the fruit gratefully and departed.

The third brother had a similar experience.

When the fourth day came, the angel disguised himself as a monk, and came very early so that he could find all three brothers at home, and he said to the youths, "Come with me. I shall improve your state of life." Whereupon they obeyed without question.

Soon they arrived at a river where the water was flowing in torrents, and the angel asked the eldest brother, "What would you like to have?" He answered, "I should like all this water to be changed into wine and to belong to me." The angel made the sign of the cross with his stick, and lo! wine was flowing instead of water, and that very moment there appeared on the banks of the streamlet many barrels, and men filling them with wine; in one word, there was a whole village. Then the angel turned again to the young man and said, "Here is what you wished. Farewell!" And he continued his journey with the others.

The three went on till they came to a field, where they saw numbers of doves, and the angel asked the second brother, "Now, what is it that you would like?" And he answered, "I should like all these doves to be changed into sheep, and to be mine!" The angel again made the sign of the cross in the air, and lo! sheep instead of doves covered the field. Suddenly there appeared many dairies; maidens were busy milking the sheep, others pouring out the milk, others again making cream. There was also a slaughterhouse, and men busy, some cutting the meat into joints, others weighing it, others again selling the meat and receiving the money for it. Then the angel said, "Here is all you wished for. Farewell!"

The angel now proceeded with the youngest brother, and, having crossed the field, he asked him what he would like to have. The young man answered, "I should consider myself the happiest of men if God were graciously pleased to grant me a wife of pure Christian blood!" Thereupon the angel replied, "Oh, that is rather difficult to find. In the whole world there are but three such women, two of whom are married. The youngest is a maid, it is true, but she is already sought in marriage by two wooers."

Journeying on, they came to a city where a mighty tsar dwelt with his daughter. She, indeed, was of pure Christian blood. The travellers entered the palace and found two princes already there with their wedding apples laid upon a table. Then the young man also placed his apple on the table. When the tsar saw the newcomers, he said to those around him, "What shall we do now? Those are imperial princes, and these men look like beggars!" Thereupon the angel said, "Let the contest be decided thus: the princess shall plant three vines in the garden, dedicating one to each of the three wooers, and he on whose vine grapes are found next morning is to be the one whom the princess shall marry!" This plan was agreed to by all, and the princess accordingly planted three vines.

When the next morning dawned, lo! grapes hung in clusters on the vine dedicated to the poor man. So the tsar could not refuse his daughter to the youngest brother. After the marriage, the angel led the young couple to the forest, where he left them for a full year.

The Angel Returns

Then God sent again His angel, saying, "Go down to earth and see how those poor ones are living now. If they are in misery, it may be you will be able to improve their condition!" The angel obeyed immediately, and, disguising himself again as a beggar, he went first to the eldest brother and asked him for a glass of wine. But the rich man refused, saying, "If I were to give everyone a glass of wine, there would be none left for myself!" Upon this the angel made the sign of the cross with his stick, and the stream began instantly to flow with water as before. Then he turned to the man and said, "This was not for you. Go back under the pear tree and continue to guard it!"

Then the angel went on to the second brother, whose fields were covered with sheep, and asked him for a slice of cheese. But the rich man refused, saying, "If I were to give everybody a slice of cheese, there would be none left for myself!" Again the angel made the sign of the cross with his stick, and lo! all the sheep turned instantly into doves, who flew away. Then he said to the second brother, "Of a surety that was not for you. Go under the pear tree and watch it!"

Finally the angel went to the youngest brother in order to see how he was living, and found him with his wife in the forest, dwelling as a poor man in a hut. He begged to be admitted into their hut, and to pass the night there. They welcomed him very cordially, but they explained that they could not entertain him as well as they would like to do. "We are," they added, "very poor people." To which the angel answered, "Do not speak so, I shall be quite content with what you have!" They wondered then what to do, for there was no corn in their hut to make real bread; they usually ground the bark of certain trees and made bread from it. Such bread the wife now made for their guest, and placed it in the oven to bake. When she came later to inspect her baking, she was pleasantly surprised to find a fine loaf of real bread.

When the couple saw this wonder, they lifted their hands toward heaven and gave thanks. "We thank thee, O God! that we are now able to entertain our guest!" After they had placed the bread before their guest, they brought a vessel of water, and lo! when they came to drink, they found it was wine.

Then the angel once more made the sign of the cross with his stick over the hut, and on that spot instantly rose a beautiful palace, containing an abundance of everything. Then the angel blessed the couple and disappeared. The modest and pious man and woman lived there happily ever after.

Why the Priest Was Drowned

A FEW PEASANTS and a priest were once crossing a river. Suddenly a tempest arose and overturned the boat. All were good swimmers except the poor priest, and when the peasants regained their boat and righted it, which they did very soon, they approached the struggling preacher and called to him to give them his hand that they might save him. But he hesitated and was drowned.

The peasants went to impart the sad news to the priest's widow, who, hearing it, exclaimed, "What a pity! But had you offered him *your* hands, he would surely have accepted them, and thus his precious life would have been saved – for it was ever his custom to *receive*."

Saint Peter and the Sand

A TOWNSMAN WENT one day to the country to hunt and came at noon to the house of a peasant whom he knew. The man asked him to share his dinner, and while they were eating, the townsman looked around him and noticed that there was but little arable land to be seen. There were rocks and stones in abundance, however. Surprised at this, the townsman exclaimed, "In the name of all that is good, my friend, how on earth can you good people of this village exist without arable land? And whence these heaps of rocks and stones?"

"It is, indeed, a great misfortune!" answered the peasant. "People say that our ancestors heard from their forefathers that when our Lord walked on this earth, St. Peter accompanied Him, carrying on his back a sack full of sand. Occasionally our Lord would take a grain of sand and throw it down to make a mountain, saying, 'May this grain multiply!' When they arrived here, St. Peter's sack burst and half of its contents poured out in our village."

Why the Serbian People Are Poor

T HE NATIONS of the world met together one day at the middle of the earth to divide between themselves the good things in life. First they deliberated upon the methods of procedure. Some recommended a lottery, but the Christians, well knowing that they, as the cleverest, would be able to obtain the most desirable gifts, and not wishing to be at the mercy of fortune, suggested (and the idea was instantly adopted by all) that each should express a wish for some good thing and it would be granted to him.

The men of Italy were allowed to express their wish first, and they desired Wisdom. The Britons said, "We will take the sea." The Turks: "And we will take fields." The Russians: "We will take the forests and mines." The French: "And we will have money and war." "And what about you Serbians?" asked the nations. "What do you wish for?" "Wait till we make up our mind!" answered the Serbians. And they have not yet agreed upon their reply.

The Emperor Trojan's Goat's Ears

THERE ONCE LIVED an emperor whose name was Trojan. This emperor had goat's ears, and he used to call in barber after barber to shave him. But whoever went in never came out again; for while the barber was shaving him, the emperor would ask what he observed uncommon in him, and when the barber would answer that he observed his goat's ears, the Emperor would immediately cut him into pieces.

At last it came to the turn of a certain barber to go, who feigned illness and sent his apprentice instead. When the apprentice appeared before the emperor, he was asked why his master did not come, and he answered, "Because he is ill." Then the emperor sat down and allowed the youth to shave him.

As he shaved him, the apprentice noticed the emperor's goat's ears, but when Trojan asked him what he had observed, he answered, "I have observed nothing."

Then the emperor gave him twelve ducats, and said to him, "From this time forth you shall always come and shave me."

When the apprentice came home, his master asked him how he got on at the emperor's, and the youth answered, "All well, and the emperor has told me that I am to shave him in future."

Then he showed the twelve ducats he had received. But as to the emperor's goat's ears, of that he said nothing.

From this time forth the apprentice went regularly to Trojan to shave him, and for each shaving he received twelve ducats. But he told no one that the emperor had goat's ears.

At last it began to worry and torment him that he dare tell no one his secret, and he became sick and began to pine away. His master, who could not fail to observe this, asked him what ailed him, and after much pressing, the apprentice confessed that he had something on his heart which he dared not confide to anyone, and he added, "If I could only tell it to somebody, I should feel better at once."

Then said the master, "Tell it to me, and I will faithfully keep it from everybody else; or if you fear to trust me with it, then go to the confessor and confide it to him; but if you will not do even that, then go into the fields outside the town, there dig a hole, thrust your head into it, and tell the earth three times what you know, then throw the mould in again and fill up the hole."

The apprentice chose the last course. He went into the field outside the city, and dug a hole, into which he thrust his head, and called out three times:

"The Emperor Trojan has goat's ears!"

Then he filled up the hole again, and with his mind quite relieved went home.

When some time had passed by, there sprang an elder tree out of this very hole, and three slender sterns grew up, beautiful and straight as tapers. Some shepherds found this elder, cut off one of the stems, and made a pipe of it. But as soon as they began to blow into the new pipe, out burst the words:

"The Emperor Trojan has goat's ears!"

The news of this strange occurrence spread immediately through the whole city, and at last the Emperor Trojan himself heard the children blowing on a pipe:

"The Emperor Trojan has goat's ears!"

He sent instantly for the barber's apprentice, and shouted to him, "Heh! what is this you have been telling the people about me?"

The poor youth began at once to explain that he had indeed noticed the emperor's ears, but had never told a soul of it. The emperor tore his saber out of its sheath to hew the apprentice down, at which the youth was so frightened that he told the whole story in its order: how he had confessed himself to the earth; how an elder tree had sprung up on the very spot; and how, when a pipe was made of one of its sterns, the tale was sounded in every direction.

Then the emperor took the apprentice with him in a carriage to the place, to convince himself of the truth of the story, and when they arrived there they found there was only a single stem left. The Emperor Trojan ordered a pipe to be made out of this stem, that he might hear how it sounded. As soon as the pipe was ready, and one of them blew into it, out poured the words:

"The Emperor Trojan has goat's ears!"

Then the emperor was convinced that nothing on this earth could be hidden, spared the barber apprentice's life, and henceforth allowed any barber, without exception, to come and shave him.

Why the Sole of Man's Foot Is Flat

ONCE UPON A TIME, when the devils turned recreants to God and fled to earth, amongst other things, they took along with them the Sun, which the Tsar of the devils stuck on the point of his lance, and he carried it over his shoulder. But when the Earth complained to God that she would soon be burnt to ashes by the Sun, God sent the Holy Archangel Michael to try by some means or other to take away the Sun from the devil. Now, when the Holy Archangel stepped down to the earth, he made friends with the Tsar of the devils, but the latter saw at once what was Michael's little game, and was always on his guard.

One day the two went together for a walk, and went on and on until they came to the sea. There they made preparations to have a bathe, and the devil stuck his lance into the ground with the Sun still upon it. After they had been bathing for a while, the Holy Archangel said, "Now, let us dive and see who can dive deepest." And the devil said, "Very well!" So the Holy Archangel dived first, and brought up in his mouth some sand from the bottom of the sea. Now it was the devil's turn to dive, but he was afraid that Michael would steal the Sun.

Then he had a fine idea. He spit on the ground, and out of his spittle grew a magpie. He told her to look after the Sun whilst he was diving to get some sand from the bottom of the sea. As soon, however, as the devil dived, the Holy Archangel made the sign of the cross, and instantly the sea was covered with ice nine yards thick. Quickly he seized the Sun, spread out his wings, and flew heavenwards, whilst the magpie croaked for all she was worth. When the devil heard the magpie's voice, he guessed at once what was the matter, and returned as quickly as possible. But when he came near the surface, he found that the sea was frozen up and that he could not get out. Hurriedly he made again for the bottom of the sea, fetched a stone, broke through the ice, and pressed on in pursuit of the Holy Archangel.

The distance between the two grew less and less. Now the Angel had reached the Gate of Heaven and had already put one foot inside, when the devil just caught him by the other foot and tore out of it a large piece of flesh with his claws. And as the Holy Archangel with the regained Sun in his hands stepped before God, he wept and lamented, "What shall I do now, disfigured thus?" Then the Lord God said to him, "Be still and fear not; henceforth shall all men bear a small hollow in the sole of the foot." And as God had said, so it came about that all men received a small hollow in the sole of each foot.

Honesty Is Ne'er an Ill Pennyworth

ONCE UPON A TIME there was a poor man who had hired himself out to a rich man and served him without any agreement. Thus he served him a whole year long, and at the end of the year he went to his master and asked him to pay up as much as he thought would be now due. Then the master produced a penny and said, "Here are your wages!" The servant took the coin, went to a rapid brook, and prayed, "Merciful God, how is it that with a whole year's work I have only earned a penny? You, O God, do know whether I deserved but so little. And I will find it out now, and throw this small coin into the water. If it does not sink, I have earned it; but if it sinks, I have not earned it." He then made the sign of the cross, and threw the coin into the brook, but, behold! it sank at once.

Then he bent down, picked out the coin, and gave it back to his master, with the words, "I bring your coin back to you; I have not deserved it. I will serve you another year." And so he began to serve afresh, and when the year had come to an end, again he went to his master and asked him to pay up so much as he thought would be his due. And the master again produced a penny and said, "Here are your wages!" The servant took the coin, thanked his master, and again straightaway went to the same rapid brook, made the sign of the cross, threw the money into the water, and said, "Merciful God, if I have justly earned it, let it float on the surface; if not, let the coin sink." But when he threw the coin into the brook, again it sank immediately to the bottom. Then he bent down, picked it out, and, once more returning to his master, said, "Sir, here is your penny back; I have not earned it yet. I will serve you another year." And so he began to serve afresh. And when the third year had come to an end, again he went to his master and asked him to pay him as much as he thought he had earned. The master, however, gave him but a penny, and he took it and thanked him, and went again to the brook to see whether perhaps he had earned it now. When he arrived, he made the sign of the cross and threw the penny into the water, praying, "Merciful God, if I have earned this penny, let it float; if not, let it sink!" But this time the penny did not sink; it floated. The joyful servant picked it out, put it into his pocket, and went away with it into a wood. Here he built for himself a tiny cottage, and led a happy and contented life.

After a time he heard that his master was getting ready to set out for a long sea voyage to a country ever so far away. He went to him and asked him to buy him something for his penny on the other side of the sea. The master promised him to do so, took the penny, and started. Whilst he was on the way, he met some children near the shore who were about to kill a cat and throw it into the sea. When the master saw this, he hurried towards them and asked them, "What are you doing, children?" They answered him, "This cat is a nuisance, therefore we are going to kill it." Then the master took the penny which his former servant had given him, and offered it to the children for their cat. The children were pleased with the bargain, and gave the cat to the merchant. And he carried the cat on board his ship and continued his voyage. Then arose a violent storm that blew the ship out of her right course, and for three months the travellers did not know where they were. When the storm abated and the master had quite lost his way, he travelled a little farther, and at last he arrived in front of a fortified town. No sooner had the ship arrived than the townspeople, hearing about a ship from strange lands, poured out of the fortress to see her, and one of them, a rich man, invited the ship's master to sup with him.

When the invited guest arrived, lo! what a sight he beheld! Everywhere there were rats and mice, and servants armed with sticks stood on all sides to ward off the horrid animals. Then the merchant said to the master of the house, "My dear friend, what is the meaning of all this?" Whereupon his host said, "It is always like this with us. We have no rest from these animals, neither during dinner nor during supper. And when we go to sleep, each one of us has a box in which he locks himself up, so that the mice cannot gnaw off his ears."

Then the master of the ship remembered the cat he had bought for a penny, and said to his host, "I have an animal on board my ship that will settle all this in two or three days." The host replied, "My friend, if you will let us have that wonderful animal of yours, and if it will do what you say it can do, we shall fill your ship with silver and gold."

After supper the merchant went to his ship to fetch the cat, and told his host that everybody might go to bed without fear now. But the people had not got the courage, and the merchant was the only one who dared to sleep outside a box. Then he let loose his cat. And she began a most awful slaughter. Mouse after mouse, rat after rat, she killed, until in the morning a high heap of corpses was piled up. Three days later not a single mouse nor a single rat was left. Then the host filled our traveller's ship with gold and silver, and the latter returned home.

When he arrived home, his old servant came and asked what he had brought him for his penny. Then the master gave him a square slab of marble, beautifully polished and cut, and said, "See. This beautiful marble I have bought you for your penny." The servant was much pleased, took it home, and made a table out of it. The next day he went out to fetch wood, but when he returned home, behold, the whole of the marble had been changed into gold, and it was shining like the sun, filling the tiny cottage with a dazzling light. The honest servant was frightened, ran to his master, and said, "Master, what have you given me? That gold cannot be mine. Come and look at it." The master went, and when he saw what a miracle God had wrought, he said, "There is no getting away from it, my dear friend: him whom the Almighty God is helping, all the Saints will help! Come with me and receive what is yours!" And thereupon he gave to him everything he had brought along in his ship, and, moreover, he gave unto him in marriage his beloved and only daughter.

Serbian Stories from Carniola

The Origin of Man

IN THE BEGINNING there was nothing but God, and God slept and dreamed. For ages and ages did this dream last. But it was fated that he should wake up. Having roused himself from sleep, he looked round about him, and every glance transformed itself into a star. God was amazed, and began to travel, to see what he had created with his eyes.

He travelled and travelled, but nowhere was there either end or limit. As he travelled, he arrived at our earth also, but he was already weary, and sweat clung to his brow. On the earth fell a drop of sweat. The drop became alive, and here you have the first man. He is God's kin, but he was not created for pleasure; he was produced from sweat. Already in the beginning it was fated for him to toil and sweat.

God's Cock

The earth was waste; nowhere was there aught but stone. God was sorry for this, and sent his cock to make the earth fruitful, as he knew how to do. The cock came down into a cave in the rock, and fetched out an egg of wondrous power and purpose. The egg chipped, and seven rivers trickled out of it. The rivers irrigated the neighbourhood, and soon all was green: there were all manner of flowers and fruits; the land, without man's labour, produced wheat, the trees not only apples and figs, but also the whitest and sweetest bread. In this paradise men lived without care, working, not from need, but for amusement and merriment. Round the paradise were lofty mountains, so that there was no violence to fear, nor devilish storm to dread. But further: that men, otherwise their own masters, and free, might not, from ignorance, suffer damage, God's cock hovered high in the sky, and crowed to them every day when to get up, when to take their meals, and what to do, and when to do it.

The nation was happy, only God's cock annoyed them by his continual crowing. Men began to murmur and pray God to deliver them from the restless creature. "Let us now settle for ourselves," said they, "when to eat, to work, and to rise." God hearkened to them. The cock descended from the sky, but crowed to them just once more, "Woe is me! Beware of the lake!" Men rejoiced, and said that it was never better; no one anymore interfered with their freedom. After ancient custom, they ate, worked, and rose, all in the best order, as the cock had taught them. But, little by little, individuals began to think that it was unsuitable for a free people to obey the cock's crowing so slavishly, and began to live after their own fashion, observing no manner of order.

Through this arose illnesses, and all kinds of distress; men looked again longingly to the sky, but God's cock was gone for ever. They wished, at any rate, to pay regard to his last words. But they did not know how to fathom their meaning. The cock had warned them to dread the lake, but why? For they hadn't it in their valley; there flowed quietly, in their own channel, the seven rivers which had burst out of the egg. Men therefore conjectured that there was a dangerous lake somewhere on the other side of the mountains, and sent a man every day to the top of a hill to see whether he espied aught. But there was danger from no quarter; the man went in vain, and people calmed themselves again. Their pride became greater and greater. The women made brooms from the wheat ears, and the men straw mattresses. They would not go anymore to the tree to gather bread, but set it on fire from below, that it might fall, and that they might collect it without trouble.

When they had eaten their fill, they lay down by the rivers, conversed, and spoke all manner of blasphemies. One cast his eyes on the water, wagged his head, and jabbered, "Eh! brothers! A wondrous wonder! I should like to know, at any rate, why the water is exactly so much, neither more nor less." "This, too," another answered, "was a craze of the cock's. It is disgraceful enough for us to be listening to orders to beware of a lake, which never was, and never will be. If my opinion is followed, the watcher will go today for the last time. As regards the rivers, I think it would be better if there were more water." His neighbour at first agreed, but thought, again, that there was water in abundance; if more, there would be too much. A corpulent fellow put in energetically that undoubtedly both were right. It would, therefore, be the most sensible thing to break the egg up, and drive just as much water as was wanted into each man's land, and there was certainly no need of a watchman to look out for the lake.

Scarcely had these sentiments been delivered when an outcry arose in the valley. All rushed to the egg to break it to pieces. All men deplored nothing but this, that the disgraceful lookout could not be put a stop to before the morrow. The people stood round the egg, and the corpulent man took up a stone, and banged it against the egg. It split up with a clap of thunder, and so much water burst out of it that almost the whole human race perished. The paradise was filled with water, and became one great lake. God's cock warned truly, but in vain, for the lawless people did not understand him. The flood now reached the highest mountains, just to the place where the watchman was standing, who was the only survivor from the destruction of mankind. Seeing the increasing waters, he began to flee.

Kurent the Preserver

Mankind perished by the flood, and there was only one who survived, and this was Kranyatz. Kranyatz fled higher and higher, till the water flooded the last mountain. The poor wretch saw how the pines and shrubs were covered; one vine, and one only, was still dry. To it he fled, and quickly seized hold of it, not from necessity, but from excessive terror. But how could it help him, being so slender and weak? Kurent observed this, for the vine was his stick, when he walked through the wide world. It was agreeable to him that man should be thought to seek help from him.

It is true that Kurent was a great joker, but he was also of a kindly nature, and was always glad to deliver anyone from distress. Hearing Kranyatz lamenting, he straightened the vine, his stick, and lengthened it more and more, till it became higher than the clouds. After nine years the flood ceased, and the earth became dry again. But Kranyatz preserved himself by hanging on the vine, and nourishing himself by its grapes and wine. When all became dry, he got down, and thanked Kurent as his preserver. But this didn't please Kurent. "It was the vine that rescued you," said he to Kranyatz. "Thank the vine, and make a covenant with it, and bind yourself and your posterity, under a curse, that you will always speak its praises and love its wine more than any other food and drink." Very willingly did the grateful Kranyatz make the engagement for both himself and his posterity. And to this day his descendants still keep faith, according to his promise, loving wine above all things, and joyfully commemorating Kurent, their ancient benefactor.

Kurent and Man

Kurent and man contended which should rule the earth. Neither Kurent would yield to man nor man to Kurent, for he (man) was so gigantic – he wouldn't even have noticed it, if nine of the people of the present day had danced up and down his nostrils. "Come," said Kurent, "let us see which is the stronger – whether it is I or you that is to rule the earth. Yonder is a broad sea; the one that springs across it best shall have both the earth and all that is on the other side of the sea, and that is, in faith, a hundred times more valuable than this wilderness." Man agreed.

Kurent took off his coat and jumped across the sea, so that just one foot was wetted when he sprang onto dry land. Now he began to jeer at the man, but the man held his tongue and didn't get out of temper. Neither did he take off his coat, but stepped without effort and quite easily over the sea, as over a brook, and came onto dry land without even wetting a foot. "I'm the stronger," said man to Kurent. "See how my foot is dry and yours is wet." "The first time you have overcome me," answered Kurent. "Yours are the plains, yours is the sea, and what is beyond the sea. But that isn't all the earth; there is also some beneath us and above us. Come, then, let us see a second time who is the stronger." Kurent stood on a hollow rock, and stamped on it with his foot, so that it burst with a noise like thunder, and split in pieces. The rock broke up, and a cavern was seen where dragons were brooding.

Now the man also stamped, and the earth quaked and broke up right to the bottom, just where pure gold flowed like a broad river, and the dragons fell down and were drowned in the river. "This trial, too, is yours," said Kurent, "but I don't acknowledge you emperor till you overpower me in a third fierce contest. Yonder is a very lofty mountain. It rises above the clouds; it reaches to the celestial table, where the cock sits and watches God's provisions. Now, then, take you an arrow and shoot, and so will I; the one which shoots highest is the stronger, and his is the earth, and all that is beneath and above it." Kurent shot, and his arrow wasn't back for eight days; then the man shot, and his arrow flew for nine days. And when, on the tenth day, it fell, the celestial cock that guarded God's provisions fell also, spitted upon it.

"You are emperor," said cunning Kurent. "I make obeisance to you, as befits a subject." But the man was good-natured, and made a covenant of adoptive brotherhood with Kurent, and went off to enjoy his imperial dignity. Kurent, too, went off, but he was annoyed that the man had put him to shame. Where he could not prevail by strength, he determined to succeed by craft. "You are a hero, man," he would say. "I am witness thereto. But beware of me, if you are a hero also in simplicity. I go to bring you a gift, that I have devised entirely by myself." He squeezed the vine, his stick, and pure red wine burst out of it. "Here's a gift for you. Now, then, where are you?"

He found the man on the earth the other side of the sea, where he was enjoying a bowl of sweet stirabout. "What are you doing, my lord?" said Kurent. "I've mixed a bowl of stirabout from white wheat and red fruit. And, see, here I am eating it and drinking water." "My poor lord! you are emperor of the world and drinking water! Hand me a cup, that I may present you with better drink, which I, your humble servant, have prepared for you myself." The man was deceived, took the cup with red wine, and drank some of it. "Thank you, adopted brother. You are very kind, but your drink is naught." Kurent was disgusted, went off again, and thought and thought how to cheat the man. Again he squeezed his stick, and again red wine burst forth from it, but Kurent did not allow it to remain pure, but the rascal mixed hellebore with it, which Vilas and prophetesses pluck by moonlight to nourish themselves with.

A second time he went in search of the man, and found him at the bottom of the earth, where the pure gold was flowing like a broad river. "What are you doing, my lord?" asked Kurent. "I am getting myself a golden shirt, and I am tired and very thirsty. But there's no water here, and it's a long way to the world – seven years' journey." "I am at your service," said Kurent. "Here's a cup of wine for you; better never saw the red sun." The man was deceived, took it, and drank it up. "Thank you, Kurent. You are good, and your drink is good, too." Kurent, was going to pour him out a fresh cupful, but the man would not allow it, for his nature was still sober and sensible. Kurent was disgusted, and went off to see whether he could not devise something better. For the third time he squeezed his stick; wine burst out more strongly, but this time it did not remain pure nor without sin. The rascal applied an arrow, opened a vein, and let some black blood flow into the wine.

Again he went in search of the man, and found him on the high mountain at God's table, where he was feasting on roast meat, which had not been roasted for him, but for God himself. "What are you doing, my lord?" asked Kurent in amazement and joy, when he saw that the man was sinning abominably. "Here I am, sitting and eating roast meat. But take yourself off, for I am afraid of God, lest he should come up and smite me." "Never fear!" was Kurent's advice. "How do you like God's roast meat?" "It's nice, but it's heavy. I can scarcely swallow it." "I am at your service," said Kurent. "Here is wine for you, the like of which isn't on earth or in heaven, but only with me." The third time the man was deceived, but cruelly. "Thank you, Kurent," he said. You are good, but your drink is better. Draw me some more, as becomes a faithful servant." Kurent did so, and the man's eye became dim and his mind became dim, and he thought no more of God, but remained at table.

Suddenly God returned and, seeing the man dozing and eating roast meat at his table, became angry, and smote him down the mountain with his mighty hand, where he lay, half dead, for many years, all bruised and hurt. When he got well again his strength had diminished; he could neither step across the sea, nor go down to the bottom of the earth, nor uphill to the celestial table. Thus Kurent ruled the world and man, and mankind have been weak and dwarfed from that time forth.

The Hundred-Leaved Rose

The man contended with Kurent for the earth. Unable to decide their dispute by agreement, they seized each other, and struggled together up and down the earth for a full seven years. But neither could Kurent overcome the man, nor the man Kurent. At that time they kicked the earth about and broke it up, so that it became such as it now is: where there was formerly nothing but wide plains, they dug out ravines with their heels, and piled up mountains and hills. When they were wearied with fighting, they both fell down like dead corpses, and lay for a hundred and a hundred years. And the mighty Dobrin hastened to the earth, bound both the man and Kurent, and ruled the world.

But the two woke up, and, looking about them, observed Dobrin's cords, and wondered who had thrown spider's webs over them. Raising themselves, they broke their bonds as mere spiders' webs, seized Dobrin, bound him with golden fetters, and handed him over to a fiery dragon, to plait the lady-dragon's hair and wash her white hands. Then said Kurent to the man, "See, by quarrelling we got tired out, and fell asleep, and a good-for-nothing came to us and ruled the world. We have handed him over to the fiery dragon, but if we contend as before, a stronger than Dobrin will come to us, and will conquer both me and you, and we shall suffer like silly Dobrin.

"But let us give up disputing. You are a hero, and I think I am, too. The hills and abysses are our witnesses, when they crashed under our heels. Hear, therefore, and follow my advice. I have a garden, and in my garden is a mysterious plant, the hundred-leaved rose. By the root it is attached to the bottom of the earth, imprisoning a terrible creature – the living fire. In vain does the creature endeavour to release and free itself from its bonds, the roots.

"But woe to us, if you pull up the hundred-leaved rose out of the earth! The creature 'living-fire' would force its way through, and the earth, and all that is on it, would become nothing but a mighty desert where the water has dried up. Such is the root of the hundred-leaved rose.

"But don't seize hold of its top, either. It is in your power to pull it off; it is neither too strong nor lofty, but it conceals within it wondrous powers – lightning and thunder. They would knock to pieces both you and the earth, and all that is beneath it and above it; the hundred-leaved rose would alone remain. But a hundred and a hundred of God's years would elapse before a new earth grew up around it, and a living race was again produced. Such is the garden of the hundred-leaved rose.

"But it also possesses extraordinary petals. I have often sat a day at a time under them, and the petals would comfort me, and sing songs sweeter than even the slender throat of a Vila singing ever uttered. But from the petals there is no danger; pluck them, and next morning they will sprout forth handsomer than ever. But up to the present time I have not injured them, but have noticed in the night how they fell and raised themselves again. And I easily understood how the stars and the moon go round, for all came up in the sky just like the petals of the hundred-leaved rose.

"Come, then; let us ask the wondrous plant, and then make peace together. The first petal is yours, the second mine, the third belongs to neither of us, and so on till we pluck all the petals. Let him who pulls off the last petal be ruler on the earth, but not for ever, for that would be a disgrace to a hero, but for one of God's hours, a hundred terrestrial years. And when the hour passes, let that one rule again to whom that luck does not fall the first time, whether it be I or you, so that we may arrange to succeed each other in a friendly manner without dispute and dangerous discord. But the beginning is difficult. Let us have no suspicion, either I as to you, or you as to me, but let all be of goodwill, and without trickery; let us ask the hundred-leaved rose, with whom there is no unrighteousness."

The man agreed to what Kurent said; one hero trusted the other. They went off to the garden, and asked the hundred-leaved rose. The man pulled a petal, Kurent pulled one, and the third petal remained unowned. "I am yours," "you are mine," "each is his own." "I am yours," "you are mine," "each is his own." So said both heroes, as they pulled the mysterious petals. But it was not the will of the hundred-leaved rose that one autocrat should rule the earth. There were still three petals, the first belonging to the man, the second to Kurent, and the third to neither, and this was the only one remaining on the hundred-leaved rose. Kurent and the man saw that it was not destined for either to rule or to humble himself. They parted in grief, and roamed through the wide world, each afraid of the other, so that they did not venture even to go to sleep at night.

An hour of God, a hundred terrestrial years, elapsed, and then both heroes met again. For the second time they consulted the hundred-leaved rose, and it arranged it so that Kurent was to humble himself, and the man, who pulled off the last petal, was to rule. The hero humbled himself to him, but the man did not know how to rule, but allowed himself to be deluded, and lay down on a plain to rest and sleep. Thus he lay for a whole hour of God, a hundred terrestrial years, and the wild beasts came up and made game of him; foxes littered in his ear, and predaceous kites nested in his thick hair.

The man was a great simpleton, but also a mighty hero, as tall as a plain, the end of which you cannot see, is long, and as shaggy as a wooded mountain. But the hour of God had elapsed, and Kurent came to the sleeper, and woke him up in no agreeable fashion. The man saw that he had slept through his term of rule, and that it was his, according to the agreement, to serve during an hour of God, a hundred terrestrial years.

Kurent began to rule, but he didn't go to sleep, but made use of his rule, and exercised his power to the full. He invited the man to dinner, and treated him in a courteous and friendly manner, that he might soon forget his servitude. Kurent kept this in view, and drew him a cup of wine straight from his own vineyard. The simpleton was tricked, and drank it up; but it tasted sour to him, so he grumbled, "Bad drink at a bad host's!" Kurent did not get angry at this, but drew him a second cup of old red wine. "Drink, and don't find fault with what is God's."

The second time the man was tricked and drank it up. It did not taste sour to him, but he said, "Wondrous drink at a wondrous host's!" Kurent drew him a third cup, of wonderful wine, which the first plant, the first planted, yielded, of the first autumn in the first created year.

The third time the man was tricked, but for ever. After drinking it up, he threw his arms round Kurent's neck, and cried out, "Oh, good drink at a good host's! Treat me with this wine, and rule both my body and soul, not only for one hour of God, but from henceforth for ever more." Kurent was delighted, and plied the man with sweet wine, and the man drank, and cried without ceasing, that he had no need of freedom so long as there was wine to be had with Kurent. Kurent laughed at him, seeing how the man's powers had decayed through wine, and that nobody could anymore contend with him for the sovereignty of the earth.

FLAME TREE PUBLISHING

In the same series:

MYTH, FOLKLORE AND ANCIENT HISTORY

Also available:

EPIC TALES DELUXE EDITIONS

flametreepublishing.com
and all good bookstores